THE FISHER CHILD

THE

FISHER CHILD

PHILIP CASEY

PICADOR

First published 2001 by Picador
an imprint of Pan Macmillan Ltd
Pan Macmillan, 20 New Wharf Road, London N1 9RR
Basingstoke and Oxford
Associated companies throughout the world
www.panmacmillan.com

ISBN 0 330 48301 3

1 3 5 7 9 8 6 4 2

A CIP catalogue record for this book is available from
the British Library.

Typeset by SetSystems Ltd, Saffron Walden, Essex
Printed and bound in Great Britain by
Mackays of Chatham plc, Chatham, Kent

TO MICK AND MARY, SEAN AND KAY

Who is dead? Who is fled?
Who lies bleeding in the ditches?

*

Two centuries counted in a single day.

Eamonn Wall

Part One

KATE

ONE

Florence, September 1997

She woke beside Dan, unsure of where she was. Half covered by the sheet, he lay belly down, his left hand beneath him, his right reaching out to where she ought to be. She had ended up halfway down the bed, at the edge, naked, her hair hanging over the side.

They hadn't made love. They had arrived late, and had drunk too much, celebrating her birthday. The waiter had a face like a youth out of a Caravaggio. They had walked in the September rain along the Via dei Calzaiuoli. Dan had stopped and kissed her in front of everyone. She was thirty-four. They had two children. Beautiful children. She loved her husband and liked her work. So that was all right, then. Another year closer to forty, but life was good.

A moped whined by outside. A young crowd, spilling out onto the piazza, had woken her at three in the morning. Gently, she pulled over the sheet to cover her, and listened hard for his soft breath.

She loved that, the way he breathed so softly in the mornings, and she reached out her fingers to touch lightly his dishevelled hair. It was still thick and brown, though speckled with grey this past year. And his belly had become a little slack. More than a little, actually. That was all right too. It was normal for a man of forty-one. Everything was in its place, and the world spun on its axis.

'You okay?' he mumbled.

She shifted up the bed and put her arms round him, the quick movement stunning her temple.

'Oh, I shouldn't have done that. Don't move too suddenly. It's not nice.'

She stroked his hair into a semblance of tidiness.

'Are we really in Florence for my birthday?'

'Last time I checked.'

He raised himself on his elbows and held her to him.

'Happy birthday, dear Kate.'

They kissed, though the taste was none too pleasant.

'Thank you,' he said, lifting away the hair falling across her face. 'Thank you for everything.'

'You old softie.'

She'd be lost without him too. Maybe she should tell him again that she couldn't imagine life without his easy-going solidity, but she held back, and basked in his compliment.

He wanted it to be her moment. Just hers.

'We stink,' she said, just to make it even better.

'Well, you can't have a good night and not stink afterwards.'

She groaned, and lay on her back, making faces at the ceiling, which had all of six inset lights. She remembered them from the night before, going out like stars.

'We should get up.'

It was six thirty. Of course, Florence was an hour ahead of London, so she had woken too early. When there was no reply, she looked at him, listening to the slow rise and fall of his breath again.

'Lazy sod.'

*

Over breakfast she found it hard to look at anything but black coffee. He was looking intently at the wooden beams in the ceiling.

'Did we pack some aspirin?'

He didn't reply.

'Be a pet and get some, will you? I didn't think it was this bad until we came down.'

She watched him leave the breakfast room. Even now, after all the times she'd told him, he refused to believe he was so handsome. Her mother had often remarked that he was the image of his Irish grandfather, and judging by the photos she'd seen, Deirdre was right. Dan had been in Wexford as a baby, and Elizabeth had liked to boast how her son was heir to half a mountainside, even when Hugh reminded her that the land had long since been sold. It was one of her foibles, and she clung to it till she died.

He returned, and she almost gagged swallowing the pills, but by the time they were ready to venture out she felt reasonably human. Dan too. And the clear sky over the piazza and vibrant colours and the splash of green lifted her completely. Her only inhibition was her lack of Italian, and that made her a whit nervous. But there was no point dwelling on it. She was here, at last, having dreamt of coming since her schooldays.

*

They walked through the open-air market by the Capelle Medicee. Leather bags and clothes, scarves, football jerseys, more leather bags. Endless stalls of leather bags. Dan seemed to know where he was going and she felt a pulse of pleasure as he took her hand. A fine Sunday afternoon, six weeks after Sara Mae was born, slipped into her mind.

The old city was buzzing now, with the inevitable mopeds creating a vaguely menacing racket as they weaved through the narrow streets. Neat ranks of them were parked in hundreds. Maybe they'd make sense in an old city, if it wasn't for the noise.

She admired an African woman dressed in a canary yellow head scarf and dark blue dress. How would those colours look on her? she wondered.

He led her down a street and they scrambled aboard a bus headed to the river. Dan had carefully studied how the system worked, and he relaxed as the machine validated the prepaid tickets first time. They were prepared for the crush too, but not quite well enough, and they glanced at each other in mild panic as the bus turned a corner and they struggled to maintain their balance. It made her feel like a student, and she laughed at the thought. His eyes shone with happiness, reminding her that he only ever seemed happy when she was happy. If she wasn't content, he wasn't content, as if her happiness was his responsibility. It wasn't right, even if it was flattering, and yes, it always touched her. But it wasn't how it should be. He ought to be happy in himself, spontaneously. And yes, she thought guiltily, it would leave her free to be happy in her own right too.

This wasn't the time to dwell on it, though, and she clung to him as he held onto the overhead bar for them both.

After a few stops, they found that they had retreated to the centre of the bus, and in the rush to get off, they gave in to the inevitable and got off too when they spotted the river walls.

She thought of *The Primavera*, the Botticelli painting which she had yearned to see since she was fifteen. It was hard to imagine she would be in its presence in a few minutes. She had tried to copy it many times from reproductions, and especially Mercury in his flimsy scarlet covering and winged boots, nonchalantly ignoring the beauties behind him.

He took her hand again as they stepped into bright sunshine and crossed the road to the river wall. The Ponte Vecchio was in the distance, and they stopped to admire it.

Being an architect, Florence was a delight for Dan. He had often spoken of how Brunelleschi had built the dome of the Cathedral, the Duomo, and she knew he would give a lot to see it, and she would be glad to accompany him; but no, he insisted these few precious hours were hers. His enthusiasm spilled out in describing buildings for her, and his face shone as he talked about the Ponte Vecchio.

It was jammed with tourists, so they continued through the crowds along the narrow road until they reached the Uffizi. They were shocked by the length of the queue. An American woman and her friend broke from it in frustration, muttering that no art, not even great art, was worth standing for four hours.

'Four hours?' Kate shook her head. 'It's too much.'

'But you've come all this way to see it!'

6

'I know. I know. But four hours. I don't think so.'

'Maybe we can book for later? Dammit, we should have booked.'

'Never mind. Do you want to go back to the Ponte Vecchio?'

'No,' he said. 'Let's go to the San Marco to see the Fra Angelicos.'

'All right. Let's do that, then.'

A street seller had a basket of posters, including a large one of *The Primavera*. She stopped to look at it wistfully. Mercury looked more handsome than she had remembered, but Primavera herself looked wonderful in her flower-patterned dress, scattering petals as she went, bringing the joys of spring. She was tall and fair and graceful, and it struck her that, like the other figures, she did not look Italian, or at least her idea of Italian. Neither did Venus, Life herself, directing operations, governing the universe. There was something about the painting that had always puzzled her and, deprived of the real thing, she looked hard at this large poster, determined to solve the mystery.

And then it hit her, and she laughed out loud. The street seller, who looked like a student, gave her a strange look.

'What's so funny?' Dan asked quietly.

'It's the apples.'

'What about them?'

'Well, they're not apples, after all. I always thought they were apples, even though it's spring.'

'Oh.' He broke into a relieved smile. 'Well, that's artists for you.'

'They're bloody flowers.'

'Yes, that sounds more like spring, I would have thought,' he said, putting his arm across her shoulder. 'And who are these three beauties here?'

'The Three Graces.'

'And the geezer in the trees making a grab for the nubile blonde?'

'Zephyr, the wind, pursuing Flora. Do you see his wings? Nice little glade, isn't it.'

7

'And that's Cupid up at the top, I suppose.'

'Yes, that's Cupid.'

'Something weird about them, isn't there?'

The street vendor was looking from one of them to the other, so Dan bought the poster.

They walked across Piazza della Signoria, stopping to see the imposing sculptures of Neptune and David. A Japanese wedding party came around from the side, preceded by Renaissance guards armed with pikes, the mother of the bride doing her best to keep her daughter's train off the ground. Suddenly tourists were clicking this romantic scene, rather than themselves, in front of the statues.

*

Once he saw the Museo di San Marco, Dan couldn't contain himself any longer and rattled on about it.

'Michelozzo built this. Well, he built part of it, restored the older monastery for Cosimo. And wait till you see the cloisters and the cells! The simplicity of it! Sorry,' he said then. 'I should let you see it for yourself.'

'Don't be an idiot,' she said. 'It's great that you know about the building. It puts the work in context for me.'

'Really? Well in that case, you might not get me to shut up.'

This queue took only half an hour. They entered the cloister and, despite the presence of tourists like herself, she immediately felt the spiritual quality of its proportions, and stopped to take it in. There were flower beds and a lovely old tree in the middle of the courtyard.

'This is Michelozzo's San Antonio cloister. And the tree is a Lebanon cedar, in case you were wondering.'

'Yes, I was wondering.'

The rhythm of the columns which supported the cloister was almost sensuous, and the tree in the centre of the garden was perfect, as if it held its exquisiteness to the earth.

They went upstairs to the dormitory cells where Fra Angelico painted his scenes from the life of Christ.

The one she most wanted to see was *The Annunciation*, which she had stared at in books many times. She assumed it was a small fresco in a cell, and nothing had prepared her for it as she turned at the top of the stairs.

'Oh my God, there it is,' she said, gripping Dan's arm.

They took the last few steps to where it was, on the outside wall of a row of cells, and stood looking in wonder at its unearthly beauty as groups came before it and drifted away.

'It's much bigger than I thought.'

'Just look at the depth of field, and the symmetry and rhythm of those columns,' Dan said.

'I never realized the angel's wings had those colours.'

'I thought angels' wings were white.'

'They're like a rainbow from another world.'

She wasn't religious as such, but the fresco gave her a woman's sympathy for the Virgin.

'She's like a convent girl,' she said.

'Maybe she was.'

'A young nun, do you mean? Look at the light from her bodice!'

'You'd almost need sunglasses. It's coming from the angel, of course. She's like the moon, reflecting sunlight.'

'That beautiful dark blue of the coat draped over her knees – and what shade of green is the lining? It's fainter than I thought.'

'It's like what you find under old wallpaper.'

'How could you say such a thing!'

He shrugged.

'Do you see the silica sparkling in the light from the window? Just look at it from side on.'

'Oh yes!' Oh yes ... This tiny detail, which she would have missed, transformed her identification with the fresco, flooding her with an excitement in which she forgot herself completely.

Many of the other frescoes were disappointing, but she loved the *Noli Me Tangere*, where Christ appeared to Mary Magdalen, and *The Transfiguration* and *The Coronation of the Virgin*, but what transfixed her was *The Mocking of Christ*. Christ was seated on a throne, blindfolded, holding a staff and orb. A disembodied head spat at him. On the steps in front of him sat a woman, presumably Mary, and on the other side was a Dominican monk, reading his office with an almost callous detachment from the drama behind him.

'That incredible light again,' she said, remembering *The Annunciation*.

'No reflection this time.'

'No. This is the Sun King, after all.'

Yet it was a king for whom one could have a contemporary sympathy. The composition, the virtuality of it, the dark psychological complexity, ensured that.

They ambled through more cells, admiring *The Ascension*, but eventually an exchanged glance agreed that, having seen the great masterpieces, the lesser frescoes only diminished their satisfaction. They came back again to *The Annunciation*. She couldn't get it out of her head: this girl had been told that she was to be the mother of God. She closed her eyes tight, trying to comprehend the enormity of such a revelation, but it was beyond her. All she could do was revere the beauty of the fresco, its light, its perfect poise, the great gift of the artist brought to bear on a sacred, ancient and living theme. She knew something of the history leading to his achievement, and had probably witnessed some of it in the cells, but it was as if it had come from nowhere, from beyond Fra Angelico himself.

They went downstairs, bypassing the shop for the moment to spend some time in the cloister. They strolled around to the Pilgrim's Hospice, the name of which intrigued her. There were darker, more conventional paintings here, and she didn't want to linger, but suddenly Dan pulled her towards him.

'What is it?' she asked.

'There's something odd about this one,' he said, looking at a small painting no bigger than a large book.

She looked at it with him but could find nothing odd.

'Did you notice that one of the sick man's legs is black?'

'Oh, you're right.'

Dan had his guidebook out again and found the reference.

'You're not going to believe this,' he said.

'What?'

'I'm not making this up, I promise. It says here that these bright sparks are the Arabian Saints Cosmas and Damian, twin brothers and physicians, and they're curing someone called Justinian who had lost his leg, by replacing it with one from a black man.'

'No!'

'Limb transplant before its time. I know someone who'd like their number.'

'They were martyred, you know. In the third century. Look, their burial is in this other one here.'

'Let's go,' he said. 'It's giving me the willies.'

They went back to the shop and, as well as cards, she bought some reproductions of *The Annunciation*, the *Noli Me Tangere* and *The Mocking of Christ*. Then they went into the late afternoon city to shop for the family.

She hadn't thought of herself as a shopper, but she enjoyed the atmosphere, the sheer Italian style of it all. They went back to the open market near their hotel. The children were easy enough to buy for. Jim wanted a Fiorentina football jersey, number 9, and she spotted a Leonardo bicycle T-shirt for Sara Mae.

'I could get used to this,' she said.

'That's what I'm afraid of.'

'Now now, don't turn husband on me.'

He was enjoying it as much as she was, or maybe he was enjoying it so much only because she was enjoying it so much. Leave it, she thought. Don't spoil this perfect time, and she drifted back into the uncomplicated pleasure of it.

'Let's have something to eat,' he said.

They ended up in a bar where they had to stand, eating a cheese roll, and the beer came from a barrel. It revived them for a while, but as the shops closed they headed back to the hotel for a rest.

As they turned from the stairs into reception, Kate caught her breath. A tall, fair young woman was at the desk, and she smiled as she handed Dan the key.

For an absurd moment, Kate imagined her in a floral dress, scattering petals on her way.

'Are you thinking what I'm thinking?' she asked him once they were in the narrow lift.

'That depends on what you're thinking.'

'Isn't she the image of Primavera?'

'Well, yes. Maybe not the image, but certainly reminiscent.'

'Isn't she beautiful?'

They reached the second floor.

'Yes. More beautiful than Primavera, in my humble opinion.' He opened the door to their room.

'Well, you've got to tell her.'

'Tell her? Tell her what?'

'You've got to tell her that she's more beautiful than Botticelli's Primavera.'

'Eh? You can't be serious.'

'I'm deadly serious,' she said, smiling.

'Florence has gone to your head, Kate,' he said as she closed the door after them. 'I'm a married man, remember? Married to you, in fact. She'll think I'm trying to cheat on you.'

'No, she won't. Well, maybe, but you've got to do it. Here,' she said, taking some paper out of her bag. 'Leave her a note.'

'This is ridiculous, Kate,' he said, taking the paper and pen from her and sitting on the bed. 'What do you want me to do this for, anyway?'

'She could have been the model for *The Primavera*, couldn't she?'

'Yes, but that was painted five hundred years ago.'

'That's the point. Imagine, there was a woman just like her, the same features, the same serenity, the same kind of beauty, five hundred years ago. Isn't that wonderful?'

'Yes, I suppose it is. It's only several generations, when you think of it.'

He wrote.

'Let me see?'

Signorina, you are more beautiful than Botticelli's Prima-vera.

'Perfect. Now go down to reception and hand it to her.'

'I think you need to be Italian to pull this off,' he said with a sigh.

Delighted, she watched him as he walked along the corridor and took the stairs instead of the lift.

He returned almost immediately and she made a face.

'You didn't do it, did you?'

'She's not on. There's a man at reception.'

'Well, just leave it for her.'

'He could be her husband.'

'So? You'd be thrilled if someone paid me a compliment like that, wouldn't you?'

He raised his eyes to the ceiling.

'Well, wouldn't you?'

'Yes, of course. So long as I didn't think he had plans to seduce you.'

'Hmm,' she said doubtfully. 'Maybe you're right. Well, we tried.'

'Let's have a nap, shall we?'

*

He lay on his front, his eyes on his arm, and she watched him for a while before taking her notebook and lying down too, propping her chin on her hand, intending to write up a diary of the morning.

Her drowsiness caught up with her, and she lay across the crook of her arm – just like Dan did, she thought, too late.

*

She woke to his touch, and looked up to see him fresh and relaxed. As he cleaned himself for the evening, she watched him through the open bathroom door. He hummed as he shaved, some ridiculous booby-boo, and she couldn't help smiling. That's what husbands were for, to make you smile. But he seemed to know that too.

13

She dragged herself off the bed when he was finished, and got into the shower. As the water soaked her, she revived, and soaping her breasts and belly felt good. Unless one of them blew it, they were going to have a fine time tonight.

*

Dan wanted to book one of the restaurants recommended in his guide but she wanted to go back to the one they had stumbled on the night before. She liked it because, like the hotel, it was plain and friendly, and while it was old, it had no pretensions about it.

The Caravaggio waiter knew their measure now, and suggested an aperitif.

Dan ordered a white wine, a Galestro, which she had never heard of. How did he know about that? Oh, of course, his guidebook. But still . . .

And he never drank white wine. It gave him heartburn, but she preferred it to red, which gave her headaches even before a hangover. So he drank beer, usually, but not tonight, and he raised his glass to toast her.

'Here's to the next thirty-four, when you'll be more beautiful than ever.'

They tinkled their glasses and smiled at each other like they hadn't done in a while. It was delicious and perfectly cool. Sometimes pleasure did amount to happiness. But then, as so often happened when she became aware of being happy, doubt slipped in. Would they still be together in thirty-four years – or even four? He'd be hitting the male menopause in a few years, after all. That old fear.

Damn!

Here she was, the one who was blowing it. She sipped some more and smiled.

'This is lovely, Dan. Was it recommended in the guide?'

'Read your menu,' he said, pleased. 'I checked it with Paola and Paolo, if you must know.'

'Oh, how nice. How are they?'

'Very well. Asking for you and wondering when we'll visit Tivoli.'

14

What a nice touch, she thought. He must have rung Paola and Paolo from London. He had it all thought out.

'The *capsula violetta*, the violet capsule, is the important bit, apparently.'

'I'm impressed.'

The waiter put their *bruschetta* before them. It was laden with tomatoes drenched in olive oil, and she crunched into it. She followed it with *prosciutto con melone*, and finished with fresh *pecorino* and *cantucci* dipped in *vin santo*. It was the words she couldn't resist, as much as the food itself. The novelty and style charmed her, her tongue happily cataloguing the succession of surprises, contrasts. She was by now quite pleasantly drunk.

An old lady came into the restaurant and Kate turned to watch her bustle in. As she appeared eccentric and poor, she expected her to be thrown out, and was surprised when the Caravaggio waiter bowed and greeted her with ceremony.

'Did you see that?'

Dan looked around for a moment.

The old lady was led to her table, and a litre of beer was placed before her. The proprietor opened a packet of cigarettes and leaned across his counter to offer it. With delicacy, she took one and the waiter lit it for her, and she puffed happily. At peace, the old lady drank her beer and smoked until her pizza arrived with the same ceremony as before. The waiter served her with finesse, and she accepted it as her due.

Kate's eyes misted over as she and Dan resumed their tête-à-tête.

As they lingered over their digestif, the old lady finished her meal and left, puffing on a fresh cigarette and escorted by the waiter to the door. Kate noticed that the waiter then spoke with quiet courtesy to a lone Japanese girl, his tenderness for the old lady still with him.

*

One part of her wanted to walk among the evening crowds along Via dei Calzaiuoli, but a stronger feeling steered them back to the hotel. On the surface, they seemed like a relaxed married couple, smiling and polite as Dan asked for their key at the desk. But too many pleasures had accumulated during the day. Though they held hands and looked into each other's eyes in the cramped lift, their calm demeanour lasted until he let her into their room and, switching on the lights, she turned to see him leaning back against the door, staring at her. She let go of everything, only her reflexes keeping her standing. He stepped forward and lightly touched her cheek, as if he was almost sure it would burn him. Her mouth was open, her tongue tip lightly pressed against her teeth. His too. He unbuttoned her skirt and it drifted over her flesh to the floor. She looked down and stepped out of it, casting it aside with her foot.

When she looked up again, his gaze had dropped to her thighs. It was too much, and she sprang at him, tearing off his jacket and shirt. In their furious tussle, they stripped each other and, stretched along the floor, they kissed each other ferociously.

She was blind ego, absorbed in the delightful pools spreading across her body under his hands. She clawed at him, caressed him too – but it was all to heighten her own gratification.

Then he slowed, and stopped, and guided her to the bed. Dazed, she followed him, shaking. She was trembling from her hair roots to her toenails. How could he have stopped? She felt weak and powerful at the same time. She knew what he wanted to do. He wanted to kiss her all over and then go down on her. He knew she liked that, but she didn't want it now, and surprised him by turning him over on his back and sucking like a vampire on his neck. He groaned, and, breathing heavily, she looked up at his closed eyes and pulled hard on a fistful of hair and tenderly kissed his lips, slipping the tip of her tongue between them. She was going to reverse what he had intended for her.

As she moved down, she shushed him with a finger on his lips, hoping as she sucked on his heart nipple that he remembered when she had done this before, and that the memory would intensify his expectation. She moved up to look at his face again. A purplish bruise was rising under her love bite. She could remember when such brutality in her would have appalled her, but now she relished it, and as a counterpoint she kissed his eyelids. He loved that, the old softie. There, she thought, licking them slowly again, that's for bringing me to Florence for my birthday. She nibbled at his earlobes, and slowly her tongue entered his ear. He gasped and she smiled. There you are, sir. That's for putting me first in everything today. Scenes from the day passed through her, all the love sacrifices he had made for her, from waiting patiently while she stared at he knew not what, to choosing a wine that gave him heartburn, for her sake. Then she embarked on her slow journey down his body, pausing often to reward him deliciously for each gesture he had made.

TWO

London, October to December 1997

They flew into dense rain clouds over the English Channel.

'Oh dear, we're home.'

She pressed her nose against the window, not really minding the prospect of low grey skies or damp clothes. Dan was stuck in an English newspaper. The sports page. She glanced at the plaster covering his love bite, and turned back to the window. He had made her go to a pharmacy to get some plasters. She had teased him about it when they woke, and he had laughed, but once he saw it for himself in the mirror, he was mortified. Fortunately he could claim he had cut himself shaving. For all his love of gadgets, he refused to use an electric shaver.

They landed smoothly, and yes, Heathrow was dull. Already she was mentally organizing the children and preparing her class for the following day. They took the tube to King's Cross and a taxi home to Islington. The rain lifted as she became absorbed in the hiss of tyres and easy familiarity with the streets. It was as if they had never been away – although not quite. Dan still held her hand as they talked through practicalities. It would be better if he collected the children on his own while she got on with things, but in the end they decided to go together just to keep the sense of occasion. Once inside the door, their luggage still in the hall, they both stopped to savour the silence and they laughed and held each other.

'Might as well enjoy it while we can,' he said, running his finger in a very nice way up her spine.

'Thank you, Dan.'

For once he had allowed her to thank him, and she closed her eyes, feeling only the pleasure of holding and being held.

They put the cases under the stairs, rang Deirdre and drove to collect the children.

'Can we put the weekend in a nutshell for them?'

'I'd rather you didn't.' He laughed.

'No, dear,' she said, looking out the window, 'I didn't mean that. I mean ... Florence! Firenze! ... They'll want to know everything. "We had the most *wonderful* time ... looking at frescoes." I can see their faces when we tell them that ...'

'Why don't we just tell them about the saints and the black man's leg?'

'Wouldn't it give them nightmares?'

'Nightmares?' He snorted. 'Our little darlings? The more gore the better they like it, would be my guess.'

*

Terry greeted them, and Sara Mae pushed out from behind him into her father's arms.

'Did you bring us presents?'

'Did we bring you presents, Sara Mae? Why would we bring you presents?' Dan said loftily.

Jim smiled and Kate ruffled his hair.

'What did you bring, Daddy?'

'Well, some lovely sweets all the way from Florence, for a start,' Dan said, letting Sara Mae down.

'After dinner, then,' Deirdre said, coming into the hall and, kissing Kate and Dan lightly, she led the family into the kitchen.

'You had a good trip, I can see,' she said, busying herself as they sat into the table.

'Oh, wonderful,' Kate said, fussing over the children. 'Unforgettable, actually.'

'What happened to your neck?' Deirdre asked Dan, concentrating on serving out the dinner.

'Eh...' Dan mumbled, smiling faintly as he felt his neck. 'I cut myself shaving.'

Despite knowing this would happen, Kate blushed like a girl. She had been the one who was proud of it, and yet here he was, bragging with the merest of smirks, while she felt as if she had been caught out in some shameful secret.

'Still can't convince you to take up the electric razor,' Terry said as he tucked into his peas. He was from Galway and his accent always came back when he was making fun.

'Naw.' There was a plop as Dan uncorked one of the bottles they'd brought home. He stood up to lean across the table and pour. 'You know me and modern technology, Terry,' he said.

'Can I have some?' Jim asked.

Sara Mae held out her glass, with her wide-eyed, irresistible look as Dan hesitated.

'Oh, all right, then,' he said, pouring, 'just a teeny bit.'

'I asked first,' Jim protested.

'Shush, Jim,' Kate admonished. 'And fill up the glass with water.'

'Well, I did.'

'You might as well give them more,' Deirdre said. 'Make them sleep. They've been wired to the moon all day.'

Dan queried Kate with a raised eyebrow. Jim was nine, but Sara Mae was only six, and she could foresee exactly what would happen. She shrugged, so he half filled the glasses.

'See?' Sara Mae beamed at Jim. 'I got more.'

'You didn't!'

'Ugh!' Sara Mae said as she tasted it. 'That's horrible.'

'I like mine,' Jim said, trying to convince himself.

Kate filled their glasses with water.

'Now try it. And stop fighting.'

'So, what did you do there?' Deirdre asked. Again, that subtle teasing.

Kate recounted their walks, the surprising rain, her joy at seeing *The Annunciation* and, as an aside, her pleasure at Dan's patience and support. This time, to her relief, there was no bravado; only a look of contentment that seemed to spread from Dan to her parents.

'We saw one very strange painting,' Dan said, addressing the adults, but then turning directly to the children. 'This poor man had his leg cut off, but two saints healed him by putting a black man's leg in its place.'

Sara Mae's face darkened. Uh-oh.

'Why did he have his leg cut off?'

'I don't know,' Dan admitted, obviously regretting he had mentioned it.

'And more to the point,' Jim said in that adult way he was trying to adopt recently, 'how did the black man get his leg cut off?'

'I don't know, Jim. He was probably killed in a battle.'

'There was a lovely garden in that museum,' Kate interrupted. 'Tell them about the tree, Dan. What was it called?'

'That's right,' Dan said, relieved. Jim was interested in trees, so he drew out the description as long as he could. The diversion seemed to work, especially as Sara Mae asked if there had been flowers too.

While Dan talked himself out of trouble, Kate saw that her mother was looking exceptionally well and bubbling with good humour. A worry had lifted, of course, when the lump on her breast turned out to be benign, and morale, more than any hormone replacement, kept a person young. Still, it was hard to believe she was actually so young at fifty-three, a grandmother at forty-four. She had been only eighteen when she met Terry, who was seven years older, and had fallen for him so quickly that Kate was born ten months later. When Kate had asked her about it, when she was fifteen or so, Deirdre had dreamily told her that it had been his Galway accent which sunk her. Deirdre's own father was still alive in Clare, so Irish accents were close to her heart. It had been a good match against the odds, just as Dan and herself had turned out to be. Terry's recurrent joke was that it was incest, a game for all the family, as Kate's grandmother, Sarah, had married Dan's grandfather, Brendan, shortly before he died in the 50s. Dan had been named after Brendan, but his mother had persisted in calling him Dan Stevie, after her brothers who had been killed in the war.

Sara Mae's eyes were drooping and Jim was becoming garrulous, despite the dilution of the wine.

'It's time we brought them home.'

Sara Mae turned instinctively to Dan and he lifted her into his arms.

As they gathered to say goodbye in the hall, Kate noticed that her father's arm was round her mother's waist.

He, too, looked much younger since the reprieve.

*

Once the children were in bed, she made some cocoa and, while Dan watched TV, she sat on the sofa with him, her feet tucked beneath her, and went through the posters and postcards of the frescoes and paintings. *The Primavera* was no longer her favourite, now that she had seen the actual *Annunciation*. How could a woman feel sane knowing she had a god growing inside her? Would she not go mad thinking about it, the meaning of it, the implications? How would she feel having it announced? Wasn't it a kind of divine rape? She vaguely remembered the old Greek stories of gods raping maidens. The sheer terror of it . . . when all you wanted to be was human and ordinary, taking your chances with an ordinary mortal – who preferably *looked* like a god, of course. She glanced at Dan. She could see he was in zombieland and fading. A yawn caught her unawares.

'Come on,' she said. 'You've to get to the site early.'

'Oh God,' he moaned, stretching and making a face.

*

Dan was gone when she got up the next morning. She had presumed that starting back after her break would be difficult, but she was fine and the children were no more sluggish than usual and, thankfully, not hungover. She sing-songed them awake over breakfast. It was a fine morning, which helped, and by the time she dropped them off at school they were in full flight.

She caught a bus and double-backed to Hackney.

*

Life proceeded as it was supposed to until she missed a period, and foul morning sickness forced her to admit she was pregnant. That hadn't been on the menu at all.

'Oh well,' Dan said when she confirmed what they'd both suspected, 'life's little tricks,' and he held her tight.

'Shit,' she said. 'Shit.'

'Yes, lots of that,' he said. 'Just when we thought the landslide was over.'

She broke from him, laughing and crying at the same time.

He leaned back his head, putting his fingers through his hair.

'It was *that* night, I suppose.'

'Yes. We've been careful ever since.'

'Ironically. Will you tell Deirdre and Terry just yet?'

She put her hand to her mouth as the old pain of her first, early miscarriage was suddenly there, as if it had never gone. Her eyes filled as she looked at him, the shadow of pain on his face too. She cleared her throat and steadied herself.

'When we're sure, I suppose. And we'd better tell the children first, really.'

'Yes ...'

'What about Hugh?'

'It can wait till he comes back at Christmas.'

'Do you think he's really going to stay in Wexford – when he's so fond of the children?'

'Well, your mother's convinced he will. He's talked about that bloody mountain as long as I can remember.'

Sara Mae came in to have her homework checked and Kate absently looked through it.

'That seems fine, darling.'

Sara Mae took her copies without comment, and switched on the TV, kneeling on the carpet to watch it.

*

She had intended waiting until she visited again, to stretch out the time as much as possible, but one evening she felt weepy and on the spur of the moment she reached out for the phone and rang Deirdre as Dan looked on.

'Deirdre? I'm pregnant.'

She wasn't surprised.

'No?'

No. She had recognized the look on her face after the weekend in Florence.

'What look?'

Oh, that contented look. The body knew when it had got its own way, even when the mind thought otherwise.

'Are you pleased?' Kate asked anxiously.

Of course she was pleased. Wasn't she?

'Yes, of course. I'm delighted. We're delighted. It's just that I'm tired.'

Deirdre called Terry to the phone. He took it in his stride, as usual. Deirdre had predicted it, he said, and Kate wasn't sure if she liked that or not. They chatted for a while.

'My bloody mother says she knew the moment we came back,' Kate said as she hung up.

'Oh?'

'She knew. The witch knew.'

'Well, she trained as a midwife, didn't she?'

'Yes, but . . .' She shivered. 'Someone knowing your most intimate business before you know it yourself . . . It's a bit spooky, that's all. Disgusting, even.'

'Come here,' he said, holding out his arm and she moaned over into its comfort. 'Forget about it. She's your mother, not some nosy neighbour. It's just one of her harmless pleasures.'

'Maybe . . .'

It bothered her, though, even if she knew it was part of a confusion of feelings she couldn't articulate.

They now felt they had to tell the children. Jim didn't look too pleased but said nothing and they didn't press him. He'd get used to it in his own time just as he had with Sara Mae. Sara Mae was inquisitive but, after a day or so, seemed to forget about it.

The following Sunday Kate came downstairs and looked into the front room to see Dan sitting in the bay of the window, which caught the late afternoon sunlight. He was playing computer chess, and his innocent hobby became part of her jumble of resentment, even as she hated herself for the injustice of it.

She had her love of music and art and he had his martial art and chess.

It took them out of themselves, and what could be more natural?

*

She settled down again. It wasn't as if she hadn't been through all this before, and experience did help in the end. The Christmas lights went up in the High Street, reminding her that the year was almost gone. At long last, she got an enlarged laser copy of *The Annunciation* and Blu-Tacked it to the living-room wall, laughing at the irony. You think of something as happening to someone else, like getting cancer or winning the lottery, and then, in the most baffling way, it has happened to you. She shuddered. Whatever about a god or goddess growing inside her, at least it wasn't cancer. At least it was life; a force for life. She looked back at the copy of the fresco, grateful that she could look at it for its beauty. Art for art's sake. And then her mind wandered back to her young pupils. A lot of her teaching them was through art. Perhaps she should show them a Christmas painting, to refer in some neutral way to Christmas. Christmas was happening all around them, even if it was devoid of religious content for the most part. Then they could paint their own Wise Kings.

She browsed through her art books, grateful for the excuse and, finally taking several, she threw them on the floor and knelt to flick through them at random.

'Mummy, what are you doing?'

'Oh!' She looked up, startled. 'Sara Mae . . . I'm looking for a picture.'

'Can I help?'

'Help? Yes! Yes, you can, as a matter of fact.'

Sara Mae knelt beside her.

'What are you looking for?'

'Oh yes, of course. Silly me. Ahhmm . . . Baby Jesus.'

'Is it for Christmas?'

'Well, yes. It's for school. My infants, really, but if we find a nice one we can put it up here too.'

Sara Mae immediately became absorbed in the search. She was a good artist, Kate thought. She was still at that age when a lot of children seemed good, but Sara Mae had something more. Perhaps she would actually be an artist one day, and the thought made her smile. She had wanted to be an artist herself, but hadn't what it took. But maybe, the next generation . . . In a book on the Uffizi, she found an *Adoration* by Dürer with a young black king. He was obviously a youth, and obviously painted from life, which intrigued her. Were there black people in Renaissance Germany? She hadn't thought of that before, associating Africans in Europe with slavery. And surely slavery didn't happen until much later?

Sara Mae tapped her on the arm and pointed to a perfect *Adoration*, and to her astonishment it had a magnificent black king.

'Oh,' Kate breathed, 'you're a genius. Who's the painter?'

Sara Mae turned over the cover. Bosch! Hieronymus Bosch!

But he was the one who painted all those mad, hallucinogenic paintings that the hippies used to love! She had no idea he had painted such a serene *Adoration*, or had forgotten.

'Thank you. Thank you,' she said, putting her arm round Sara Mae.

'Would you like me to find another?'

'No, love. That's fine.'

'Okay,' Sara Mae said brightly, escaping from her arm

and skipping away to go to her room, leaving Kate faintly disappointed.

She looked closely at the handsome black king. He was younger than he looked at first sight, but he wasn't a boy, like in the Dürer, but a fine, noble man – most convincingly a king. She looked in amazement at his superbly painted white finery, and the ring of precious stone hanging from his right ear.

Magi. The word stopped her. It was one she had always taken for granted. Mage was the singular, wasn't it? She took down her *Concise Oxford*.

Magi pl. of MAGUS.

'Magus, let's see . . .'

1. a member of a priestly caste of ancient Persia.
2. a sorcerer.

A sorcerer! The Magi were sorcerers?

3. (the (three) Magi) the 'wise men' from the East who brought gifts to the infant Christ. (Matt.2.1–12) [Middle English via Latin and Greek from old Persian magus]

Sorcerers. She looked up 'sorcerer'. No surprise there. She browsed back until her eye fell on

mage. 1. a magician. 2. a wise and learned person. [Middle English, Anglicized from MAGUS]

She looked at the Dürer and Bosch reproductions. So the Three Wise Men were magicians. She checked 'magician'. No, it came from a different root, but perhaps 'wise' and 'magician' meant, or could mean, the same in ancient times. Magician in a much higher sense than doing party tricks. After all, she reasoned, science was descended from alchemy, and that largely from magic, and certainly the things that science and technology could do in the here and now seemed like magic a lot of the time. And when she thought of it, the Magi were astronomers – how else could they have known about the Star of Bethlehem? She looked at Bosch's Mage again. This was a man wise beyond words, and surely a benevolent sorcerer.

Dan came in from his Tae Kwon Do, looking tired and absent-minded.

'Have you seen this?' she asked, holding up the Bosch to him. 'Sara Mae found it for me.'

'Hmm!' He looked at it more closely.

'What do you think?'

'Sara Mae has a good eye.' He *hmmed* again before going to put his things away. 'You should do a thesis on it,' was his parting shot from the stairs.

Did he mean on this painting, or Renaissance art – or on black subjects in Renaissance art? she wondered, remembering the picture of the saints healing the amputee with a black man's leg. She looked at the blow-up of *The Annunciation* on the wall. She was so ignorant of the meaning of things. The meaning of symbols and the meaning behind words she took for granted, the associations they linked back to, their history. Just as the Virgin was ignorant. Yet the Virgin had one advantage over her: she was humble in her ignorance, and in accepting her fate.

The next day she had a colour blow-up made of the centre panel of the Bosch *Adoration* during her lunch hour. It came out very well, so she decided to get a close-up of the black Mage.

What was it he held in offering? Gold, frankincense or myrrh? The sumptuous words came back to her like a mantra. And what was that bird, standing on the dispenser, and was it eating a berry or vomiting blood? Was it a phoenix? Suddenly she was glad she would show it only to children, who were hopefully more ignorant than herself.

Deep in such thoughts, she walked back to the school and was startled to see a tall black man in his white native costume striding towards her. She stopped and stared as he walked past, then coughed hard to cover her embarrassment. Thankfully he had been so absorbed in his own thoughts that he hadn't noticed, or so she hoped, but she found herself looking about her for a security camera.

'This is ridiculous,' she said aloud.

Back in the din of the school, she chatted with her colleague Fiona over tea and sandwiches, for once grateful for the banal normality of their conversation. She liked Fiona. She had a brother in the army in Germany, and she'd come out with some anti-Irish remarks when the IRA had killed British soldiers there, but no worse than what Dan had gone on with. Still, despite her accent and her Englishness, it was one reason Kate used her married name, which everyone, even her own children, pronounced Kin*sell*a. That got on Hugh's nerves. But to use her own name, O'Flaherty, would most probably be like waving an Irish tricolour.

When Fiona wandered off, Kate took the laser copy to the toilet, the only place in the school that was reasonably private.

How magnificent he was in his white robes! And it was a pearl hanging from his right ear. He wore a ring, but she couldn't make out what it represented. His necklace was gold. His collar had a white – what did they call that? a fraise? – a white fraise flowing back from his neck which accentuated his grace.

The bell rang, and as her eyes lingered on the picture she noticed, discreetly behind him and at the very edge of the centre panel, his black page, dressed in red.

She thanked Margaret for looking after them over lunch, and gathered her bits and pieces.

'Now, children,' she said as they settled into their tiny tables. 'As you know, it's coming up to Christmas.' She looked at the black and coloured faces among them. Few, including the white children, were Christian, of course, but then, the Magi weren't Christian either. And they talked about the feasts of other cultures, when they came round the calendar, so why was she nervous? Would they notice what had struck her so forcibly – was she using them, in fact? She looked into their expectant faces and knew it was too late to drop the subject.

'So I thought you might like to see a picture of the Three Wise Kings from the East, coming to adore the baby Christ.'

Their innocent faces brightened with interest. Why, she asked herself again, was she so nervous? She took a deep breath as she unrolled the copy of the centre panel and stuck it to a board. They talked about it for a while, she emphasizing that the Kings had come from the East and from Africa. The implications only dawned on her as she spoke. Dürer and Bosch, at least, had no problem with depicting an African as not only a king, but an astronomer. How interesting. The realization encouraged her to show them the blow-up of the black king.

'Now,' she said. 'I really like his clothes. What do you think?'

There was a chorus of approval.

'He's cool,' an Asian girl said, and Kate laughed, delighted.

'Yes, he is, isn't he? Would you like to wear clothes like that, Charles?' she asked a conservatively dressed black boy.

'No, miss.'

'Why not?'

He shrugged, and Kate felt nervous again. 'Well, why should you?' she asked, shrugging lightly herself and moving on quickly.

'He looks very sad,' a girl said out of the blue. Kate swung round to the picture as if the child had discovered it was pornographic.

'Do you know, you're right, Sally! He's very sad.' And he was looking into the distance, as if mentally he was elsewhere, far away.

'Why do you think that is?'

'Because he's far from home,' a Turkish girl said.

'Yes. Yes, Afife. I think you're right.' Afife often had a similar look, which she got from her father.

Far from being beyond them, the children understood the picture better than she had done, and she shook her head, surprised by them yet again, as they bent over drawing paper and began to create their own Wise Men. She felt she had accomplished something intangible but very real, and it buoyed her.

*

Christmas crept up, as it always did, despite the rush and crush that she hated. A few days before it, Hugh rang. Dan answered, and mimed to her that he was back from Ireland. Good. She liked her father-in-law, and the children adored him, and the more grandparents they had around at Christmas the better.

She brought home her blow-up of *The Adoration* and Blu-Tacked it onto the wall beside *The Annunciation*. She stood back to admire it, then looked closely at the blow-up of the black Mage. She kept noticing fascinating details and this time it was the ornate silver thurible and its gold chain. On its surface, three figures were lining up, the first on bended knee to offer gifts to a king. Why were there three – and not four, or two?

Hugh arrived on Christmas Eve, laden with presents and full of the joys of life, chasing the children round the front room until they were screaming with delight. Kate and Dan looked at each other. It would probably take the children hours to settle, but apart from them, the man was nearly seventy and he was acting like a seven-year-old. Of course, he would suffer for it later, but he would take himself to Deirdre who would indulge his aches and pains.

Over supper he enthused about the house he now joint-owned with a cousin and his cousin's partner, or lover as he called her.

'Well, Kate, you never saw the like. It's all made of glass. Sitting out in the middle of a bog and you wouldn't know it was there until you were up against it. And then, inside, it's as bright as a shilling, all year round.'

'And it's solar powered,' Kate confirmed.

'All solar powered,' he agreed in wonder. 'In the middle of a rain-swept bog. Mungo's young fella, Aidan – you met

31

him – plugs in his computer when he's there – a little yoke not much bigger than a magazine – and he sits there, and not a word of a lie, the whole world comes to him. In the middle of an Irish bog!' He threw back his head and laughed. 'Hah!'

'He has a notebook?' Jim asked, impressed.

'No, Jim lad. A computer,' Hugh explained patiently.

'No, I mean a notebook computer, one you can carry around under your arm.'

'Oh, I get you. Is that what they're called? Well now. That's what he has. He says to me, "What would you like me to find for you, Hugh?" So I think for a second and say, "Get me a map of the London Underground." And do you know what? He has it there before my eyes in full colour quicker than you'd get a map out of your pocket.'

'Wow.' Jim was fascinated, and Kate and Dan looked conspiratorially at each other.

'What do you think of that, Sara Mae?'

She beamed at her grandfather.

'And you should see the flowers Nuala has,' Hugh said.

'Really?' Dan asked stiffly.

'Them flowers they grow in glasshouses: take any one of them and you could grow them in that house no bother.'

'I see.'

'You should give up building shopping centres, Dan.'

'Gotta make a crust, you know.'

'Ah crust, me arse! The future is solar!'

Kate nearly choked on her Stilton, but stifled her laughter for Dan's sake. Poor Dan. The future might be solar, which he knew a lot about, in fact, but he had to do what supported them in the here and now.

'Nuala is the architect, isn't she?' Kate managed.

'That's right. She's shacked up with Mungo.'

'What does "shacked up" mean?' Sara Mae, like Jim, enjoying her grandfather's merriness, wanted to know.

'They're living together,' Dan said curtly. 'What's a solar architect doing in the middle of a bog? There can't be much demand for her services around Hollyfort and Croghan.'

'Give it time,' Hugh said. 'Give it time. No, she commutes

all over the place. Uses the computer yokamabob to get clients.'

'The Web,' Jim said.

'The very thing.'

'And what will you do all day?' Dan asked mildly. 'Water Nuala's flowers?'

'Well,' Hugh said, taking a generous draught of wine, 'my compost heap is doing nicely, thank you, so I should start my organic garden in the spring.'

'Are you really going to settle there? After all these years here in London?' Kate asked him.

'Yes,' he said, sobered by the question and glancing at the children. 'You'll come and visit me, won't you?' he rallied, addressing Jim and Sara Mae.

'Oh yeah!' Jim said. Sara Mae beamed. They had never been, but they loved the idea of Ireland, especially since Hugh had gone back.

'Ah,' he said, turning to Kate. 'I know you've Irish blood, but you and Dan are English. I appreciate that. But even though I've spent a lifetime here, I've never really settled. Well, I thought I had, but now that Elizabeth is gone I'd like to die there. Sure in all the time I lived here, I never got an English accent, even.'

'You have a little,' Sara Mae said, looking at him from an angle.

'Have I, pet? Well, that's nice.'

'We were thinking of going to the grave on Boxing Day,' Dan said quietly.

'Aye. Aye. We'll do that, so.'

He got tired quickly after that exchange, so Dan drove him to Deirdre and Terry's.

*

When he got back, Dan was quiet. They had the house to themselves as the children were in bed early in anticipation of Santa. Jim was dubious about the man in red but was sensibly hedging his bets. Kate poured them a glass of wine.

'Did he get to you with the solar-house propaganda?'

'A bit. Well, more than a bit, perhaps. He wants to see Karl and Marta on Boxing Day as well. Do you mind?'

'No. Of course not.'

'Their grandkids will be over there too, so we can bring Jim and Sara Mae and let them wreck someone else's house for a change.'

'Excellent.'

He clinked his glass against hers.

'Well, I suppose we'd better unpack this computer and set it up for the Internet.'

'We can send Nuala an email.' She giggled.

'Ask her is it sunny there at the moment.'

'And if her batteries need charging.'

They laughed so much they almost spilled their wine. Then Dan got serious again as he started to unpack the computer.

'Now that he's gone high-tech on us, if he finds out this was made in Ireland, we'll have more of his *insufferable* Irish super-race guff.'

Kate smiled.

'Come on. Let's get on with it. If it doesn't work, we can blame the Motherland.'

'Indeed. What will we do with my old, clapped-out machine?'

'Best put it in the attic till we can find some charity to give it to.'

'My thinking, exactly,' he said. 'I've everything backed up, of course.'

'Of course.'

It took them much longer than they anticipated, despite Dan's familiarity with computers, but by midnight, thanks to a disk which came with it, Kate had composed emails to her brother Johnny in Sydney and her sister Annie in New York. Dan pressed the *send/recv* icon, which activated the agonized cackle of the modem, and suddenly the emails were gone on their way.

'Should we look up the tube map?' he asked.

'You can if you like. I'm bushed.'

'I'll just make sure I know where to find it.'

She looked at his intense face, never having seen him so competitive before. Within seconds, he had the tube map.

'Impressive,' Kate said. 'Now, can we go to bed?'

*

She remembered why Christmas was worth it when the children burst in on them the next morning. Once he was conscious, Dan pinched her and discreetly mimed locking a door. He had forgotten to lock the door to the front room, and he slipped away while Sara Mae babbled on about her talking doll and her books and her body paints and . . . and . . . and . . .

*

Dan acted like a little boy all through breakfast, and when everyone was finished he stood dramatically.

'Baaraam!' he intoned, and it caught their attention. 'My ladies and gentleman. Follow me!'

When he unlocked and threw back the door, the computer was already on with a picture of the Ice Queen on the screen, wherever he'd found it. The children stood there, speechless, until Jim broke the spell.

'Oh, mega!' he shouted, running over to it and grabbing the mouse.

'And it has the Internet . . .' Dan trailed off.

'Let me, let me,' Sara Mae screamed.

Dan winked at Jim and he surrendered the mouse to Sara Mae.

'Now click twice on this,' he said, guiding her to the browser icon. 'There you go.'

'She'll take all day,' Jim said, frustrated.

'Watch this, Jim,' Dan said. 'Now click here,' he guided her, and the email program launched. 'Now click *send/recv*, and Sara Mae watched in awe as the modem went through its tortuous procedure. Two emails arrived almost immediately.

'You've got mail,' Dan shouted to Kate, laughing.

'Really? Already?'

'There you go, Sara Mae, you got email for Mammy. Now, Jim, you take over,' and Sara Mae gave way without a murmur, still, no doubt, wondering how she had got email for Mammy.

'Shall we get the tube map?' Dan prompted, and before he could blink it was on the screen.

'Oh cool!' Jim shouted. 'Wait till Granddad sees this!'

'Shall we print it off for him, Jim?' Dan suggested innocently. 'In colour?'

'A colour printer?' Jim asked, delighted.

'Sure.'

'It was worth every penny,' Dan said to Kate with quiet satisfaction.

*

When Jim handed his grandfather the colour version of the London tube map and Hugh's face fell in surprise, Kate didn't have to look at Dan to feel his quiet triumph, and yes, it had been worth every penny. The computer and all its amazing feats easily outshone the bags of toys and books they had ritually brought to show their grandparents.

'So you're in the Information Age too,' Deirdre said quietly, but with feeling, to Kate.

'Yes, I suppose we are,' Kate said, trying to suppress a smile.

'Not planning on building a solar mansion, by any chance?'

'No. No, I don't think so.'

It was a happy evening, and even Dan rose to wit, something he rarely did in Hugh's presence.

'If I drink any more the baby'll be pickled,' Kate protested when Deirdre tried to ply her with a fourth glass of sherry.

'Oops!' Deirdre giggled, being quite tipsy, and put her hand to her mouth. 'I forgot you were pregnant. How are you feeling, anyway?' and she went into a fit of the giggles again.

'I'm fine, Deirdre. Just fine.'

*

When she got up the next morning, she felt off-colour, but struggled on. Dan was already up, and when she looked in the children's rooms, there was no sign of them either. Frowning, she stopped in the middle of the stairs, listening to the unaccustomed silence in the house. The kitchen was as she had left it the night before. Frowning even more, she looked into the front room to see the three of them, still in their dressing gowns, rapt in front of the computer screen.

'Come on, you lot! We've to collect Hugh in an hour!'

*

Hugh was subdued as they drove to Highgate, the car heady with the scent of flowers. He listened to the children ranting on about the Web, commenting gently here and there.

There was a light mist falling when they got to the grave. Dan put on gloves and cleared away the weeds, and the children put the flowers on the grave. Then they all bowed their heads in silent prayer. Hugh traced Elizabeth's name on her headstone, which had replaced the one erected for Charlie in the 50s.

ELIZABETH KINSELLA
beloved wife of Hugh, mother of Dan,
died November 14, 1992, aged 75.
She joined her beloved son,
CHARLIE KINSELLA
1951–1954.

Kate looked up to see the tears streaming down Hugh's face, and she tugged Dan's sleeve.

He eased the children away from the grave.

'Leave Granddad alone for a while.'

They moved to the shelter of another tree, watching Hugh's lonely figure stooped by the grave.

'Maybe you should be with him,' she said gently to Dan.

'No, he's fine.'

Perhaps, but was Dan fine? she wondered. His face was ashen. All she could do was hold his hand.

*

Hugh cheered as they drove to Karl and Marta's, and joked with the children again.

Marta sat by the fire, shawls round her shoulders and lap, and smiled, her false teeth doing a leisurely waltz in her mouth, and she nodded to the grandchildren who surrounded her. Jim and Sara Mae were shy at first until she called them over to her in her weak Eastern European voice and they soon settled as they did on these occasions.

Marta's daughter and son-in-law dispensed drinks and the inevitable Boxing Day fare, and Kate and Dan chatted to them, leaving the two old cronies to banter between themselves. Karl must have been over eighty, but his tall thin frame was still erect, his fine cheekbones still strong-looking despite his sunken cheeks.

'Are you really going to live in a sunhouse, you old fool?' Kate overheard.

'Ah, Karl, when you think of what we used to build, and then look at what they can do now!'

Kate was offered more sherry. Ah well, baby, she thought, I hope it makes you happy too.

'We were at the grave today,' she overheard. She both wanted and didn't want to hear what the two old boys were talking about. She turned to look at them. Karl nodded, taking his pipe from his mouth and putting his arm round Hugh's shoulder. The two men bowed their heads in silence, remembering Elizabeth, and if what Deirdre had told her was true, then perhaps a great deal more besides.

*

Kate and Dan stayed up late that night watching a film on TV. While she was making some hot chocolate before they went to bed, Dan called her urgently from the front room. He had switched to the satellite news channel.

'It's the volcano in Montserrat,' he said as she stood at the door, watching in awe as the dome of the volcano collapsed, sending lava and a huge cloud of ash hurtling through a valley towards the sea. 'It's had it this time, that's for sure,' Dan said quietly.

Nothing could survive it. No town, no landscape, much less a frail human. The flow had destroyed the deserted communities of St Patricks, Gingoes and Morris, and severely damaged Trials, Fairfield and Kinsale, south of Plymouth, the report said.

'Morris is gone.' Kate shook her head, trying to grasp the idea.

'That was Delly's mother's place, if I remember rightly – wasn't it?'

'Alice. Yes. She was born in Morris. My God.'

'Does she remember it?'

'Of course. She was in her thirties when she came to England. Just after the war.'

'Maybe you should ring your mother.'

'Is it too late?'

'Ring her.'

Deirdre was immediately alert when Kate asked if she had seen the news.

'Morris is gone,' Kate said.

'Oh Christ.' Kate had rarely heard her swear. 'Completely?'

'If it was in the path ... I never knew lava could flow so quickly. I mean, faster than any car. Will you ring Delly?'

'In the morning. She probably knows already anyway. Thank God everyone was evacuated. Bad as they were, the flows last summer probably saved lives in the end.'

'Can you imagine what it must be like? Your most cherished place – where you were happiest – gone?'

'No. I can't.'

She put down the phone and went back to the kitchen, made the hot chocolate and brought it in to Dan without a word.

'Is there anything we can do?' he asked.

'No.'

He switched off the television and put on a Beethoven piano concerto.

'Thanks,' she said and, unable to think, she drank her chocolate, letting the music fill the void.

THREE

London, December 1997 to May 1998

Deirdre rang. Alice was in shock at the destruction of her home town in Montserrat, and hadn't spoken since she was told. Deirdre was so upset that Kate left a note for Dan and drove over with the children.

Sara Mae insisted that she know why her day had been disrupted, so Kate tried to explain in the car.

'You're named after your great-grandmother – you know that, don't you? My grandmother?'

'Yes, but she was Sarah with an "h".'

'That's right. Well, Sarah used to keep lodgers, and one of them, Alice, became her best friend, and her daughter, Delly, was your granny Deirdre's best friend. You know Delly.'

'I think so.'

'She's black, isn't she?' Jim asked.

'Yes, that's right. Alice was born in Montserrat.'

'Where's that?' Sara Mae asked.

'In the Caribbean.'

'Where's that?'

'Near America,' Jim volunteered.

'That's right, Jim.'

'Where's that?' Sara Mae was enjoying herself now.

'Stop it or you're dead,' Jim said.

'Well,' Kate continued, suppressing a smile, 'Sarah fell in love with Brendan, your dad's grandfather, and they got married.'

'Are you and Dad related, then?' Jim asked, frowning.

'No, Jim. It's confusing, I know. But we're not.'

'Good.'

'I don't understand!' Sara Mae shouted.

'All right, Sara Mae, calm down. Just ... calm down, and I'll explain. Sarah grew up in a place called Kilrush, in County Clare, in Ireland. She fell in love with a young man there and got pregnant. She had to come to London to have her baby, and so your granny Deirdre was born here, during the war. When Deirdre was six or seven – about your age, Sara Mae – Sarah met Brendan Kinsella, your daddy's grandfather, and they fell in love and got married. Do you understand that?

'I think I do.'

'Yes. Well. Alice was bridesmaid when Sarah married your great-grandfather.'

'And Delly was bridesmaid for Granny!' Sara Mae said loudly.

'Yes! How did you know that, Sara Mae?'

'I guessed.' She giggled.

'Huh!' Jim looked out the window.

*

'Oh, you were good to come,' Deirdre said. 'I'll just get my coat.'

Kate hadn't bargained on this but she ought to have known Deirdre would want to see Delly and Alice. Alice lived with Delly, which was convenient.

'She's expecting us,' Deirdre said busily as she got into the car, barely acknowledging the children.

'How is Delly coping?' Kate asked as she checked the traffic before turning off the road.

'How would you feel if I was struck dumb?'

Kate didn't answer and the children fell quiet, obviously sensing Deirdre's anxiety.

'You should see more of Charlene,' Deirdre said.

Charlene was Delly's daughter, the eldest of four children and Kate's contemporary. Deirdre had often mentioned this from a sentimental desire to forge a direct descent of female friends.

'Don't you like each other, or what's wrong?'

Alice had started it, and Sarah had colluded, and perhaps, now that she thought of it, the attempt to force the girls together had put them off, especially when their mothers joined in the attempt.

'Of course we like each other. We have different lives, that's all.'

*

Delly greeted them with a strained smile, but Deirdre hauled her into her arms and they swayed together.

'You poor thing,' Deirdre said. 'You poor thing.'

Delly brightened after that and made a fuss of the children.

'It's so nice to have children in the house,' she said. 'She loves children. Charlene is bringing Michael, her little boy, today. Maybe she'll perk up with all the children around her. Jack!' she called. 'Look who's here!'

Jack was a smart man, just sixty, but an old sports injury had brought on arthritis and he shuffled more than walked, and this with his grey, clipped hair made him look older than he was. Kate smiled broadly. She had forgotten how fond she was of him, how kind and natural he had been to her as a child, and when he was animated, as he was now, you forgot about his infirmities. And after he had kissed Deirdre, ever mindful of protocol, he kissed her cheek with special warmth, Kate thought. Then, hands on knees, he made the children smile.

'Will we go up to see her now?' Deirdre asked tentatively.

'Have some tea first,' Jack said.

'Yes, we have some nice fruitcake. You like fruitcake, don't you?' she asked the children, and they nodded. Oh yes, meek and mild. Smiling, Kate guided them into the kitchen, which was overheated but cosy.

'Did you tell her we were coming?' Deirdre asked.

'Yes, but she didn't react at all,' Delly said as she made the tea. 'I've managed to get her up, and she'll go to the toilet on her own, but otherwise she just sits in her room and stares out the window.'

'How old is she, Delly?' Kate asked.

'Eighty since October – but she won't see out this spring.'

'Don't say that,' Deirdre said.

'And what did you get for Christmas?' Jack asked the children.

'A computer,' Sara Mae said brightly, shifting in her seat.

'Yeh, and the Web,' Jim said.

'The Web! Well now, that's all beyond me.'

'We might as well not have got them anything else, Jack.'

'Ah, to be young,' Jack said, smiling at Kate.

*

After tea they went upstairs to see Alice. Sara Mae touched her crinkled black fingers, but she didn't notice. Deirdre hunkered down before her and took her hand.

'Alice,' she said softly. 'It's me, Deedree, your white daughter.'

But there was no response and Deirdre rose and turned away, tears in her eyes.

*

As they were leaving, Charlene arrived with her husband Steve, their baby in her arms. The child diverted Deirdre but Kate was struck by how like her Mage Steve was. Tall. Regal. Another woman's husband, she thought, as Charlene moved between them, smiling.

'I haven't seen you in so long!' Charlene said. 'How are you?'

'I'm fine, Charlene.' She peeked at the child. 'What's his name?'

'Michael,' she said, looking down at him proudly.

'He's lovely, Charlene. Really lovely.'

44

'Yes, he is, poor darling.' She looked up at Kate again, her face bright. 'I've a long way to catch up with you, Kate.'

'You're doing just fine, Charlene. Just fine.'

*

Deep in thought, Deirdre was silent on the way home until Kate stopped the car outside her house.

'It's not that she would ever have gone back,' Deirdre said then. 'Like Hugh did after all this time. It's just that now the dream is gone.'

'Maybe she'll get over it. It's early days.'

'No. You don't get over it when your dream dies.' She got out of the car and walked up the path without saying goodbye.

*

Once, when she'd had a few gins, Deirdre told Kate that her most intimate times with Terry were when she shared a bath with him. Kate was uncomfortable hearing about her parents' sexual lives, which had flowered in the 60s, and fearing worse to come, she had silenced Deirdre. But later, when she'd allowed herself to think about it, she liked the idea. Dan was so easy-going that he never objected when she wandered in to use the loo while he was soaking, so it wasn't such a big step to drop her clothes, and lie back into his open legs and arms. The secret was not to do it too often. A bath, after all, was a private time, to dream as well as wash.

A few nights later, Deirdre rang, depressed, having gone alone to see Alice, and she talked on about how she had been a mother to her, and told her about the time Alice and Sarah had hauled Delly and herself out of the bomb-sites where they had been up to no good with some wild boys. That was a new one on Kate. Yet as Deirdre talked on, Kate couldn't help feeling pleasant about visiting Alice. As soon as Deirdre left down the phone, she went into the front room and took down her book on Bosch, opening it at her photocopy of *The Adoration*. Yes. Yes, he looked very like him. Perhaps

she should have stayed friends with Charlene after all . . .
And then again, maybe not. There was no harm in dreaming,
though, was there? The children were in bed and Dan was
in the bath, relaxing after a tough day on the site. She
felt almost too languid to move, but nevertheless she went
upstairs. The bathroom door was closed and she half turned
back, but she went to the door, pressing her nose against it.
There was a leisurely splash, and she spoke softly.

'Do you mind?'

There was another splash as he reached across to unlock
the door. She stood on the threshold for a moment, smiling
at him as they looked at each other, then, assured, she stepped
in, locked the door, stripped and lay back blissfully onto his
chest.

'You're blooming,' he said, his chin on her shoulder.

She looked down and pulled a current over her belly.
He kissed her damp neck, and she closed her eyes, loving
it. She admired her smooth, wet skin, how it contrasted
with Dan's. The contrast was erotic in itself. Yet even as
she felt that nourishing closeness, Charlene's husband,
Stephen, slipped into her mind. Irritated, she rid herself of
his image.

'Are you all right?'

'Yes.' But she wasn't. 'Oh dear. I'm sorry to ask you this,
Dan, especially when we're so cosy, but would you ever be
unfaithful to me?' She had meant to ask it gently, almost in
fun, but it had come out like a demand.

'What? No, of course not. What brought this on?'

'Are you sure?'

Her hair was stringy from the water and steam, and he
pulled it back from her neck before answering. 'Not unless
I was certifiably mad . . .' And then, as if it were an after-
thought, 'Or unless you ran off with a black man.'

Her eyes shot open, but then she laughed softly and
relaxed back against him again.

'Well then, we ought to grow old faithfully!'

She stared at the ceiling. All right, it had been amusing
that he had read her mind – but it was a fluke, wasn't it?

'Why did you say "black man", specifically?'

'Well, you haven't stopped ogling black men in those paintings since we came back from Florence.'

'I haven't been *ogling*.' She laughed.

'Yes you have.'

'No I haven't. It's just that . . . well, I didn't know they were in Renaissance painting at all, before we saw them in Florence.'

'Oh it's much more than that . . .'

'No it's not!' She turned to face him, splashing water onto the floor, and saw that he was intolerably amused. She pinched his nose hard.

*

They brought Jim and Sara Mae to a children's party before the holidays were over. Jim baulked at what he called 'that muck', but Sara Mae stood patiently while her face was coloured over with paint, a forgotten Christmas present. She wanted flamingoes on her cheeks, for reasons best known to herself, and Kate left that bit to Dan, who did a fair job. She didn't want to put Dan through all the noise of a children's rampage, but he came and talked to Alan, the birthday boy's father, and they consoled themselves with Scotch, so that was all right.

*

It had been in the back of her mind for a while, but now she knew she wanted to have the child at home. With the experience of two births behind her, she felt confident of emulating her mother, who had birthed all three of her children at home. Dan had been present at the births of Jim and Sara Mae, so he was used to the blood and sweat of it, and liked the idea.

'It's much nicer to be able to say "I was born in that house" instead of "I was born in that hospital", isn't it?' she said.

Her doctor frowned but put her in touch with a midwife and the back-up arrangements were made.

'We can do it in the bath,' she said as she snuggled up to Dan that night.

'We?'

*

She was tired in the evenings as her pregnancy progressed. She was still working, and coping with the demands of the children, so she forgot about the black figures in the paintings until Alice died in April.

'I'm relieved, to tell you the truth,' Deirdre said on the phone. 'She couldn't go on like that. And it's a release for Delly too.'

'Will Hugh come over?'

'Hugh? Oh yes. I'll ring him now.'

So Alice was dead. As long as Alice was alive, Deirdre could somehow cling to her mother's past. And maybe it was fanciful, but maybe it also gave her access to that part of her past that was in her mother's memory, and from her point of view. Now there was no one who could say to Deirdre that she was a lonely child. Or anything about Sarah as a woman. There was no one to say that she was a beauty in her prime, or 'Yes, young madam, she struggled to do her best for you in difficult times.'

She had photos of them somewhere. Yes – they were in the bookcase in the front room. She leafed through an album that Deirdre had made up for her when she was twenty-one, and found Sarah's wedding. Deirdre had got the photo restored and enlarged. A smile crossed Kate's face as she contemplated this old moment. How handsome Dan's grandfather was, even though he was ill and hadn't long to live. They must all have known that, except Deirdre and Delly, perhaps. And yet they looked as if they hadn't a care in the world. Sarah looked wonderful and very glamorous. And Alice too. And the pair! The inseparable pair, Deirdre and Delly, the great double act, always up to mischief according to their own boasting, playing in the bomb-sites like wild cats. A mother's nightmare – but what fun it must have been! And Hugh. Young and nervous, his hair creamed back.

She shook her head. Looking at him like this, it was hard to imagine they ever existed at that age, beyond what she could know of them physically. Why was it so hard to imagine them being young? Even in their forties? That was even harder in a way, somehow. That moment, when the camera clicked shut, out of all the moments of their lives ...

Kate hated funeral homes, so while she took the morning off, she drove directly to the cemetery. She was early, so she had time to visit Sarah's grave and was surprised to see it freshly tended to and a mass of colourful flowers. Poor Sarah had borne her pain like a saint, never once mentioning it to her, at any rate, though it was etched into her face. Like Alice, it was a happy release in the end. She touched the black marble, as if to comfort her grandmother, and hoped that if there was such a thing as an afterlife that she was happy and free of pain.

In the distance she spotted another funeral and watched the ritual, until Alice arrived. It was sunny but out of nowhere a shower squalled across as the mourners followed the hearse to the grave. Hugh was among them, in the black suit he had bought for Sarah's funeral.

'Hello, Hugh,' she said, walking alongside him.

'Ah,' he said, spontaneously putting an arm round her shoulder.

'Hello, pet,' Deirdre said across him.

Kate ground her teeth. She hated being called that, but Deirdre was in her Mammy loves her little girl mood and there was nothing to be done about it.

'How is Ireland?' she asked Hugh.

'Smashing.' He smiled. 'Have you ever heard a corn-crake?'

'No.'

'A rare sound these days, I'm told. Which is a shame because it's a glory. You hear them just before it rains, you know. Two shrill notes. Then you look up a minute later and, sure enough, a band of rain is coming from Croghan at a rate of knots.'

'It's a rain alarm system, then.'

'The very thing.'

They gathered around the grave and were handed shaded candles. Kate looked into Steven's face as he handed her hers, and smiled weakly. That man! She took a deep breath and looked around her. The priest began the funeral prayers. She tried to think of Alice but all she could think of was Steve, or rather he occupied her mind, like an atmosphere. She was relieved when Delly started to weep as the coffin was lowered, and Deirdre followed suit, both Terry and Hugh moving to comfort her. Steve had his arm round Charlene, who was holding the baby, and despite the fact that there were other family friends, both black and white, Kate felt isolated. Charlene must have noticed her standing apart from everyone as the mourners moved away from the grave, talking quietly, as she came alongside her, without her child now, and smiled.

'I'm sorry about Alice, Charlene. I was very fond of her.'

'Yes, I know. She was very fond of you too. You must be due soon, Kate?'

'Yes, next month.' Kate smiled.

'Are you coming back to the house?'

'No, I'm afraid not. I really ought to get back to work.'

'Oh. What a pity. I was hoping we could start to get to know each other better.'

'You mean now that they're not trying to force us together any more.'

Charlene laughed, showing her beautiful teeth.

'Yes. Yes, exactly.'

Kate kissed her on the cheek.

'Maybe you'll come over when the baby is born.'

Kate smiled to herself on the way home. She liked Charlene and it made her think she could be loyal to her and so prevent any foolishness with her husband – even in her mind. And that was a big relief.

*

She took maternity leave and, as it had been before and the time before that, it was hard to get used to being in the house all day long without a schedule, and all her friends worked, so she had no one to visit and have a cup of tea with. It was a fine spell of weather so at least she could sit in the garden and read. She found herself staying longer in the supermarket, or being half pleased at the queue in the doctor's surgery when she went for her check-up. But she liked the evenings when Dan and the children were home. There was a long stretch in daylight and the TV was left off until after dark, which made the house unusually quiet. Even the children seemed more content and didn't fight, happy to be in their own company.

On a warm evening in early May, a week or two before she was due, she looked out the kitchen window onto the back garden. Sara Mae was playing some role game with Celine, her friend from next door. Presumably Jim was upstairs doing his homework. Dan was at the table behind her immersed in a journal. All was right with her world and she felt very lucky.

She went into the front room, idly thinking she might play some music, and was surprised to see Jim at the computer, not making a sound.

'What are you doing, sweetheart?'

He looked around.

'I'm messing with an image I got off the Web.'

'The Web? Oh yes. The Internet. And how are you doing that?' she asked, pleased that he was being creative and open about it, but the words 'Internet' and 'image' together made her uneasy.

'Well, I got this cool image viewer called Irfan View—'

'Where did you get it?'

'Off the Web. It's freeware.'

'Free.'

'Yeh. Freeware. So then I got this image of Africa taken from space off the NASA site, and that's free too, in case you're worried.'

'Go on.'

'So I open that up – here, like this – and now I can do anything with it: sharpen it, blur it, change the colours –

anything! But this is the best of all: you can cut pieces out and paste them into another part of the picture, or crop whatever you want to keep.'

'What does "crop" mean?'

'Well, say you just want the Sahara part of the picture, you highlight the Sahara, like this,' he said, electronically outlining the area, 'then go to the edit menu, and choose *crop*.'

'Can I try?'

'Sure,' he said, excited now, and he clicked *undo* on the menu and the picture returned to its original state.

'Let's see,' she said, sitting in. 'How about Ghana? It should be about here,' she said, pointing the cursor which she was accustomed to by now.

'Okay,' he said, 'put the cursor to the top left of where you want to crop, and keep the left mouse button down and drag it down and across.'

'Like this?'

'That's it. See the outline? Keep going. Yes! That's it. You're good at this, Mum.'

Delighted, she drew the cursor down and across until she had the outline of what she presumed to be a part of Ghana.

'Now what do I do?'

'Click on the *edit* menu, yes, that's the one. Now go down to *crop*, and click.'

She did so and the rest of the picture disappeared, leaving Ghana.

'Oh! That's clever!' She looked round at his beaming face. 'Jim?'

'What?'

'Promise me you won't look up naughty pictures?'

'Oh Mum!' he groaned. 'You're just like all the adults. I'm not interested in that stuff. Besides, I'd need a credit card.'

'Yes, well . . .'

How did he know that? She left him to his satellite image, and went upstairs to lie down and listen to music on the radio. Credit card, indeed! It made her feel old, suddenly.

Her nine-year-old child, so knowing, teaching her about the contemporary world, instead of the other way around. She put her hands to her swollen belly. What sort of world would this one grow up in? That was the frightening thing about being a parent in times like these. You couldn't even guess at what lay in store. What was so dreadful was that because you didn't know, you felt you weren't equipped to protect them from such baffling challenges. Still, they seemed to take it on like animals in the natural world without as much as a blink. So where did that leave her and Dan? Facilitators, vessels of the future, that was all, really. She reached across and turned up the music, something by Strauss.

FOUR

London, May 1998

The birth went as she had imagined and hoped, and was much easier than before. It was a girl, with powerful lungs, born in the bath as the sun rose. The midwife handed her to Kate and, once she had let her hold her for a while, cut the cord. She was flooded with happiness, a kind of distant happiness which nevertheless enveloped her. Dan was leaning on the side of the bath, and Deirdre was leaning on him, their mouths open in wonder as if they had never seen the like before. Their faces looked like shells, all the same. They were almost exhausted, just as she must have been, but the drama which filled that little room kept them euphoric.

It was full, bright daylight by the time the midwife had gone and the children were allowed into the bedroom to see their new sister. They came up to the bed slowly in the muted light, Sara Mae's eyes wide in awe, and Kate leaned forward with the child. She could not help smiling when Jim frowned. He would be disappointed that he hadn't a brother. Sara Mae touched her peaceful brow lightly.

'She's very dark, isn't she?'

'All babies are in the beginning,' Deirdre said.

Hugh, who had come over from Ireland, stood in the door.

'Come in, Hugh.' Kate smiled. 'See your new grand-daughter.'

'Was I dark when I was born?' Sara Mae demanded.

'Yes, pet. For a while. A kind of red.'

Hugh laughed unconsciously as he stared at the child and shook his head.

'It's well known I was never a judge of new babies but, as far as I can tell, she's a beauty, God bless her,' he said, delicately touching her bunched hand with his little finger, before pressing a pound coin into her grasp.

'I seem to recall Elizabeth telling me you thought Dan looked like a piglet when he was born,' Deirdre said with a superior air.

'A piglet!' Jim snorted.

Hugh smiled sadly.

'No, that was our firstborn. That was Charlie.'

'Oh I am sorry, Hugh. How stupid of me.'

'Don't be sorry, Deirdre. There's no need. It was a long time ago.'

Kate smiled at her new child again, marvelling at how, just as Jim and Sara Mae had done, she held onto her grandfather's good luck coin. Jim and Sara Mae still had theirs.

'A piglet!' Jim shook his head again in bafflement, and they all laughed, including Hugh.

'Listen, young fella,' Hugh said. 'What would you say to you and Sara Mae having breakfast with me 'fore I leave?'

'Are you going back today?' Dan asked.

'You popped just in time, missus,' he said over his shoulder as he left with the children.

'Popped, indeed,' Deirdre said.

'Goodbye, Hugh,' Kate called, just as Delly and Jack appeared at the door.

'Delly, Jack – come in,' Kate said.

'We won't stay a minute, but when Terry rang us, we just had to come over,' Delly said.

'You're very welcome. You know that,' Deirdre said.

'I know you must be exhausted, dear. Jack said not to come, but I was so excited.'

Jack left a wrapped gift on the side table alongside the one from Deirdre and Terry.

Delly bent to look at the child and her smile suddenly faded before she forced it wide again.

'Oh, look at the button nose on her!'

Kate broke into a sweat. Deirdre had remarked on her nose earlier. The midwife had pronounced her perfect but maybe she had missed something about her nose. And yet, when Delly touched it with her finger it seemed perfect, and she told herself to relax, she was imagining things.

'Jack, take a peek and we'll be on our way. The girl needs her rest.'

Jack winked at Kate as Delly embraced Deirdre.

'How many is this, Deirdre? Seven? Eight? You're leaving me far behind.'

Deirdre blushed with pleasure and pinched Delly's cheek.

'God bless her,' Jack said, before kissing his fingertips and placing them on the child's forehead. 'You too, Kate. See you soon.'

Deirdre ushered them out of the room, leaving Kate, Dan and the baby in silence. She was suddenly overwhelmed with tiredness as Dan pulled the blinds shut, but she hauled herself out of bed and gently put the baby in the wicker crib beside the bed.

'What are we going to call her?' he asked. They had agreed to wait until the child was born.

'Later,' she said. 'Come on, you must be as tired as I am.'

'No,' he said. 'I'll have some breakfast and take a nap in the spare room later.'

She was too tired to argue, and lay back into bed, almost unable to pull the sheet over her. He took it from her and covered her, and kissed her on the forehead.

'Don't worry. I'll look in on you both from time to time.'

*

She woke out of a deep sleep, confused, but instinctively sitting out to pick up her crying baby and put her to her breast. It had begun already. Dan put his head in the door, saw that all was well, and closed it after him again.

'You were hungry, weren't you?' she said softly. 'Drink up, little one. Drink up.' She gazed down at her in the semidarkness. 'What *are* we going to call you?' she wondered aloud. It wasn't as if they hadn't discussed names, but there was no hurry.

Satisfied, the baby drifted off again on her breast, and she couldn't help smiling, tired as she was, and brushed the scant wisp of black hair with her finger. Even in this light she looked dark. Mediterranean – Italian, even! She smiled again and laid the baby down with balletic tenderness, before lying back into bed.

She woke again to bright afternoon sunlight. Dan had left tea and toast on the side table and had opened the blinds. The presents from Terry and Jack were unopened alongside Hugh's coin.

'What time is it?' she groaned.

'She's black,' he said flatly.

'Yes, she's very dark,' she said, stretching.

'No, she's not dark. She's black.'

She felt the blood drain from her body.

'Is she dead?' she whispered, unable to contemplate what she was asking.

'No,' he said, his face tight and ashen. 'No, she's fine. But she's black.'

Kate shook her head as she saw the baby in clear daylight; then she stared.

'The doctor . . .' she managed to say after a long time. 'Get the doctor.'

'I rang him this morning. He's due in about twenty minutes.'

Her nose, she thought. Her nose. It was something to do with her nose. Somehow she lifted her hands to draw back the sheet and open the buttons on the child's Babygro. Her body, too, was black, a chocolate colour.

'This can't be. This can't be . . .' She looked up weakly at Dan. 'Wake me. Please wake me.'

He stared at her, then seemed to wake himself. He picked up the cup of tea and brought it to her lips.

'Here. Drink this.'

She obeyed, and sipped, but his hands were shaking and some of it spilled onto her knee. It wasn't hot any more, but warm enough to believe it could be hot. He put the cup down and wiped her knee with tissue.

'I'm sorry,' he said as he wiped.

He sat beside her and they both stared at the child.

'How could this happen?' she said, more to herself than to him.

'You tell me, Kate.'

'Oh God,' she said, turning to him. 'Oh God.' His hands were shaking on his thighs. She couldn't take her eyes off them and her mind went blank.

There was a knock on the door.

'Kate?' Deirdre opened the door. 'Dr Murray is here to see you . . .'

She frowned, seeing them like that, but ingrained courtesy made her step aside for the doctor and close the door after her.

'Kate! Dan! I believe congratulations are in order!' the doctor said breezily, putting down his bag and extending his hand to her. He was an old Irish doctor who Kate had known all her life and who knew her every physical detail since she'd been a few hours old, so it was a relief to see him and she limply accepted his handshake. He turned to Dan then and shook his hand, but by now he was concerned, looking from one to the other.

'Are you two all right?' he asked quietly.

'She's black,' Dan said again.

'Hmm?' He reached for his bag and took out his stethoscope. 'Put her on the bed for me, will you, Kate?'

The baby woke and began to cry as she picked her up. Dan stood out of the way and she laid the child on the bed and undressed her for the doctor. He tested her heart and lungs, then her eyes and ears, and then her limbs. Then he checked her umbilical cord, already withering outside its fine silk knot.

'She's perfect, God bless her,' he said, and dressed the now placid baby himself.

'How could she be white this morning and black this afternoon?' Dan asked. Kate looked at him, nodding. That was the question she wanted to ask.

'Melanin, in a word, Dan. It takes some time to manifest itself, as it were, in a newborn. You'll have to get used to it, I'm afraid. In fact, she could be blacker still by tomorrow.'

Dan's head dropped, and Dr Murray looked at Kate. He moved the baby to make space for her on the bed, and Dan left the room.

*

'You're avoiding the question, Bill,' she said as he examined her.

'And what's that?'

'Did I have sex with a black man?'

'Kate, my role is to make sure you and your child are well. That's all I care about. Now, any tears below?'

'No. I didn't, Bill. I only had two real boyfriends before Dan, and I haven't looked at another man since.' Even as she said it, Steve's strong figure slipped into her mind. But she hadn't got pregnant by looking at him.

Dr Murray looked her in the eye for the first time.

'It's possible that one of your ancestors, or one of Dan's, was black. It's rare, but it does happen.' He took her hand and patted it like the old father figure he was. 'You've no objections to a black child, have you?'

'No. No, of course not.'

'You don't feel like neglecting her? Anything like that?'

'No!' She surprised herself by the energy of her reply.

'Well, then. It doesn't matter what other people think – and I suppose you'll be forced to explain things to a lot of people. What matters is that— What are you calling her?'

'We haven't decided.'

'Oh. Well, what matters is that she's healthy. And she is, I can assure you. If you're worried about what Dan might be thinking just now, we can arrange a paternity test without too much bother, I should think.'

'Will you speak to him, Bill?' she asked as he put his instruments away. He winked at her.

'Man to man.'

'Thanks.'

'Now you get some rest,' he said in his best doctorly manner which at another time would have amused her. 'You need all the strength you can muster, and more, I would imagine.'

She turned to her child as he left, feeling better and now more hopeful. There was still a huge amount to get used to, but if Dan could somehow accept that she hadn't been unfaithful, that this little stranger was the fruit of their night in Florence, then she was sure all would be well in the end. She stared at her for a long time, trying to absorb her features in a way that she hadn't quite done with Jim or Sara Mae. Perhaps she wanted to believe it, but she was almost sure she looked like Dan in some way.

Deirdre knocked softly and opened the door a little.

'Kate . . . ?'

'Come in, Deirdre.'

'I had a snooze, and – ' she stepped in – 'the children are home and they're fed, so I thought I'd pop up to see . . .'

'Dan told you, I presume.'

'Yes. I thought I saw signs of it this morning, but . . .'

'It seemed impossible.'

'Yes. You see what you expect to see, sometimes.'

'Mostly, perhaps.'

'Yes. How are you?'

'I'm better since Bill came.'

'Tsk. He's a wise old goat, isn't he?'

'Did he speak to Dan?'

'Yes. But in private.'

Deirdre delicately took away the covers from the peaceful child.

'She's beautiful, Kate.' She smiled dreamily.

'What's so amusing?'

'It's not amusing . . . When we were young, I fantasized about having a black child, and Delly fantasized about having a white one.'

'Really.'

'Because of Dell— I'm sorry. I know how difficult it must be.'

'There are things to sort out. That's all.'

'Yes. Of course.'

The children came in, breaking the awkwardness as Deirdre fussed over them.

'She's black,' Jim said.

'Yes, Mammy. Why is she black?'

'Well, the doctor says it was because one of her ancestors was black.'

'Was one of my ancestors black?' Jim asked darkly.

'Perhaps.'

'What's an ancestor?'

Deirdre explained and, satisfied, Sara Mae peered at the baby.

'She's pretty.'

'No, she's not,' Jim retorted.

'Jim!' Kate reprimanded.

'Not yet . . .' He faltered. He looked towards the window, his face intense. 'What am I going to tell my mates?'

'Tell them you have a new sister,' Deirdre said.

'Is she really my sister?'

'Yes,' Kate said firmly. 'She's your sister. Now go and do your homework before you go near that computer. Go on, the pair of you.'

Kate seethed as they left.

'Is it something in the male mindset that has to make everything neat and tidy?'

'I'm sure that's what it is,' Deirdre said.

'She's here. She's flesh and blood. She needs to be fed, changed. Can't they see that is the first and last of it? But no. The only thing on their mind is what others might think.'

She sobbed into her hands, and Deirdre rushed to embrace her. What had been so deeply satisfying was now meaningless, reduced to physical duties. She felt so tired and empty. She pushed Deirdre away and, taking the baby under the sheets with her, turned her back to her.

'I'll let you rest,' Deirdre said softly, and left.

Kate tried to force herself to stroke the baby's downy hair, but she was too distressed, and stared at her instead.

*

She woke to the cries of the baby and instantly sat up and took her to her breast.

Deirdre came in with her dinner, leaving it at the end of her bed, and she remembered how hungry she was.

'Where's Dan?' she asked as she watched the pink lips on her nipple.

'He went to work this afternoon. I said I'd stay.'

'What time is it?'

'Eight.'

Fear trickled through her heart. The site was well advanced and he hadn't been home later than seven for more than a month.

'Maybe he's making up time,' Deirdre said.

Yes. Yes, that was it, she told herself to steady her nerve.

Deirdre had thoughtfully left her a magazine and when she had finished her meal she sat up to read. She had read a few lines when first Sara Mae and then Jim came in to say goodnight.

'What's she called?' Jim asked.

'Well, she hasn't a name yet, Jim,' she said. 'What do you think?'

'Meg,' he said.

'Meg! That's a great name. It fits her like a glove.'

Jim tried to hide his pleasure, and Sara Mae stood back and looked at him in amazement.

'Meg,' she breathed.

'We'll have to see if Daddy likes it, but I love it,' Kate said, leaning forward to kiss Sara Mae, who then skipped off, muttering the name to herself.

'Goodnight, Jim,' she said, kissing him on his forehead. They both looked at the baby before he left, he with what she guessed was a mixture of bafflement, and pride at naming her.

Meg. She smiled at the pleasure of it. This was the thing about children, she mused, especially for men. You can't imagine what they'll be like, or rather they always turn out differently to what you expect, but then they get their own identity and you grow into them.

She tried to read again, but hadn't the concentration. Where was that man?

It was almost ten o'clock when she heard him come in and her heart beat painfully as she waited for him to come up and look in on her.

She had forgotten he had to leave Deirdre home, but when he returned she was forced to wait again. After half an hour she couldn't bear it any more and got up, anxious about leaving Meg, but driven to see Dan. Standing up suddenly made her dizzy, and she swayed, realizing that she was weaker than she thought. She steadied herself against the bed, and put her feet into her slippers and put on her gown before making her way cautiously downstairs.

He was in the kitchen, looking exhausted and twiddling with a pencil at the table, with only a side lamp on.

'Dan?' she asked softly.

He went on twiddling with the pencil.

'Dan, please . . .'

He concentrated harder on the pencil.

'Dan, don't do this to me. Whatever it is you're thinking, I'm completely innocent.'

Still there was no reply, and she stared at him in despair.

'Come to bed,' she pleaded. 'Or go to bed, as you please.'

'Later.'

At least he had spoken. She took a deep breath.

'The children want to call her Meg.'

'Good.'

'I think it suits her.'

'It sounds good.'

'That's it settled, then. We'll call her that.'

'Yes.'

This gave her the courage to ask the central question, but still she had to swallow hard before she could ask it.

'Did Bill mention the option of a paternity test?'

He smiled faintly but didn't answer. She had gone too far, but she was too tired to appreciate nuances, and felt tears trickle down her cheeks before she turned and went upstairs again. Tired as she was, she wept until her pillow was drenched.

FIVE

London, May to June 1998

He didn't come to bed that night, and in the morning she woke to Deirdre holding a tray laden with breakfast.

'Everything's under control,' Deirdre said. 'Dan left the children to school on his way to work. You just eat up and rest. Get your strength back!'

Between feeding Meg and the absence of Dan, Kate had been awake for most of the night, and felt drugged as she struggled to sit up and accept the tray. Deirdre touched her forehead.

'You've a slight temperature.'

'Have I?'

'Eat up and don't *worry*. Everything will be fine.'

'He wouldn't speak to me last night.'

'Oh? He said you'd decided on the name.'

'The children liked it and we agreed. Did he say anything else?'

'No, Kate, and I didn't ask. Meg . . .' She looked down at the baby. 'What a pretty name, for a pretty, pretty girl. Ah . . . she's lovely,' she said.

Kate nibbled on her toast and sipped the strong tea.

'Will you be all right for a few hours? I'll come back and make you lunch.'

'No, Deirdre, I'll be fine. Honestly. Can you collect the children?'

It was arranged. Deirdre touched Meg's nose again. She turned at the door.

'He just needs time, Kate.'

'Yes. We all do.'

He'd arranged to take time off, she brooded, as he had done when the other two were born. But he'd dumped it all on poor Deirdre – who didn't mind but that wasn't the issue. She stank of breast milk and sweat. There was another smell in the cocktail, but she finished her breakfast, letting her cry for a while before getting up to change her. They both slept then, and around noon she felt well enough to bring her into the garden. It was sunny and very warm for the end of May, so she settled under the tree.

'You've been there for so long. Maybe centuries. Why did you choose to come out now, and upset the apple cart?'

Yes, Meg had upset everything, her nice life, her happy marriage, her feeling that everything was settled and content.

'Is that why you came?' She thought back over what she knew of her family's history, and Dan's. Their lives were full of struggle and difficulty. 'Why am I thinking of you like this? Why am I thinking of you as a burden instead of a gift?'

She looked around her, knowing how lucky she was to have such a home, inherited from Hugh and Elizabeth, and how she had taken it for granted for so long, but if she and Dan were to remain estranged she wasn't sure it would mean anything to her. Did he only need time? Was Deirdre right? Somehow she doubted it. She tortured herself with such questions, distracted only by Meg.

She tried to think back, to see how she had come to this. Her life had seemed perfect, so easy, but now she knew what loss meant.

The loss of Alice's childhood home had killed her, even if she had never wanted to go back. She thought about Alice's funeral. It was over too soon, somehow, like all modern funerals. They ought to go on for days, raging at the heavens, keening like the old Irish, with long solemn prayers murmured by old people who knew them by heart, with lots of whiskey to keep them going.

Her heart had skipped a beat when she'd looked up to see

Steve in front of her – but she didn't want to think of that now. It raised too many uncomfortable questions.

Sarah's grave was blazing with flowers. Deirdre must have done a quick tidy in case someone went to see it.

She missed her grandmother with a surprising, longing ache. Sarah had known all about loss. Come to think of it, she had known all about being a fallen woman which, absurd as it might sound in late twentieth-century England, was how Dan thought of the mother of his black child just now. She shook her head, baffled.

Sarah, too, had lost her country, for all intents and purposes, when she had to leave Ireland, pregnant outside of marriage with Deirdre. Yet she had borne it all, even the agony in her hip, with a light dignity, always thinking of others before herself. Was that her secret?

She had been widowed for nearly forty years, and now that she thought of it, Kate was appalled by that. She had taken Sarah's solitude for granted, but the thought of enduring loneliness for forty years was shocking. When Deirdre had left home, Sarah never complained at the rareness of her visits, caught up as Deirdre was in the freedom of the 60s. When Kate was leaving for Spain, Deirdre had told her how grateful she was to Sarah for that, and encouraged her to forget about her family and home for a year or so, to find out who she was. Looking back, though it had been the loneliest time of her life, that kind of freedom was wise and wonderful at that age, and she hadn't regretted it, despite everything.

Everyone was grateful to Sarah, but at what cost to Sarah? Had anyone even told her how grateful they were to her?

Her house was full of books and, in a rush of affection, Kate remembered the glow on her grandmother's face as she told her grandchildren old Irish fairy tales – but then she went cold as she remembered one of them.

'Oh, there you are,' Deirdre called, shielding her eyes against the sun. 'Stay there, and I'll bring us out lunch.'

Deirdre was like a rock. What did she really think of Meg,

though? If it came to that, what was at the back of her own mind about her daughter? She looked at her again, puzzled for the hundredth time. Deirdre came out with a laden tray, smiling so broadly that Kate couldn't help but smile in return. Her mother was – what was the word? Indefatigable. Yes.

'How is she?' Deirdre asked, glancing at Meg.

'She's fine.'

'Did you sleep?'

'A little.'

They settled into the meal.

'Deirdre, did Granny tell you any of the old Irish stories?'

Deirdre paused, her sandwich at her mouth.

'No. She didn't. But she told them to you, didn't she?'

'Yes.'

'Well, grandparents are supposed to have more time for these things, but I'm afraid I've none to pass on.'

'I was just thinking of one when you arrived. Something about a changeling. You know, the fairies take the real child and replace it with one of their own. Do you know it?'

'No,' Deirdre said, her sandwich forgotten. 'I can't say I do. Are you saying that's what Meg is – a changeling?'

'No, of course not. No. But I wonder why such stories exist. I can't be the first woman who thinks her child is a stranger, and that my own child is . . .'

When she recovered she took a sip of tea.

'It makes you wonder, that's all.'

Deirdre concentrated on a patch of flowers, letting the moment pass.

'Deirdre, did you miss having a father around?'

'Yes.' She looked around her. 'Yes, I did. Terribly. I used to dream about him. My real father. He sent me five pounds every birthday. That was a lot of money in the 40s and 50s, especially as he had another family. I had to get a coat out of it every year. That was so important to me, to get that damn coat. It was like obeying the commandment of a god.'

The cup remained poised at her lips.

'But then, as you know, Dan's grandfather came along, and I adored him.'

'And was he a god?'

'Maybe. I hated him at first, mind you. He and Sarah drank an incredible amount – an Irish cliché, both of them.'

'Sarah? A drinker?'

'Oho, yes,' Deirdre said with feeling. 'There was a very dark side to Sarah when she was younger. It was only much later that I understood why. Sometimes life is unbearable,' she said, looking directly at Kate.

'I never knew that.'

'But then they gave it up, for some reason, and he became like a real father to me. I loved him so much. Adored him, really. I was heartbroken when he died. Hugh seemed to grow up after that, and more or less filled the void. It's amazing how he grew more like his father as the years went by. He was very good to me. In fact he was the man in my life for a long time!'

'Did you have sex with him?'

'What? Good Lord, no!' She laughed at the absurdity of the question, and drank her tea.

'Well, I ask because there's about the same age difference between me and Dan.'

'That's true.'

'Did you ever consider it?'

'Yeesss . . .' she said reluctantly.

'Go on,' Kate prompted her, glad of the distraction.

'It crossed my mind. But he was married, remember, to a woman I liked a lot, and your husband, his son, was already born.' She shuddered. 'When you think of what might have happened!'

'You mean my husband might have also been my half brother?' Kate laughed, relieved to laugh.

'It was a teenage crush, nothing more. I doubt if it ever entered his mind. And if you ever tell him, I'll kill you on the spot. It's getting a bit chilly, isn't it? Shouldn't we go inside?'

'That's right, change the subject,' but it had clouded over, so they went inside.

'I wouldn't change old Terry after all this time,' Deirdre said, putting the dishes in the sink. 'Do you know what I like about him?'

'What?'

'Now, I wouldn't recommend this too often, but once in a while it's lovely to lie back against him in the bath, his wet arms round me.'

'I know. You told me.' Kate settled Meg in the pram.

'And he doesn't mind if I fart, and I don't mind if he farts.'

'Deirdre, I don't want to know.'

'We eat much the same, you see, and drink much the same, so they smell much the same.'

'All right.'

'Sometimes we hold back so we can fart together and get the most enormous bubbles.'

Kate ran out of the room.

'It's such a laugh. You should try it some . . .'

Kate put her head back round the door.

'Yes, you were saying?'

'I was saying . . . that when this little tiff blows over, you should try it some time.'

Without a word, Kate lifted the child and went upstairs to find some peace.

*

Deirdre came up to her after a while.

'I'm sorry. I didn't mean to make light of what you're going through.'

'That's all right. I know you didn't.'

'I'll let you rest. Don't worry about Jim or Sara Mae.'

'Thanks.'

*

She took Meg into bed with her and slept between her demands for most of the afternoon. Yet she still felt exhausted by evening when Jim and Sara Mae brought her supper.

'Is Daddy home?'

'Not yet. But Granny says not to worry, she'll stay till he comes in,' Jim said.

Tired as she was, she reflected on his tone. He had been trying, now and then, to sound adult for about a year now, and it had been by times comical and touching, but this was different. In the absence of his father he was trying to be a man.

Where was he?

Then she remembered that it was Dan's martial arts night, and seized on it as an excuse for him, knowing it was no excuse when she needed him to be around, if nothing else.

The children stayed while she ate, Sara Mae fussing over Meg, Jim standing back, looking at her warily.

'Did you tell your mates?' Kate asked him.

'Yeh.'

'And what did they say?'

He shrugged and made a face.

'Nothing?'

He nodded.

'There – you see?'

'Wait till they find out she's black!' he said passionately.

She blushed. It all came back to her in the end, of course.

'You have black mates, don't you?'

He nodded again.

'Well, then,' she said, as if that settled it. She put down her knife and fork.

'Are you finished?'

'Yes.'

He picked up the tray and was gone and relieved to be gone, no doubt.

She looked at Sara Mae, whose lips were comically shut, and she shuffled from foot to foot, impatient to be asked too.

'Did you tell your friends about Meg?'

'Oh yes,' she said.

'And what did they say?'

'Sally said the future is black.'

Kate laughed out loud, to Sara Mae's delight. What a relief! But Sally was half Jamaican – what about her white friends?

'And what did Emma say?'

'She wants a black sister too!'

'Really. You could be starting a fashion.'

Sara Mae giggled before leaving, happy, no doubt, that she had one up on Jim. Thank God for Sara Mae, she thought. Of course it meant that the children's parents, whom Kate was friendly with, knew all about it now. And news would spread quickly to Jim's mates. But it had to happen sometime, so it might as well happen now.

'Oh!' She shook her head wearily and stood out of bed. She felt light-headed, but persisted and went to the window to look onto the world. It was a beautiful evening and the garden was dusky. A bird flitted between the trees, distracting her. Was it a robin? She hadn't seen one in such a long time, and strained to spot it, but just as suddenly it flew out of the garden without her being sure, leaving her vaguely frustrated. She would have liked to hear the whirr of its wings, at least.

Meg cried and she fed her again, trying to relax in case she picked up on her misery. A kind of love, where she would protect the child from what was happening, occurred to her. Yes, that was it, or at least would do for now.

Meg drifted off and Kate watched her for a time. She relieved herself, and had a shower, which lifted the spongy feeling behind her eyes, and dressed before bringing Meg downstairs.

Thankfully, Deirdre was watching TV with the children, and she sat in beside them, determined to recover normality, if only for an hour.

Deirdre was putting Sara Mae to bed when Dan came home. Jim quizzed him immediately about his Tae Kwon Do, but he replied in monosyllables, and when Jim asked without conviction if he could take lessons soon, he just said no.

'Hello,' Kate said.

'Hello,' he replied, but without looking at her.

Hurt cut through her again, and she was blinded by tears as she looked back at the TV. He went to the kitchen to make himself something to eat.

'Mam, why won't he let me go?' Jim knelt on the sofa, his body contorting with frustration.

'You're too young, Jim.'

'But there's lots of boys my age doing it!'

'Jim,' she pleaded quietly. 'Go to bed. Please.' She rubbed her eyes with the insides of her hands and a broken sigh escaped her.

'Your eyes are bloodshot,' he said, forgetting himself.

She tried to smile. He looked anxiously towards the kitchen, then back to her.

'Goodnight,' he said quietly.

'Jim?' He turned. 'Will you give me more lessons on the computer?'

'Sure.' He shrugged.

'Next week, perhaps, when I have a little more energy.'

'Sounds good.'

'Are you off to bed, Jim?' Deirdre asked, almost bumping into him.

'Yes, Gran.'

'Goodnight, then, pet,' she said, bending to kiss him. Jim shuffled off and she sat on the sofa.

'Sara Mae went off with a smile. She's ... Your eyes are bloodshot.'

'So Jim told me,' she said, biting her lip. 'He's still shutting me out, Deirdre.'

'This has got to stop. Dan?' she called.

'No, don't ...'

'No, this has ...'

They heard a chair scraping the floor in the kitchen and he appeared at the door, chewing his food and holding a cup of tea. His face was dark with stubble and there were black lines around his eyes. Deirdre stood to face him.

'Deirdre . . .' Kate protested feebly.

'Dan, you and Kate are going to have to start talking about all of this.'

'Mind your own business, Deirdre.'

Kate stared at the TV, unable to bear the exchange.

He turned and left but after a moment's shock Deirdre called him back. He stood at the door again, his food swallowed. He took a drink of tea.

'Dan, it is my business. You're destroying my daughter, who's just had a baby and hasn't the strength, physical or otherwise, to fight you. All right, all right, she's your wife and I have no business interfering between man and wife. But even if I didn't care about anything else, I'm minding your children – which I love doing, by the way – while you indulge in a selfish, childish sulk. So it is my business. It's affecting my life too.' She was white, and trembling, but determined.

'In all the years you've known me, have I been selfish?'

'No. To your credit. But you are now, just when Kate needs you most. And it's not a pretty sight.'

Kate turned to find him staring at her, and she stared back into his haunted gaze, her heart pounding, time speeding up for her as she dared to hope that Deirdre had brought him to his senses, but he turned and left again. Stunned, she watched as Deirdre picked up the phone and dialled.

'What are you doing?'

'Terry? Will you pick me up? Straight away? Thanks. I'm not sitting in the same car as him tonight, that's for sure,' she said as she replaced the phone on its cradle with difficulty. She sat beside Kate again, breathing hard.

'Don't worry,' she said then, calming and holding Kate's hand. 'I'll be here in the morning to look after things.'

'Thanks.'

'I hope I haven't made things worse.'

Kate shook her head.

'I said some hard things.'

They turned to watch the TV. From where Kate sat, things couldn't be worse.

*

Terry knocked, and immediately Deirdre stood, then leaned down to kiss Kate on the forehead.

'I'll see you in the morning, pet.'

The door closed behind her, the car moved smoothly away, and Kate turned off the TV with the remote control and sat in silence, her mind as blank as the screen. Meg needed changing. The task gave her enough will to turn out the lights and go upstairs and, when Meg was fed and settled and her own ablutions were seen to, she gingerly opened the door to the spare room where she assumed he was in bed. The light from the landing showed a neat bed and, puzzled, she turned on the bedroom light. The room was untouched. His absence scared her a little, and the incongruity of the chair on the landing, which she hadn't noticed before, chilled her. Something made her look up, and she saw that the trapdoor to the attic wasn't quite shut.

He was in the bloody attic. She dimly remembered there being a bunk up there, but mostly there was junk, like in any other attic, mostly old stuff belonging to Hugh and Elizabeth.

Oh God, she thought. He's gone mad. Maybe both of us have gone mad.

In bed, she stared at the ceiling, baffled. He was up there, probably brooding, when he should be lying beside her, his breath softly rising and falling. She had thought this rift was as if he had walked out on her, but this was worse. He was there and not there. Maybe it was like when a loved one was missing, presumed dead – but you could never be sure until you saw the body and gave it a decent burial. She chided herself. It wasn't as awful as that, but she knew she'd prefer if he were really gone.

*

Deirdre and Dan called an uneasy truce, and she let him bring her home at night.

Charlene wanted to come and see the baby, but Kate begged Deirdre to put her off, and she promised she would.

'All your friends will be queuing up to see you soon,' she said.

'I don't want to see anyone,' Kate said. 'Have you told Johnny and Annie?'

'I told them you had a girl,' Deirdre said.

Annie rang that night, and Deirdre didn't make her any the wiser, using her weariness as an excuse to keep the call short.

*

Their separate lives took on a pattern but, despite the stress and depression, she recovered her physical strength. It was as if her body was letting her get on with her heartbreak, but it needed to be strong for the new life it was nourishing.

When she looked in the mirror she was still pale, and Bill had warned her not to overdo things, especially in her emotional situation, but at last she could stand in her body in a determined way. She had never felt like this. Life had happened after a more or less pleasant fashion and, in an odd, vague way, she was grateful for this difficulty. She was going to see it through. Neither of them was bad or mad, though blocking out reality as he was doing was a good imitation. It couldn't last, she told herself. All of this was happening to make them stronger. Even as she thought it she knew she was fooling herself, but she persisted in half believing that this was what marriage was about, after all. When one partner was weak, the other could be strong, and she was going to be the strong one for a change. It was liberating, she insisted to herself.

She set about being strong and saw that he was intrigued when she smiled at him, as if nothing had happened. The children noticed too, and almost magically the atmosphere in the house improved. It was a strain for her, but if it was working, however slowly, then it gave her the courage to continue, despite her unease that she was avoiding the truth as much as he was.

If only she could persuade him to take the paternity test
– well, things would never be the same, of course, but they
could be mended, somehow.

*

She was washing up when the phone rang. An unfamiliar
voice asked her if she was Mrs Dan Kinsella.

'Yes? I'm Dan Kinsella's wife.'

Her new strength drained away as a nurse told her that
Dan had been in an accident. It barely registered that he
wasn't seriously injured. In a daze she wrote down where
he was, and replaced the phone, breathing quickly. She had
almost lost him. Her horror had barely turned to relief when
anger welled up in its stead.

'You bastard. You'd rather die than face me. You'd rather
die than face your child, your own flesh and blood.' She
took up the wet dishcloth and flung it against the wall. 'You
bastard!' she shouted.

Meg wailed immediately and she turned to stare at her
before she came to her senses and rushed to pick her up.

'Oh I'm sorry, my poor darling. Did I frighten you?' she
cooed, rocking her in her arms. 'Did I frighten you, my pet?'

Meg wasn't to be consoled, and her tiny lungs pushed out
a piercing wail.

'There, there,' Kate said, becoming distracted. Maybe she
was mad after all, she thought as she resisted an urge to drop
the baby, head first, and end all this misery, but she waited
till Meg calmed as she held her close to her heart. Her heart
was thumping, almost buffeting Meg and, as she watched her
brow unknot, she was caught up in her, talking nonsense
about her father, how he would have to wait for them, seeing
as he was so silly – all of her frustrations came out softly like
a lullaby. She enjoyed a few minutes of peace with Meg
before ringing Deirdre.

'You sound very calm,' Deirdre said.

'Yes, it's just a flesh wound.'

'Where?'

'The right foot.'

'Something tells me you think he deserves some pain.'

'It's not that. It's just that he preferred to get himself injured or worse than speak to me.'

'If you're going to see him,' Deirdre said after a few moments, 'I'll mind Meg. She's too young to bring into a place like that.'

'Thanks, Deirdre. I'll feed her before I go, so she should be fine.'

'By the way, I got a letter from Hugh this morning. He says his cousin Mungo's son, Aidan, can restore the old photos he left with you. Are they still in the attic?'

'The attic? Yes, they must be.'

'Good. I'll get them from you some day this week. He wants me to send them to this Aidan fellow.'

'I've met him. Why didn't he just write to Dan?'

'It was in passing, I suppose.'

*

Kate faltered at the ward door. He had become an abstraction for her since Meg was born, especially in the past week or so. Meg had grown large in her life and, because he rejected her, he had grown small. But now she wasn't so sure. Nervously she looked into the ward and as quickly withdrew, as if she had been spying on a stranger. A nurse glanced at her as she passed on the busy corridor, embarrassing her, and before she had time to think she was at his bedside, leaving her gift of fruit and a gadget magazine on his locker.

'How are you?' she asked, without being able to look at him directly.

'Sore,' he said.

'What happened?'

'Someone got mugged and I chased the junkie.'

'Did he attack you?'

'No. I tripped and cut my ankle on something. Don't ask me how. Not very heroic, I'm afraid.'

'Not in the end. How long will you be in?'

'I don't know. It's not serious.'

'So they told me.'

They had run out of things to say. She looked around the semi-private ward. The other men were a lot older. She surprised herself by being curious about them. They were all up and about, attached to drips.

'Is there anything I can get you?'

'No, I'm fine.'

'Well, I'd better get back to the baby. Deirdre is minding her but she's too young to be left for long.'

He didn't answer, so she left, managing to hold back her tears until she was in the car park.

*

'Well?' Deirdre asked, looking up. She was rocking Meg in her arms, and Kate took her from her.

'Was she any trouble?'

'None. Not a bit. Well, how is he?'

Kate opened her shirt and watched Meg suckle.

'Kate, look at me.' She obeyed. 'Your eyes are bloodshot. Again.' It was meant to be an admonishment, but Deirdre couldn't rise to that. 'He still won't talk to you, obviously.'

'No.'

'Hold your nerve, Kate.'

Kate didn't answer. She knew it was all over. She'd had nothing to say to him, and it was all over. They had been happy for ten years, but now it was gone. She'd have to find the courage to begin again, discover a new way of thinking of herself. She looked up. Deirdre was staring at her.

'I see you've a lot of thinking to do. I should leave you to it. Call me if you need me.' She touched Kate's face, trying to smile, and left.

The thought of a future without Dan was stunning. Even if their way of interacting had become habit, it had been a comfortable habit. She didn't have to think before doing something for him, or with him. The comfort of him. The memory of them together in the bath came back like a fantasy, both of them so happy, at peace with themselves and with each other, and her tears overflowed. She couldn't get around the idea that this would never happen again, that she would have to lay down new habits of thought. How could she function like that, with three children, one of them new and strange and difficult if only because of her colour? How could he be so loving at Meg's birth, she asked herself desperately, and be capable of leaving her stranded like this within hours? How was that possible? But that was why, she told herself, that was why it was gone, like a puff of smoke. She sobbed, and Meg started to cry.

'Oh I'm sorry, pet. I'm sorry.' She hushed her until she was calm again.

When Meg was asleep, she found a pen and paper and sat at the kitchen table, looking at the sheet for a long time before writing.

What is it like? Is it like being condemned to death for a crime I didn't commit? No. Not like that. I must be careful not to describe it as worse than it is in reality, because that belittles the greater suffering of others.

She thought hard.

It would mean that as much as I am suffering, it isn't worthy to be thought of in the same way as being condemned to death for a crime I didn't commit. So what I can truthfully say is that my heart feels raw, that I'm frightened and insulted.

She looked at 'insulted'. She hadn't expected it but it was the right word. Her integrity hadn't even been allowed the dignity of being questioned before it was condemned. Her sense of fair play told her that she should look at his point of view, but no, she didn't want to do that. Maybe later but not now. She had been insulted to the root of her being as a woman, and knew that if she let that pass, if she did not experience it for what it was, then she was finished.

Although a fresh wave of pain passed through her, seeing this made her feel stronger.

Her thoughts drifted. Charlene's husband was there, vaguely, but where thinking of him would have made her smile before, it was the innocence of her pleasure which had made it pleasurable. How like a young girl she had been, like

Deirdre had been with Hugh, and this was almost as painful a loss as her lost belief in Dan's love.

She took out the hoover from under the stairs and hoovered the entire house. Then she slept for an hour before going to collect the children. When she brought them to see their father, while Sara Mae chatted to him endlessly, she noticed that Jim stood back. He was aware of the rift and she saw that his torn loyalties made him tense.

*

Dan came home sooner than expected, in a taxi.

'They don't keep you any longer than necessary,' he said when she opened the door and stood aside to let him limp past her. She had been cooking the children's dinner so she made some for him too. Sara Mae was thrilled to have her father back. Jim played it cool.

'Does it hurt?' he asked, just as it seemed odd that he hadn't spoken.

'Yes, it does, actually. The painkillers wear off too quickly. But it's better than it was.'

'Oh. Right.'

'Thanks for asking.'

After dinner he took a few bottles of beer from the fridge and watched TV with the children in the front room. She stayed in the kitchen washing and tidying up, but really to avoid him. In the end she joined them a little while before Sara Mae's bedtime, hoping to keep things more or less normal for the children.

'Should you be mixing drink with your medication?' she asked. He was on his third.

'Two or three won't make much difference,' he said, 'when I'm not driving.'

'Sara Mae? Bed,' she said wearily.

'Oh! Just another ten minutes,' she pleaded.

'Do as your mother tells you,' Dan ordered quietly, to Kate's surprise. Sara Mae leaned forward to kiss him, and meekly accompanied Kate upstairs.

Jim went up after a while, without prompting, leaving

them alone. Her heart beat painfully as she tried to find the courage to ask the question that burned through her in its reasonableness.

'Dan, will you have a paternity test done?'

'Why should I do that?' he asked after a while. He was pale-faced and angry.

'Because,' she said, trying to control her own anger, 'it would prove that I didn't fuck a black man or any other man for that matter.' She was shaking.

'Excuse me,' he said, rising and going to the phone. He dialled long distance. She felt the only way to stop shaking was to do violence to him. She looked around for something to throw.

'Hello? Hugh? Oh, you heard. No, it's not serious. No. They're fine. Listen, I need to recuperate in some fresh air. Yes. Would you mind? Are you sure? See you some time tomorrow, then. Good luck. Bye. Bye.'

'What are you doing?' she asked. 'What are you bloody-well doing?'

'I need some open space.'

Jim stood in the door, staring at his father as he turned from the phone.

'Jim!' Kate breathed.

'Are you leaving us?' Jim asked, his voice trembling too.

Dan suddenly looked exhausted and old.

'I'm going to stay with your grandfather Hugh for a while. That's all. Now go to bed, there's a good man.'

'Goodnight,' Jim said.

'Goodnight, son.'

'Goodnight, Jim,' she said.

Dan stood where he was, distracted. Her anger had gone, somehow, replaced by something like regret. She got up and took his keys from the mantelpiece.

'Here,' she said. 'Seeing as you're not leaving us, you'll need these.'

'Thanks,' he said, accepting them. He looked so dazed she would have pitied him had she the emotional energy.

'Shall I make you up a bed down here?'

'That would be a big favour,' he said gratefully. 'I'm obliged.'

She shook her head, perplexed again. There had been such softness, maybe even tenderness in his voice. She cried on the way upstairs to get the bedclothes and pillow, but composed herself before she came down and made up the bed.

'Thanks,' he said again.

'Goodnight,' she said.

'Goodnight.'

In their bedroom she threw his pillows as hard as she could against the wall.

*

He was gone in the morning when she got up. Jim said nothing about it over breakfast and Sara Mae seemed oblivious, assuming, perhaps, that he had gone to work, so Kate felt obliged to explain. Sara Mae said nothing, but swivelled her eyes to the extreme left as she thought about it, then resumed her breakfast.

She felt remote from what she was saying as she rang Deirdre mid-morning to tell her.

'He's working things out, like I told you he would. The Kinsellas always go back to that mountain when there's a crisis. Look at Hugh, throwing up his life here to live out his days in full view of it.'

'But he had no crisis, had he?'

'Elizabeth's death?'

'True, but that was six years ago.'

'Time means nothing when you lose someone you love, Kate.'

Kate bit her lip.

'He's still refusing to take a paternity test,' she said quickly. 'I asked him last night and he didn't want to know.'

'He will.'

'What makes you think that?'

'He loves you.'

'He has a funny way of showing it,' Kate said, her voice breaking.

'Oh my dear,' Deirdre said softly. 'Oh my poor child.'

*

She lay on the bed for most of the rest of the day with Meg, staring at her, and eventually fell into a deep sleep. The phone rang, and as she struggled to wake she knew she had only slept for a few minutes, and resented the call even as she fumbled for the receiver.

'Kate? It's Charlene.'

'Charlene . . .'

'Mum told me the good news, but I thought I'd wait a while before I rang. Did I wake you?'

'Yes.'

'Oops. Silly me.'

'No, it's all right.'

'Her name is Meg, isn't it?'

'Yes. Jim thought of it.'

'How clever of him. It's a lovely name, Kate. Is it too soon to call around and see her?'

'Oh, Charlene, I'm . . .'

'Are you in the dumps?'

'Yes.'

'I know that one.'

'Do you?' Did she? Did she – *really*?

'God, yes! I didn't want to see anyone for months. Listen, I'm going to let you get back to your nap. I'll ring you in a few weeks.'

'Thanks.'

'Take good care of yourself, Kate.'

'Yes.'

'Bye.'

Kate replaced the phone, yearning to be unconscious again.

*

Somehow she got herself together for the children's sake. Jim was still quiet, which worried her.

'Is there anything on your mind, Jim?'

'Will Dad be gone for long?' he asked, having hesitated so long the question was a surprise.

'Oh, a week or so,' she said as airily as she could. Jim nodded, and was about to leave the room when, out of desperation to distract him, she called him back.

'Will you give me another lesson on the computer tonight?'

'Sure.' He smiled. 'But don't tell Sara Mae. She'd want to stay up.'

'Done,' she said.

*

Jim smiled again as Kate came downstairs, his two sisters safely in bed.

'Are you ready?'

'Yes, let's go.'

He had the computer on, and clicked to launch them onto the Web, impatient at the tormented whine of the connecting modem.

'Okay,' he said. 'You click here to bring up your search engine. That's what looks for things for you.'

'Where?'

'Just here. Like this.' It appeared on the screen. 'There it is. Now, what do you want to find?'

'Bosch,' she said. The name had been in the back of her mind but now she was certain. 'Hieronymus Bosch.'

'Here,' he said, making way, 'it's best you type it in.'

'Here?' She typed it in the appropriate box. 'Now what?'

'Just click *search*,' he said, the mildest hint of impatience in his voice.

A raft of results appeared on the screen.

'Oh look!'

'Click on one,' he said.

'Oh look,' she exclaimed again, really excited now as a

site with a number of Bosch paintings appeared. She clicked on *The Adoration of the Magi*, and slowly the image appeared from top to bottom.

'It's a triptych,' she said, surprised.

'A what?'

'Look, it has three panels.'

'Oh.'

'I didn't know that. Could we save it and crop the black king, I wonder?'

'Sure. Save it and we'll do it off-line.'

'Will you do it?'

'Okay, but you'll never learn unless you do it yourself.'

She could learn later. Just now she was mesmerized by the black Mage, who looked even more noble in the context of the triptych.

'It's done. Now, would you like to choose another?'

'Oh. Yes.' She took the mouse from him and clicked on *The Garden of Earthly Delights*, which a note said was in the Prado Museum in Madrid. Once again, the image appeared slowly from the top of the screen down.

'Oh dear! It's huge. I've only ever seen sections of it.'

'Well, that's the Web for you,' he said proudly.

She looked at it closely, and her mouth dropped, as among the cavorting, sensual yet strangely asexual naked bodies which crowded the picture were at least four black figures, probably female.

'Is it interesting?' he asked.

'Fascinating. Jim, can we save this too? And then I want you to show me again how to crop.'

'Forgotten already?' he asked, too satisfied, saving the picture and severing the connection.

He launched the image editor and outlined the black king.

'Now,' he said. 'Just go to *edit*, and *crop*.'

'Ah.' Now she remembered. She did it and the king appeared in his splendid isolation. 'Now, can we make him bigger?'

'Yes, but not too big, or we'll lose definition.'

'Indeed!' A metaphor there, somewhere, no doubt.

'About 330 by 670 pixels, I would say,' he said.

'Really? I'm impressed.'

He smiled proudly. And he was right. It was perfect.

'Why are you so interested in black people?'

'What?'

'There's lots of black people in that other picture too.'

'The Bosch?' she asked, to gain her time.

'Yeh. That one.'

'Yes, I'm very interested in black people in Renaissance pictures. I have to admit that. Have you heard of the Renaissance?'

'No.'

'Well, it means "rebirth". About five hundred years ago, artists began to paint more pictures, and better pictures, than they had for over a thousand years. But I didn't think there were black people in Europe five hundred years ago. And yet, here they are in these paintings.'

'Why?'

'I don't know,' she said. 'I don't know, and I wish I did.'

'Do you want me to do the same with the other one?'

'No. No, I think I can do it myself now. It's the only way to learn, as you pointed out.'

'You don't want me to see those nudies, that's all.'

'I think it's time you went to bed.'

'I get the hint,' he said.

'Good.' She smiled and tossed his hair, and then she kissed him on the forehead and held him gratefully for a moment.

''Night,' he said, breaking away.

She turned to watch him leave, then chewed on her lip for a while before turning back to the computer. She opened *The Garden of Earthly Delights*. It, too, was part of a triptych, she remembered. The picture receded to the horizon, a carnival of naked figures, giant fruit and birds, and exotic, maybe mythic animals. Sprites and angels flew overhead.

She smiled as she picked out a figure, upside down in a pool of water, a giant strawberry between his legs. There was another, circular, pool with bathers in the centre, and a larger one in the distance with more bathers cavorting around heavenly domes and spires. The figures were too small to make out properly, so she doubled the picture in size. As Jim had warned, it lost some definition, but now she saw that there were more black figures. As she worked her way up the picture, with growing excitement she found more, bathing in the middle pool and in the pool at the top. Then she looked again at the pool to the left of the picture and her mouth dropped again. Not believing her eyes, she cropped and enlarged it.

A white man and black woman, sitting on a giant mallard in flight, were sensually embracing. In the pool itself, beside a white couple, a white woman was leaning back into the embrace of a black man beneath a giant, indifferent finch.

She sat back and stared at the scene. This had been painted around 1503, if she remembered rightly. She couldn't articulate what was happening, but neither could she rid herself of the feeling – a strong feeling . . .

She wanted her identification with the painting to convince her that Meg's ancestors had been like that couple, wrapped in each other's arms.

'What a stupid idea,' she said aloud. It was some artist's religious fantasy, that was all. Christ figured in the first panel of the triptych, and hell filled the third. It was an allegory.

Yet she yearned for the scenes to be normal and unremarkable. Until she had been to Florence, she had never heard of Africans in Europe in the fifteenth century, much less of a coupling of the races, which, to Bosch at least, seemed the most natural occurrence in the world. Was she racist in being surprised? A long history of domination, brutality and murder stood between her and this idyllic picture. It was amazing that such an idyll existed at that time, if only in the mind of a genius like Bosch.

She heard Meg's cry on the baby monitor as she turned off the computer, deep in thought, and hurried upstairs. As she nursed her in bed, she stared at her, still grappling with her otherness. How had her ancestors come together? Had it been rape or love? She held fast to the tender image of the Bosch picture, hoping against hope that it had been in such a paradise. Perhaps it had been. After all, when Bosch painted his great, mysterious painting, Europeans had just discovered the New World, and Europe was innocent of the trade in slavery, as far as she knew. Was that why she was troubled? Did she know, even without knowing, that she had taken within her most intimate self the tortured history of Meg's blood? When a child grows inside you, what does it mean? she wondered. She had half asked herself the question before, but with Meg it confronted her with its full force. Meg was like a messenger from a distant past.

Had she sought these paintings out, or had they sought her? That was the strong feeling, the ludicrous question which bothered her. Or had she simply become open to a voice which had always been there, through time, and regardless of time? She changed Meg and settled her.

Perhaps it meant that it was long since time that she stopped living as if there was no more to her life than being content and mildly bored with the sameness of her daily routine. It might even mean that she was a little mad because of the pressure she'd been under, and all would fall back into place when Dan returned to his senses.

'No,' she said as she watched Meg's eyes close. 'No, everything's changed.'

*

Meg woke her in the middle of the night and, as she was feeding her, she thought she felt a presence in the room and a frozen sensation gripped her. She was terrified, and dared not look across to the window.

Go away, please, she pleaded silently. Leave us alone.

Whatever it was, they or it would not have her child. They would have to kill her first.

She worked up the courage to look at the window. Nothing. She reached over to the bedside lamp and turned its beam towards it, then took a deep breath and breathed out in relief. She was overtired and her imagination and, yes, her loneliness, were playing tricks. That was all.

*

When she woke the next morning her dream of being surrounded by giant but benevolent birds was still vivid. It took her a while to recognize them as the birds from Bosch's painting, and she would have liked to dwell on them a while and take comfort from their support, but already it was time to get the children up.

She was having a mid-morning cup of tea when the door bell rang insistently. Her heart jumped. What more could be wrong? But it turned out to be Deirdre.

'I'm sorry, I'm so excited I can't find my key. You'll never guess what I've got!'

'No, I wouldn't.'

'Proof!' Deirdre said as she marched past her into the kitchen.

'Proof? Proof of what?' Kate asked, following her.

Deirdre waited till she had caught up, then dramatically produced a photocopy of a document and slapped it on the table. It was the birth certificate of a Millicent Harrup, born in 1872.

'What's this?' Kate asked, puzzled.

'You see the address?'

'It's in the East End, isn't it?'

'Exactly. And do you see where it says "Father"?'

'It says "father unknown".'

'Exactly.'

'So?'

'Millicent is one of Dan's ancestors. He had an aunt Millie, do you remember? And Millicent's father is unknown.'

'I'm sorry. I'm still not with you.'

'He must have been a black sailor, or docker, maybe. A sailor. A black American sailor. Think of all the black children of GIs, during the war. This is what happens, you know. He must be the one. I'm sure of it.'

'Oh, Deirdre.'

'You don't think so?'

'It's possible ... but I don't think it's proof, Deirdre. I'm sorry.'

'Oh,' Deirdre said, crestfallen.

'Would you like a cup?' Kate asked anxiously.

'Yes,' Deirdre said, frowning.

'You went to all that trouble.'

'Oh don't mind that! It was fun, actually. Though it was frustrating when the trail went cold. I wanted to go back further, but there was nothing. I suppose her mother was an innocent girl who came up to London and got into trouble with the first handsome boy she met.'

'Most likely,' Kate said, pouring the tea.

'But it is possible, you'll grant me that,' Deirdre said hopefully.

'Yes, it's possible.' She smiled and touched her mother's hand. Just possibly – Millicent was one of Meg's ancestors. But what if her black genes were from the other side?

Why it hadn't occurred to her before now she couldn't say but, as she watched Deirdre lift her tea to her lips, she remembered that her mother made no secret of her liking for black men, which, indeed, she had inherited.

Kate blushed at the thought. It was possible that the mystery of there being no known black relative on either side was solved. It was a relief, in a way, and she wanted to get up that second and ring Dan, telling him that all was well. And why did Deirdre go searching among Dan's ancestors? To cover up? After all, she had her own marriage to protect.

'Don't let me forget Hugh's photos, while I'm here,' Deirdre said, taking a biscuit. 'They're still in that yellow box, aren't they?'

'Yes, I think so.'

Deirdre insisted on going up the ladder to the attic herself, and found them quickly.

They looked through them in the kitchen.

'I'll send these off today to Aidan. Look, this is my

favourite,' Deirdre said, 'your grandmother's wedding to Dan's grandfather.'

'I have a copy of that one.'

'Have you? Wasn't Sarah glamorous? She bought that dress when we were in France on holiday.'

'You used to go every year when you were small, didn't you?'

'Yes.' Deirdre smiled dreamily. 'Yes, we did. How she managed it, I don't know, but I often bless her memory for it.'

'Deirdre . . . ?' Kate swallowed hard, fiddling with one of the photos.

'Yes?'

'Did you . . . did you ever do it with a black man before you met Dad?'

Deirdre paled, and Kate felt terrible, but she had to know the answer. Deirdre recovered, and reflected a moment, so that Kate was sure she was going to say yes.

'Hmm,' she said. 'No. I often wanted to, but I never did.' She pursed her lips. 'Your father is your father.'

Part Two

HUGH

SIX

Co. Wexford, 21–24 June, 1798

Hugh Byrne's heart thumped like a blacksmith's hammer as he looked down Vinegar Hill at the English army. Every time he had been through a battle, at Oulart, Enniscorthy, Ross, Tuberneering, he thought he had mastered his fear. The flush of survival did that to a man. But now he knew he would never master it, and this was very different from before. A blind man could see that the English meant to finish it this time.

There must have been ten thousand rebels on the hill, counting women and children, but they had few weapons to match the English, who had lined up their cannon. They hadn't a hope. Along narrow roads and in small fields their pikes were deadly, but up here they could only pike fresh air.

The bombardment had gone on for hours, and many people, including women and children, were already dead before the battle had begun. He feared mutilation more than death. He had seen his share over the past weeks: legs and arms blown off by shot, men dying in agony from gangrene.

Enniscorthy was on fire. Billy Byrne of Wicklow had led reinforcements down to protect the bridge which led directly to the hill, and the word was that he was holding it.

He was shaking now. The more he thought about how hopeless it was, the more he shook. *Up the Monaseed men*, he mouthed, to help his nerve. *Up the Monaseed men*. He couldn't see his brother Tom. He wished he could at least see him. He looked over at Miles Byrne, a distant cousin, tall, cool, and a chief even though he was only eighteen like himself. Though he was saying nothing now, he knew Miles was still lepping that their leaders, or generals as they called themselves, had left their people exposed and defenceless on this hill, having some gentlemanly idea of facing the King's army. The English were not so stupid as to be gentlemanly in war. The Wexford men had won every time they fought on their own terms, he thought, forgetting Ross. But now an awful lot of them would be dead within the hour, including himself, most probably. It would be worse than Ross.

He thought of his family, of the meetings outside the chapel of a Sunday morning with the neighbours, and how he had come to be here. The thirty-first year of their lease would be up in September, and some Cromwellian git would be entitled to take their land, and his family would starve. His anger came back to steady him. His father was in despair, but not him. Not Hugh Byrne of Monaseed. The blood was thick in his neck now. *Up the Monaseed boys!* He looked over at Miles, who a second later looked around at him.

'Are you all right there, Hugh?' he shouted.

'Never better!' he shouted back.

'Good man. Up the men from Monaseed!' he shouted to the rest of them.

'Up Monaseed!' they shouted in unison, and Hugh felt strength flow back into him. There were men from Gorey and Ballyellis whom Hugh was acquainted with in the column. He knew they would all fight like hell, despite the cannon and hail, as they had elsewhere.

The order was given to attack the enemy's left flank, and they manoeuvred under fire before charging, their pikes like ferocious extensions of themselves. Many fell immediately, as if a scythe had cut them down. A man fell to his left and Hugh glanced at him but kept charging with the rest, his fear displaced by a desperate fury.

Then something slammed against his head, spinning him

around, and for a moment he felt stupid and weak, before collapsing into darkness.

*

He woke to a terrible stench and scattered screams. At first he thought he was struggling out of a nightmare, then began to focus on what was happening around him. They had been defeated, as he and Miles had feared they would be, and the King's soldiers were killing off the wounded. They'd find him too, and bayonet him where he was. The soldiers were a distance away, moving methodically across the field, so he dared to move his toes. They worked, so at least his legs had not been blown off. He could see his left hand and moved his right carefully. It was still there. He flexed his buttocks so that his pelvis moved. He flexed his stomach muscles. Unless he was in a delirium, or was dead after all, he wasn't seriously wounded. He was surrounded by the dead. Bodies mutilated by cannon and shot were scattered, some of them in heaps. His tongue was swollen and his lips were broken. If the soldiers didn't kill him, the sun would. He was near a ditch. If he inched towards it, perhaps they wouldn't notice. He managed to swivel his hips in what he hoped were unnoticeable movements, before rolling over into the ditch. He lay face down. He had no illusions. If the soldiers didn't get him, the militia, with no pikemen left to fear, would show him no mercy. He lifted his head and cursed them, swearing he would bring three of them with him if he had to die. For the second time that day, his fury drove him on, but a few yards up the ditch he came across the bodies of a woman and girl child. The girl had been stabbed in the heart, the woman's throat slashed. The child was in the ditch, her mother hanging over, her arm outstretched. He stared at them. He had seen so much of this over the past month. His anger made him forget himself and look over the ditch. The killing was still going on, and they must have had hundreds still to finish off. He had to fight a desperate urge to find a pike and run at them, killing as many as he could before they got him.

Reason and the fear his anger had masked prevailed. They'd shoot him before he got within an ass's roar of them. And he knew he was sick of killing, having killed his share. And no matter how hateful a man was, it was no small thing to kill a human being but, and he asked God to forgive him, defeated or not, he would kill at least two more, if only to lay the souls of these poor innocent creatures in the ditch to rest.

He made it out of the field, and now the hedgerow gave him cover. But he had to be careful. They were in command of the hill and could see for miles, and would think nothing of sending cavalry after him, eager as they were to wipe out every last man.

He waited till nightfall and made his way to the Slaney river. His vague plan was to follow the river until he came to the Bann, a tributary, and follow that as far as Hollyfort and make his way to Monaseed to say goodbye to his parents and sisters. If Tom was dead, as seemed likely, then he was the only son, but there was no way he could stay in Ireland now. Not in Wexford, anyhow. If they didn't hang him, or worse, there was no way they would re-let the farm to a United Irish family, be they Protestant or Catholic.

He kept going until he was a safe distance from Enniscorthy, then stopped to rest. He had a terrible headache and, putting his hand to the left side of his forehead, felt a gash that was badly swollen. His face was caked with blood. He must have been hit by shrapnel. The man who had fallen beside him had saved his life.

He washed his face in the river, then stiffly got out of his clothes and eased his body into the cold water. As he stood against a tree on the bank to let himself dry, he felt like an old man. When he was dry, he pulled on his clothes again, and although hunger clawed at him, exhaustion won.

When he woke the sun was well up. It was perhaps almost noon. He could have slept longer were it not for his hunger. He hadn't eaten since the night before the battle, and that had been a watery stew. He saw a cabin a distance away, then saw three or four in a cluster. There was no way of knowing if they were friendly, but he chose the one near a copse in case he had to duck away in a hurry.

An old man answered, pulling open the half door.

'Do you have any bread to spare, sir. Or a potato?'

The old man looked up at Hugh's wound, then opened the other half of the door to let him in. The room was dark, the tiny window barely admitting daylight, and the hearth was cold. When he was accustomed to the gloom, he saw an old woman staring at him. She was standing beside a scattered bundle of straw.

'What ails you, son?' she asked.

'The hunger, mam.'

'Is that all?'

'I can tell you no lie, mam. I was part of the Wexford army that fell to the English at Vinegar Hill just yesterday.'

'All is lost, so,' her husband said.

'I fear it.'

The couple looked to each other and then at the floor. The man turned to Hugh, the meagre light catching the tears in his eyes, but his voice was low and steady.

'I've three sons went off with the farmers and gentlemen to fight three weeks ago.'

'God bless them,' Hugh said.

'Then the militia started their killing and raping, so their sisters and wives and children went looking for them, and I fear they found them.'

'Was everyone killed be the cannon?' the old woman asked.

Hugh felt weak. His wound, hunger, and the loss of this family combined to thin his blood, but he steadied himself out of courtesy.

'A lot were, mam, far too many that I saw with my own eyes. But I was taken down near the start of the fight, and saw nor heard nothing else till it was over.'

He desisted from telling them of the slaughter after the battle. They were suffering enough as it was. The woman bent to her pot and gave him three small potatoes.

'Thank you kindly, mam,' he said, the saliva flooding his mouth.

'I'm sorry, sir, but we've no buttermilk.'

'Spring water will do me well,' he said, his mouth full.

A shadow fell across the floor and the old woman stared. Hugh and the old man turned to see a bedraggled woman holding a child. Her eyes stared like glass balls.

'Mother of God!' the old woman shouted, and hobbled across to her. 'Ye're alive!' and she embraced the woman and child.

'The others?' the old man asked quietly, his voice breaking.

The young woman did not reply and, staring at her and the child, they escorted her to the makeshift table and stools, and seated her. The child started crying. The mother ignored it for a while, the old couple looking at each other, before she bared her breast, still staring, and the child found the nipple.

Hugh's second potato was still in his mouth. He had forgotten his hunger. He swallowed involuntarily and coughed as some of it brushed against his windpipe. It seemed to break the spell as the young woman turned her eyes to look at him.

'You must be hungry,' he said, handing her his third potato. She took it and ate, but as she did so her mind seemed to turn blank again. Then she startled them by speaking.

'The rebels got away. I saw them heading for Wexford.'

'Jesus,' Hugh said, his head flooding with hope.

'The others?' the old man asked again. The young woman looked into his face. Then she broke into a terrible sobbing.

Hugh backed out of the cabin into the heat of the sun, dazed and bewildered. Then, instinct reminded him that he was exposed, and he backed into the copse. He wanted to run away, but knew that he could not. No matter where he ran, the horror he had seen, the suffering endured by people like these, would run with him. He was losing his breath, and he fought to calm himself, but he was overcome and collapsed into a soft bed of green fern.

He found himself blinking at a ladybird making its way along a blade of grass. His first thought was that the Wexford army had got away. He rolled over onto his back. The sky was blue above the treetops. It was a haven in hell, and the thought of staying here until the creatures of the grass consumed him appealed greatly. They got away, he thought again. The idea stuck in his mind, like a phrase from a foreign language, and for some time meant about as much to him.

Turning on his side, he reached for the slim trunk of a hazel tree and dragged himself up. How many were butchered like the mother and child he'd seen in the ditch? The demented woman in the cabin had a fair idea, he'd wager. The Orangemen wanted to wipe them from the face of the earth and with the help of their English masters they were on their way to finishing their work. He shook his head in frustration. Could they not see that the United Irishmen was for Protestants as well as Catholics and men of no religion at all? And that most of the United Irish leaders were Protestant, for sweet Jesus' sake, both in Antrim and Wexford?

They got away. The import of it hit him. His family would be thrown off their land when the lease ran out at summer's end, and they would be no better off than the poor wretches beyond in the cabin. Unless the boys had really got away to fight again. It wasn't a defeat, then, but a retreat. At a terrible price, as he himself had seen. But the dead were dead, he thought, grinding his teeth, and he couldn't raise them out of the ground, and if the United Irish didn't win in the end, the scourge that had driven them out to war would go on forever.

He longed for a pike in his hands again, and felt naked without it. But where would he find them? The woman had said Wexford, but they wouldn't stay long there if they had any sense. Towns didn't suit the pike. The narrow roads and small fields of the Wexford countryside were made for it. Miles Byrne had told him that and Hugh saw the truth of it. So where would they go? The towns suited the English and their garrisons. The country and the mountains suited the Irish. The mountains. That was it. He looked to the west, over to Mount Leinster. He looked north. He couldn't see it, but he was sure they'd head for Croghan Kinsella. Or Mount Leinster. Which? Both? Yes, that made sense. There were a lot of Wicklow men among the rebels. They'd want to go to Croghan and beyond into the Wicklow mountains. The south Wexford men would head for Mount Leinster.

Pleased with himself for what he considered thinking strategically, a word he'd heard a lot of in the previous month, he headed out across the fields, relying on the sun to keep him in the right direction.

Oulart Hill, where they had defeated the Gaelic-speaking Cork militia, was his first stop, both to give him courage and to use as a milestone. The Gorey road was just beyond it, and with any luck he'd catch up with them, as they were probably slowed down by the wounded.

He was right. A few miles before Ballycanew he found them, his brother Tom among them, and it seemed to raise their spirits as much as his. Some men had died from their wounds along the way, and their pikes were in the cart with the wounded and some women and children. There must have been a couple of thousand men on the road, their pikes like a small forest.

'We thought you were dead,' Tom said, holding him at arm's length.

Tom was Hugh's eldest sibling, there being two sisters after them. Hugh was the taller, and more solidly set.

'I thought yis were all dead too,' Hugh said, feeling young and strong again. 'Have yis anything to ate?'

'Ne'er a bit,' Tom said cheerfully. 'We'll ate when we get to the White Heaps.'

'Well, the White Heaps can't come soon enough, so.' It pleased Hugh that he'd been right about their destination, the White Heaps being a strategic hill alongside Croghan, and the pleasure helped soften his hunger.

Tom told him that their force had been twice the size when they left Wexford, and that several thousand more had headed south, but due to disagreement among the leaders and a weariness of war among the men, they were now much reduced. Many of them, including the leaders, wanted to trust the English and surrender, Tom told him.

'But that's the thinking of an idiot,' Hugh said. 'They killed every living thing in Enniscorthy. I saw it with my own eyes. The only choice is to leave the country or fight.'

'Is that so?' Tom had gone pale. 'I was thinking of going home myself, but I see what you're saying.'

'Maybe in time,' Hugh conceded. 'But not now. Another general, maybe. Not this one, that's for sure.'

It was disheartening to hear Tom talk this way, as he knew him to be next to fearless. He had fought like a man possessed in the past month and, moreover, had saved the lives of many of their friends. And yes, Hugh remembered with a shiver, he had saved his life too, at Ross.

The column stopped abruptly, so that many walked into those ahead. Word passed back that six women had been found at the side of the road, their bellies ripped open.

Furious, they rushed to Gorey instead of skirting it. Outside the town, they encountered troops of the garrison and charged, scattering them. They stormed the town without resistance as the rest of the garrison had fled, no doubt to Arklow. The loyalists had evacuated too, and when it was discovered that the prisoners in the Market House had been taken out and shot, tired and hungry as they were, many of the men gave chase.

The women's bodies were brought back to Gorey on a cart and Tom and Hugh helped to bury them with the dead prisoners.

'You'd think,' Tom said bitterly as they dug with the others, 'you'd think, if nothing else, they'd have the sense to save their ammunition for a fight.'

'Since when has killing anything to do with sense?' a Wicklow man asked him. 'You should know that by now as well as any of us.'

Tom stared back at him, but said nothing, knowing the truth of what he said.

They recited prayers over the graves and found something to eat in the deserted houses, and rested in whatever shade they could find.

'Do you think we could slip home for a few hours?' Hugh asked Tom.

'You go,' he said. 'Tell them I'm safe.'

'I thought you wanted to go.'

'I'm too angry, Hugh. I couldn't face my mother like this. You go, but be careful. Ten to one that hellhound Hunter Gowan is killing all around him out in Hollyfort. Go by Craanford. And keep to the ditches. Or maybe you should wait till night.'

A few hours later the men who had given chase returned, looking grim. The garrison troops had made it to Arklow, but they had caught up with the loyalist stragglers and slaughtered at least fifty of them in Coolgreany.

There was hardly a word spoken as they set out across the country to White Heaps. It was dark as they reached the summit, exhausted.

They stayed in White Heaps the following morning and, while the leaders argued over what to do next, they ate a meal of the mutton their musketeers had shot. Hugh looked around him at the sweeping landscape below. He could see the familiar blue peak of Croghan to the west, Ballymoyle Hill to the north, and even Arklow to the north-west and Gorey to the south. Their meal was interrupted by firing from the direction of Croghan, but the shots were much too far away to be effective, and after a while the yeomen left. No one in the camp seemed to be bothered by the attack, and by mid-morning they had set out for Wicklow and Garrett Byrne's house in the mountains.

'I'm going home,' Hugh said to Tom. 'I'll join up with yis later.'

'Fair enough,' Tom said. 'Mind those yeo fools aren't still about.'

They were at the back of the column, and as Hugh stood

still it marched on without him. There were close to two thousand men, some with guns but most with pikes. There were no stragglers, and the upheld pikes moved as one, like a slow, spiky river moving downhill.

Hugh wondered if he should leave his pike at the camp, but in the end he took it and set off. Having skirted the lower reaches of Croghan, he headed across the side of Annagh Hill to Monaseed, keeping close to the ditches by the heather line. The heather smelt so fresh it raised his spirits.

No doubt the yeomen had gone to Mount Nebo to alert Gowan to the rebel camp, so he had to be careful, but he reasoned their focus would be on White Heaps, so he was safe for a while at least.

There were loyalists in Monaseed, so he bypassed it and headed uphill. He had been so cautious his journey had taken a couple of hours and he had a raging thirst.

He spotted his sister drawing a bucket from the spring, and all he could say after so long an absence was, 'Mary, give us a sup of that.'

She dropped the bucket, spilling it back into the spring, and stood still.

'Is that Hugh?' she asked quietly.

'Aye, Mary, it is.'

She turned, her face contorted with emotion, and jumped into his arms, making him drop the pike.

'We thought you were dead,' she sobbed into his chest. 'And Tom?' she asked, drawing back.

'He's gone on with the others into Wicklow.' He took the overturned bucket, recouped some water and drank.

They walked back to the house in silence. He didn't know how he felt being back. It was strange, that was for sure, and the old stone farmhouse his grandfather had built looked smaller, and his sister looked younger.

'Bridie has baked some bread this minute,' she said, 'so you're in luck.'

He turned to her and, for the first time, he smiled.

'Bedad, that's luck, all right.'

'You were always lucky, Hugh,' she said, smiling to herself.

She ran ahead, bringing Bridie and their parents to the door. He stood in the middle of the yard, his pike at his side, and they stared at each other. He knew they all, including himself, realized that he was different to the boy who had left them more than a month before. His mother wept silently.

'Tom's in Wicklow?' his father asked.

'Aye.'

'Hide the pike for him, Mary,' his father said.

Mary took the pike from him with both hands.

'You're welcome home, lad.'

He nodded and they made way for him to go inside. His mother and Bridie ushered him to the table and Bridie coated a thick slice of hot bread with butter and laid it on the table with a jug of buttermilk.

'So yis were bet at Vinegar Hill,' his father said.

'A hape of men were killed, right enough. Women, too. But we weren't bet. Most of us got away.'

'We heard tell you were brought down in a charge.'

'Aye. I didn't see God's light for hours. It was all over when I opened my eyes.'

'A ball did it.'

'Or shrapnel, maybe.'

His mother reached over and touched the scar. It still hurt.

'And we heard tell yis brought a gross of loyalists down in Coolgreany,' his father said, a bitter tone entering his voice.

'After they'd ripped the bellies out of innocent women and shot prisoners in the market square before they ran,' Hugh retorted.

'Are you sure yis got the ones that pulled the trigger?' his father asked.

Hugh didn't reply.

'Were you one of them that . . . were in Coolgreany?' his mother asked.

'In Coolgreany? No. Meself and Tom helped bury the prisoners and the women.'

'That, itself,' his father said.

Hugh didn't want a row, so he didn't reply.

'Hunter Gowan and his merry boys paid a courtesy visit more than wance since you were here,' his father said with bitter irony.

'Show him your neck, Lar,' his mother said.

He didn't have to. Hugh stared at the scab across his father's neck and knew immediately he had been half hung between the shafts of an upturned cart. It was a favourite torture. Then he lifted his gaze to his father's watery blue eyes, which were full of pain and disapproval.

'Eat your bread,' his father said then.

Hugh chewed on the bread for a while before taking a draught of buttermilk and swallowing it. He looked at his father, not as his father but simply as another man.

'It's a quaren hard thing for a man to be half hung,' he said.

'It is, by Christ,' his father said with feeling, but he was mollified by the acknowledgement. He struggled with himself before blurting, 'And it's a quaren hard thing to face into cannon and ball, and you only with a pike.'

Hugh nodded. His father's unexpected recognition of what he'd been through hung in the air as his family stared at him, and he found himself unable to explain how he had faced death again and again.

'You look tired, Hugh,' his mother said.

'I am, Mother.'

'Then go and get yourself some sleep. The girls will keep a watch for the militia.'

In a daze, he climbed to the loft and fell onto the first feather mattress he had seen since leaving home.

*

When he woke it was twilight, and he felt as tired as before. There was hot water on the hob waiting for him to wash, and a hot stew also. It was a big thing for him to have these comforts, having foregone them for so long, and yet he had to force himself to enjoy them.

Bridie lit the candle from the fire. He looked up at her and she smiled before sitting at the hearth. Several weeks of camp, march and fighting had made this domestic normality seem beyond his reach, and yet he yearned for the time when it was taken for granted.

When he had finished his meal, his father took down a jug of whiskey, handed him a mug and poured. Hugh put up his hand to stay him. They drank in silence for a while.

'Did you kill many men?' his father asked then.

Hugh looked over at his mother and sisters, but they were staring into the dying fire.

'I did . . .'

'In a fair fight.'

Hugh thought back over Oulart Hill, Ross, Enniscorthy, Wexford, Carraig Rua, Vinegar Hill. For some moments he forgot where he was as he recalled the death and carnage, of pike and old muskets against cannon and well-equipped and organized garrisons. And then he understood what his father, a man of conscience, was asking him. It was hard enough for him that his sons had killed a human being, but now he was wrestling with the distinction between war and murder.

'I killed no man that had no gun or sword in his hand,' Hugh said. 'There were some that did, but not me.'

Hugh's father nodded several times.

'Good. Good. A fair fight. Man to man.'

For the first time, Hugh pitied his father. Like many who had chosen peace at any price, he had suffered terribly. He looked over at his mother and sisters again. They were lucky to be alive, and he knew that for all their hardships and terror and need of inhuman courage, the fighting men had it easier in the end.

They talked until the candle was almost gutted, his father drawing from him many details of which he had no wish to speak, but his tongue was loosened by the whiskey and he kept a distance from his story to help him tell it without breaking down.

Lying in bed, the scenes of agony and death paraded before him and, for the first time since he witnessed it, he wept.

*

They called him out of his troubled dreams, and he washed in the soft early morning light and put on his Sunday best which his sisters had thoughtfully aired. Then as a family they walked across the fields to the thatched chapel in Monaseed. It was a risk, but his father insisted. Immediately he stepped in he knew that for some young girls he was the centre of attention, another United Irishman back from the war along with five or six other men he noticed out of the corner of his eye, standing at the back for a quick escape. He was far from taking pleasure in it and had a strong feeling that his family and the older neighbours were of the same mind, and understood that there had been too much suffering, and there was still too much at stake, for light-hearted interest in him or any other of the returned men. So he kept to his own thoughts and knelt gratefully as the priest's Latin washed over him.

'*Dominus vobiscum.*'

'*Et cum spiritu tuo.*'

It was only when the priest named those murdered by the yeomen, and those men who had not returned, that he raised his head. Then the priest led them in prayer for their souls.

It was no surprise that they had been on the rampage, with no one now to stop them, but the priest mentioned those all over the north of the county, and until Hugh had ventured out with the United Irishmen, the next parish might have been on the other side of the world. Still, there were relatives and neighbours on the priest's list, and news of this was still the hardest to bear.

When Mass was over, the congregation huddled outside the chapel, gravely exchanging news. Hugh gravitated to the stragglers of the dispersed Monaseed corps, young men like himself and fathers of grown sons like Ned Maher, on equal terms.

'Bedad, Hugh,' Ned said in greeting, 'you made it. I didn't think you'd get up from the slap you got on Vinegar Hill.'

'Any sign of Miles?' Hugh asked him, putting his hand on his shoulder.

'He'll make it,' Ned said. 'Never fear.'

'What do you think of Gowan shooting Mick Behan in his bed, in front of his wife? His own neighbour?' Sean Kirwin asked darkly.

'They'll hunt us all down, one by one,' Mick Kavanagh said. 'We shouldn't be here at all – we're only a danger to our families.'

'Ah, we're safe enough for now,' Ned Maher said, trying to make light of it. 'Sure they don't get up before noon.'

They laughed, and the tension drained away.

'As for that walking shitbag beyond in Mount Nebo,' he continued, 'may his fourteen daughters all give birth to good Catholics.'

'Better still if he finds himself looking at the sharp end of a pike,' Mick Kavanagh growled, breaking in on the continued laughter.

Bridie tugged at Hugh's sleeve and drew him away. He assumed she was urging him home for breakfast, but when they were a discreet distance away, she stopped him.

'Cathleen Maher was asking for you,' she said.

'What?' His heart pumped painfully at her name. He looked around to see Cathleen, tall and fair-haired, standing with her mother among the women, her eyes downcast.

'She says she'll meet you here after supper, if you like.'

He looked back at his sister in consternation and knew he was blushing like a girl, but although she was smiling she at least had the decency to look away.

'Well?'

'Aye,' he said faintly.

'You will, then?'

'Aye.'

'Hugh!' Ned called him again and, relieved, he went back to him.

'You were with the army that hit Gorey, I hear. Where is it now?'

'Above in Garrett Byrne country.'

'And how many of them were in it?'

'Near as makes no difference to two thousand.'

'Now, wouldn't we all be safer with them than on our own here? Did they camp before heading into Wicklow?'

'At the White Heaps. Perry wanted to wait for Father Kearns's men, but Byrne wanted to go into the mountains.'

'Maybe we can wait for Father Kearns there. Or maybe the Goldmines river might be better,' Sean Kirwin said.

'Settle your family affairs. We'll meet on White Heaps tomorrow at dusk.'

They dispersed and Hugh rejoined his family to walk home. As Bridie and Hugh fell behind, Bridie cleared her throat.

'Cathleen will meet you below the chapel after supper,' she said.

*

His father brought him to see the sheep and to check the two fields of barley. He had hardly noticed what the earth was up to in the last month, preoccupied as he was with war, and had taken the onset of summer for granted. Now it was good to stand with his father and take in the normal beauty of it all. There was a light breeze against the incline of the ground, the green barley yielding to it in lovely, easy waves.

'It's looking like a good crop,' Hugh said.

' 'Tis, right enough,' his father said.

They lapsed into silence again, gazing on the fresh green of the fields, and the grey-blue of the uplands beyond them. That the fight to keep it theirs was almost over, and that soon they would have no right to walk on land that had been theirs for generations, was left unsaid, and they turned as one and left for home.

'I doubt if there's a lovelier land on earth,' his father said, before disappearing into the cowhouse. Steeling himself, Hugh found a sprong and tidied up the dungheap, doing his best to keep such thoughts out of his heated brain.

SEVEN

Wexford and the Atlantic, 24 June to December 1798

'Myself and Hugh are going for a walk,' Bridie said after supper.

'Oh? Who with?' Mary asked, burning with curiosity.

'That'd be telling ye!' Bridie retorted.

Her mother signalled her to hush.

'Have yis ever seen Hugh shine so with the cleanness?' Mary said, giving vent to her frustration.

Hugh felt himself redden and glanced at his father, but he seemed oblivious as he rhythmically crushed his tobacco between forefinger and thumb.

'She's a good girl,' his mother whispered in Hugh's ear.

It was a relief to get out into the open evening and, once out of sight of the house, Bridie skipped ahead of him.

'And who has you in such good humour?' he asked.

'Sean. Sean Kirwin,' she said.

'I didn't know yis were walking out.'

'Oh,' she said, turning to him, 'I've missed him even more than I've missed you and Tom. Hugh, I can't believe yis are all back safe.' Her face darkened. 'I've prayed hard to God and His Blessed Mother day and night.'

He stopped, and they looked into each other's eyes.

'Well,' she said, 'enjoy her.'

'Enjoy him, you,' he said awkwardly. She laughed, but her eyes were sad. He watched her go up the lush laneway until she turned a corner and was gone.

He crossed a field to avoid the crossroads at Monaseed. Cathleen wasn't at the chapel and he grew even more nervous as he waited. This was worse than before a battle, and he walked up and down, clenching his damp fists to steady his galloping heart. He was about to go when she arrived.

'Hello,' she said.

'Hello.' He was relieved to see that she was as nervous as he was. 'Are you well?'

'All the better for seeing you,' she said, trying to make light as he had often seen her do in the company of friends, but she was shaking, so he took her hand until they had both calmed.

'I dreamt about you often,' he said.

'Did you?' She tried to smile but then sadness clouded her face and she looked away from him.

'My father and Mick say they're going out again tomorrow night, but he wouldn't say anything about you. Are you going too?'

'Aye, Cathleen. I am.'

'Must you?' she asked, tears flooding her big green eyes. He nodded.

'What'll I do if yis're all killed?'

She touched the wound on his forehead.

'Come away from the chapel,' she said, taking him by the hand and leading him through the fields to a perfect hiding place amid the whin bushes, their yellow flowers in full bloom. She lay down and pulled him down with her into her arms.

*

Hugh had never known a woman before, and as he lay quietly on top of her she stroked his hair, her face turned aside. He was still inside her, and he marvelled at her heat. He was in awe of her beauty and of what they had done. Baffled at the melancholy he felt in the midst of such happiness, he rested his head at her neck, staring at the grass.

'The sun's going down,' she said softly. 'I must go home.'

He didn't move for a while, but then he got off her suddenly and they modestly covered themselves again, and stood together. She looked at him for a long time, and he was hard set to know what she was thinking.

'Goodbye, Hugh,' she said then.

'I'll walk you back.'

'No,' she said, 'it's only a few fields.' She shook her head as he made to protest. 'I want to remember you in this moment.'

Cathleen hesitated before she turned and walked away towards the low-lying sun, until she nimbly crossed a ditch and disappeared.

On his way home, he kicked the side of a rabbit path. This wasn't how he'd imagined their parting, and he kicked the verge again. If it wasn't for the memory of her wet heat, their love-making could have been one of his fervent imaginings. He made a cup of his hand, missing the fullness of her breast in it.

Maybe he should surrender like so many others, after all, if some half-just English general could be found. He would have to hide out for a while, till the yeomen settled, but then he could go to Ned and ask him about marrying his daughter. There'd be no problem with Ned, who he had stood with in every skirmish and battle. Ned knew he was sound.

Suddenly fearing he was being watched, he looked around him, and as he did he thought he heard shots. But he had stepped on some dry twigs. That was all. He had heard too many shots in the last month. They rang in his ears at night.

He was crossing a field and nearing home when he heard the clatter of hooves along the road. Without thinking he ducked behind a ditch as he knew it was a gang of yeomen and a pain assailed his heart. They were coming from the direction of his house.

The clatter died away, but still he could not move. Then he was running, taking the road to get home quicker, praying that they had been looking for him and Tom only, but then he remembered the shots. In his happiness he hadn't been thinking.

He stopped outside the house, intimidated by the unnatural silence. The tracks of horses were all over the yard, with a heap of fresh horse dung in the middle, midges hovering over it. His legs wouldn't move, but breathing heavily, he forced himself into action and, slipping into the outhouse, he took down one of the reaping hooks from a rack. The hook steadied him, restored him to the battle-hardened man he was.

The door was ajar, and he pushed it further open. A bluebottle made the only sound as he stepped inside, ready to kill. There was no waiting yeoman, and his reaper dropped to the floor as his eyes became accustomed to the gloom and the carnage took shape and the stale, bloody, shitty smell of death reached his nostrils.

'Oh God. Oh God, no.'

He rocked his head in his hands, back and forth, back and forth, muttering *no* again and again as if the word would reverse what he had seen. And then he was consumed with one thought. He picked up the reaping hook and walked steadily to the two fields of barley. He hesitated for a moment to make sure they were theirs, then he started, grasping the green stalks, handful by handful, and cutting them at the root.

Night fell, and he continued by touch, unmindful of his protesting back, and he did not stop until both fields were cut.

When he had finished, he found it hard to straighten, and he walked back to the house bent like an ancient.

'Ah, yes,' he said to himself, repeatedly. 'Ah, yes.' He knew what he was going to do. The reaping had given him time.

He felt his way through the dark, remembering their bodies were on the floor. He touched a forehead, already cold, and knew that it was Bridie's. His hand travelled down her face and to the rough, congealed gash in her neck. He almost passed out, a feverish sweat drenching him, but he managed to crawl to the hearth and find the tinder box in the cupboard built into its side. He knew the table was upturned, so he scrabbled about the floor until he found it lying against his mother.

His hands were shaking so hard, and his eyes so hampered by sweat that it took him a long time to get the candle lit. He put it in the window, and slowly the dead took shape.

Mary was sitting against the upturned table, her hands at her side as if supporting her, her head propped on her shoulder, stiff where it had fallen, and he dragged her away so he could right the table and forms.

He sat on one of the forms, and for the first time saw that Sean Kirwin was among them, shot through the temple. His father had been shot through the heart, but the women, he saw, his guts wrenching, had had a more lingering, terrible death, their throats cut. He got sick.

The bluebottle which had been silent in the dark started to buzz again in the candlelight. Its flight took up his consciousness until it settled on Sean's wound. Watching the fly walk into the fatal hole made Hugh snap into alertness. He moved the form to the back wall, and laboured to haul his family onto it, sitting them up as much as their stiffened bodies would allow. Sean would not fit, so he propped him up beside them. The two men stared at him, but try as he might he couldn't straighten his mother's or his sisters' heads. It was no use, their hair hung over their faces and they could have been anyone. In desperation he tried to pray, but gave up and looked at them one by one. Then he leaned down to kiss Mary's head, and told her corpse that he was asking God to forgive her the few mild sins she may have committed and to bring her quickly into His arms.

At last he had found a way to pray, and did so over each of them, and he kissed and caressed each head and face, including Sean's.

Then he gathered every burnable material he could find, inside and outside the house, and stacked it in front of them, packed it around their feet, and set alight some kindling with the candle flame. The flames grew stronger until, with a *whoosh*, they surrounded his darling family, and Sean, his comrade, their clothes catching fire. As the flames engulfed them, a wondrous thing happened. They sat up straight, their heads held proudly. He stayed for as long as he could, watching their end, and he smiled as the flames beat him back. It was a small thing to do for them, but it gave them their dignity at the last.

He stayed in the yard, watching the house burn until the roof collapsed, then, conscious that even at this late hour it would bring the neighbours running, he found his pike and set off across the fields. He needed to be near water, so he made for the Bann river below Hollyfort.

He thought it must have been after midnight when he reached it, and he walked across the shallows and through the tall fern and young oaks, before he settled beside a pool.

Sean must have left Bridie home, and that was their undoing. If he had been home, if Cathleen hadn't detained him so sweetly, then he himself would have been dead too, most likely. Even as he thought this, the image of them burning never left him, and the fire burned on in his head all night, even when he must have slept. He got up at dawn, and noticing a large, shadowy trout slipping through the pool, he tried to pike it, but it was hopeless. He drank from the pool instead, before taking off his clothes and getting in, grateful for the cold, clean water.

It cleared his head, and he stood on the bank as he waited to dry. He had to find Tom and tell him what had happened. His grief was turning to anger and he knew there was no question of surrender now, not till ten yeomen or soldiers died at his hands for every one of his family and for Sean. A sob escaped him and he bent over, his hands clenched like claws, his eyes clouded.

He dressed in a daze and stared at the river for a long time before heading north along its banks towards the source on Croghan Kinsella. It took him a few hours and the sun was well up when he left the Bann and headed to White Heaps. He found some shelter and ate some of Bridie's bread, weeping as he ate, but then he stopped.

'No more crying,' he blubbered, 'no more crying. Thank you, Bridie girl, for sustaining me this day.'

There was nothing to do but wait for the others to arrive. He hoped they took a long time, as he didn't feel like talking to anyone, the funeral fire pushing against him as if the memory of it was physical.

All that kept him sane was his hour with Cathleen, the memory of her tenderness like a golden feather on scales weighed down by death. At least it was there. Her touch, her deep, surprising kiss, the way she pulled him into her. He hadn't known what life was like till that moment when another human craved to join with him. He'd known what death was, sure enough, and he knew it better now.

*

Ned arrived with six others, including his son Mick, after dark. Hugh rose to greet him and stood with his pike at his side, the way he had stood in front of his family an eternity before.

Ned and his men stopped dead.

'It's me, Ned. Hugh.'

'Jesus above,' Ned said then, 'we thought you were gone to the next world.'

'Were yis above at the house?'

'You know, then?'

'I know. Sean Kirwin was the unlucky one. Not me.'

'Oh Christ. Poor Sean. A decent, brave man.'

They were quiet as they absorbed this news.

'My Cathleen's mourning for you, Hugh,' Ned said then.

Hugh didn't reply but lit the fire from the deadwood he had gathered. Two of the men had rabbits slung over their shoulders and they set about skinning them.

When they had eaten and were settling for the night, Ned handed him some whiskey.

'I was keeping this to dress wounds,' he said, 'but have some, you. It'll help you sleep.'

*

The army that had forayed into Wicklow and Carlow returned the next day with many wounded in the carts. They had attacked Hacketstown with no success and many losses. Hugh looked through the ranks and carts for Tom, asking the women if maybe he was wounded, but there was no trace of him. He turned to see Ned staring at him in pity and he went cold.

'He died like a lion, Hugh,' Ned said.

The blood drained from Hugh's head, and Croghan fell on its side.

When he came to, he was lying in the shade, and Ned and two women were beside him.

'Here, have some of this,' Ned said.

Hugh accepted the whiskey, and felt it burn into him.

'I loved him,' a woman said, her face twisted with emotion. 'I loved him dearly.'

Hugh stared past her, and for the next two days as the camp busied itself about him, despite the constant company of the women, and despite the attempts of Ned and his other friends from Monaseed to engage him, he refused food and only drank because Ned persisted with a bottle of water. Hugh looked at him as he drank, like a child woken from a deep slumber. He ate that night, and the following morning he took his pike and fell in with the rest as they marched across Annagh and Connahill, stopping for a while in Monaseed. The woman who had said she loved Tom had stayed by him on the march.

'Did they get a chance to bury Tom?' he asked her.

'Sure we told you that,' she said, upset.

'Well, tell me again.'

'They did,' she said. 'He's buried in a bog outside Hacketstown. Lord be good to him, he was one kind and brave man.'

'Would you know where he is if you saw the place again?'

'Of course I would. How could I ever forget it?'

'Thank you,' he said. He knew she needed comfort, but he hadn't the strength to offer it as she cried quietly to herself.

The column proceeded. They were to attack Carnew in the hope of acquiring weapons and ammunition. Aye, Tom was a kind man, but he had torn men to pieces and there was nothing kind about that. He thought of his father's anxious questioning about killing, and knew he was beyond caring about how a man died.

They stopped by the old deerpark wall at Ballyellis. The word spread fast. The Ancient Briton cavalry was on its way through Monaseed, giving them chase, with some local yeos bringing up the rear.

'Well to the rear,' Mogue Loughlin said, spitting.

Holt, who knew his tactics, organized them quickly, placing the musketmen behind the wall, the pikemen behind the high ditch on the opposite side. The women and wounded were moved a safe distance with the horses, and the upturned carts were used to block the road and the gaps in the ditch.

Hugh's heart beat heavily as it always did before a fight, but he was smiling. It was a perfect trap.

'Will you look at that black devil with the drum,' a Wicklow man beside him said as the cavalry came into view. Hugh looked in amazement at the small drummer, the first black man he had ever seen.

'God damn your soul, Anthony King,' the Wicklow man said.

Hugh looked at the Wicklow man.

'He tortured my brother in Wicklow gaol,' he said, but the words had hardly left his mouth when the leading horses, unable to stop, ran into the barricade, and amid the commotion the musketeers opened fire. Before he knew what was happening, Hugh and a thousand pikemen were over the ditch, trapping the cavalry. A terrified Briton in Hugh's sights managed to unsheathe his sword, but he couldn't control his rearing horse and, with a terrible scream that carried the death throes of his family with it, Hugh lunged at him and piked him through the top of his belly and into his heart.

He was dead before he hit the ground, the pike still in him, Hugh's hands still on the handle, and in a mindless fury now, Hugh dislodged the gory pike head and turned to join the attack on a tough Welshman, still mounted and trying to fight. But it was an uneven tussle as another pikeman brought him down, his arterial blood spurting, and he, too, was dead in seconds, Hugh's and other pikes hacking him as he fell. Hugh forged on and the scene repeated itself again, and still again and, blind with sweat, he looked around him in the midst of the carnage, frustrated at not being able to fight a man head on, but those that hadn't got away were almost all killed. Riderless horses were rearing in terror and now posed the only danger, the confusion giving sufficient cover for a few soldiers to clamber over the wall and get away.

'Where's King?' the Wicklow man shouted behind Hugh.

'Who?' Hugh shouted back, scanning the corpses and dead horses, his head hammering.

'The black fella,' he screamed. 'Don't let him get away.'

Hugh swung round and, without thinking, followed the Wicklow man over the wall, unmindful of the big drop to the field, but already there were dozens of pikemen racing after the Britons who were running in several directions, the screams of those when they were cornered flashing his family into his head again, and he pushed himself still harder. The black man was a good runner, but not as good as the Ballyellis man who caught up with him.

'Don't peek me, don't peek me!' the black man shrieked as the Ballyellis man raised his pike to kill him, but the pike came down on him as Hugh and the Wicklow man arrived.

'Leave him to me,' the Wicklow man shouted, and plunged his pike into him, and Hugh, still in a fury, pulled back his pike and drove it between his legs.

'That's the end of your breed, by Jesus!' he shouted.

Covered in blood and sweat, and gasping for breath, the three men looked at each other fiercely, but then they looked down at the black man again. He wasn't yet dead. He was moaning softly, and Hugh thought of how Cathleen moaned while he moved inside her, and looked in awe at the dying man.

'Will you look at those for grand earrings,' the Wicklow

man said, and for the first time Hugh noticed that King had a gold ring in each ear. The Wicklow man took out his knife and knelt beside him, and slowly cut off the right ear. King moaned a little louder, as if this new pain only reached his brain as the Wicklow man handed his lost ear to Hugh. Stunned, Hugh accepted the bloody flesh. And as his second ear was being cut away, King's moans reached a climax before stopping suddenly. The Wicklow man handed the other ear to the Ballyellis man, who turned away in disgust, but Hugh could not take his eyes off it. The Wicklow man got up, put it in his pocket, and walked away.

'Let him die in peace,' the Ballyellis man said, pulling at Hugh's arm, but despite being cursed and cajoled, Hugh would not leave with him.

He knelt beside King who was fading, but his eyes still held intelligence.

'May God ... May your God forgive you your sins, Anthony King,' he said.

A bugle sounded and the horses which had been galloping aimlessly around the field did their best to get back into military line, much to the hilarity of the pikemen and musketeers who were exuberant. When Hugh turned back to Anthony King, he was dead.

He stayed with the corpse until after the column had continued on to Carnew. He had nothing to bury him with, but no doubt there would be carts sent out from Gorey to collect the dead, and he set out to follow the column. Halfway across the field, he paused. He still had King's ear in his hand. He looked from the ear to the corpse, and back again, then put it in his pocket. Not knowing what he was thinking or what he would do, he threw his pike in the ditch and headed across country in the opposite direction, making his way through a ravine and up its flower-covered side.

*

In half an hour he was standing in front of Cathleen as she was putting clothes on a bush to dry. She looked up and shrieked, and he made some gesture to calm her but it only made her worse as she put her hand to her mouth, shaking her head violently.

'I didn't die above in the house fire,' he said. 'That was poor Sean. Sean Kirwin.'

She started to calm, but when she took her hands away from her mouth she was as pale as the dead, and it occurred to him that his clothes and person were spattered in blood.

'We had a fight with the—' he mumbled, pointing vaguely in the direction. 'Beyond in Ballyellis. We bet them,' he said simply.

She roared at him then, and he thought she was rushing into his arms, but she pushed him with such force that he fell back several steps before he painfully hit the hard ground.

Her fright and rage spent, she was sobbing quietly now, and he watched her as he sat up, perplexed. He got to his feet and went to her and touched her lightly on the shoulder. She fell against his chest, despite the bloodstains and stench of battle, and cried ever more bitter tears. He looked up to see her mother.

'I heard guns going off. Was there a fight?'

'There was, missus.'

'I told Cathleen we should get down on our knees, but she said I was dreaming. Are Ned and Mick alive?'

'They are, missus. Not a bother on them. We lost no men at all.'

'So yis bet them.'

'We did. We wiped them out.'

'Good. The Lord have mercy on them. Their mothers will be grieving now, God love them. Well, they'll be out for revenge, my boy, so either you go with the men and get killed in another fight, or you take the car that's going to Dublin from Buckstown tomorrow night. That, or get yourself hung.'

Cathleen broke from him, completely self-possessed. She waited till her mother was back in the house, then turned to him, speaking evenly.

'I'd rather see you gone than hung, that's for sure. I'll see

124

if I can get some old clothes of my father's and wash the ones that're on you. They'll dry in no time in this heat.'

He kept the ear in a rag, and when he'd washed and put on Ned's clothes, he handed her out his own and she told him where to hide in a cattle shelter a few fields away. She was civil to him, but distant, as if they had never been intimate, and it was her mother who brought him supper and his fresh clothes, giving him instructions as to where to meet the carman and who to contact in Dublin.

'She told me to tell you God speed,' she said, turning away.

'She'll always be in my thoughts, Mrs Maher.' He meant it, but didn't feel it. He hadn't settled enough to feel anything, but he knew it was the truth all the same, so he felt compelled to say it.

'Aye, lad. Well, you'll always be in hers, I've no doubt.'

And then she was gone.

He knew he could not stay in the country he had fought for at such cost. Unless he counted Cathleen's reserved love, even if his life wasn't in danger, there was no reason for him to stay.

*

But he could not have foreseen, as he worked as a labourer building a house for his cousin in Booterstown outside Dublin, or supped with his cousin's family in Newstreet in the city, that within ten days his cousin would have him smuggled to the strange city of Hamburg, a place rich beyond his imagination up to then. Neither would he have guessed that Hamburg was a haven for United Irishmen, and that others would follow him to that great port; nor that he would take his chances with an English merchantman that would dock in Bristol and then Cork, before setting out to the New World.

He marvelled at all of this, which happened in so short an interval, as he drank in for what he believed to be the last time the fading coast of Ireland, before the ship tacked south towards the Azores to pick up winds that would carry them west.

EIGHT

Montserrat, late 1798–1802

All went easily for some days. While travelling to Hamburg in calm summer waters, he had learned to furl and unfurl sail, and now, being quick at whatever he was sent to do, the mate, though he showed no favour, was only harsh to him in speech, and Hugh thought of making the sea his life, away from cursed, disputed land. At night he amused himself by watching the moon dance about the sky as the ship rolled over the waves. Then, off the north-west coast of Spain, they were assailed by a thunderstorm, the lightning making day of night, the lit sea swelling around them like a succession of moving hills, and once again he knew the sour taste of fear. As he stood by his watch, he thought that he would accept his fate, but if they survived, he would never set foot on a ship again. The decision calmed him.

By dawn the sea was quiet. The men had talked of hurricanes in the Caribbean, where they were bound, but the season had passed. There would be no more storms on this voyage, though he would almost wish for one as they crossed the doldrums, with barely a lungful of air to draw breath.

*

They dropped anchor off Montserrat at dawn. As Hugh came on deck, he stopped to look at the beauty of the island, set like a green stone in the turquoise sea, its mountains pinning it to the ocean floor. During the voyage Will Thomson had told him he had been here before, that it was an

English colony won back from the French of late, but that it was an Irish island. The mate woke Hugh from his wonder with a roar, and he set to work.

As the boats approached them from a stony beach, carrying small mountains of barrels, he saw that a few among the crews were white, but mostly they were black.

'I only ever seen one black man before,' Hugh said.

'Where you been all your life, lad? Them's not men. Them's slaves. And not just any slaves,' Will said, as if to challenge Hugh. 'Them's the slaves of the Irish.'

'The slaves of the Irish...' Lord Edward Fitzgerald, the United Irish leader who had been killed resisting arrest, had kept a black slave in his mansion. Hugh had heard that in Hamburg, but had thought nothing of it. Now he was confused.

They exchanged cargo, and the islanders rowed back. They were a good distance from the shore, but Hugh could see one group wade out to take the barrels from the boat and carry them to the white checker on the stony beach, as another group waded out with barrels of sugar cane and coffee, and other goods he had never heard of. They worked that way, back and forth.

'Are there any black women?' Hugh asked Will.

'Oho, boy, you can bet your sweet life. I had me a black woman once,' he said, leering, but Hugh didn't rise to that. He was having second thoughts about settling here. He didn't like the idea of slaves. He liked even less the prospect of working among black men every day, keeping the face of Anthony King forever before him.

When the merchandise was exchanged and secure, the captain was rowed ashore. The owner of the Paradise Estate was a friend, and that's where he was going to dinner. Or that's what Will said. He didn't know any more when the man was serious or joking. They got permission to go ashore, and he got his money and possessions. He hesitated over the whiskey jar which held King's ear, wondering if he should throw it into the sea, but he still needed it to remind him he had killed in revenge. As their boat was lowered into the

127

water, he threw in his meagre bag, made sure he sat beside Will, and waited till they were rowing steadily towards the beach.

'I think I want to stay in this place, Will. Do I have a chance?'

'He'll put you in the log as a runaway sailor, but as long as the captain has a full crew, he won't give a whittle if it's you or any other man. There's always some young buck what wants to leave.' He looked ahead as he pulled hard on the oar. 'Leave it to me, Hugh boy. Leave it to me.'

The slaves had gone, to his relief. He wanted to be among his own people, the Irish, in this paradise. He wanted it so badly that he was prepared to ignore the awkward question of slaves, and if he had to think of the slaves like Will did, as beasts of burden, then so be it.

They went to the tavern and drank rum. The heat had turned heavy away from the sea and the day had clouded over. An ale was what he needed. The rum had gone to his head and he could hear himself slurring. Will found an islander to replace him and the deal was done. Will had promised the lad he would teach him the ropes, and they would weigh anchor before the mate knew what had happened. To whistles and jeers, Hugh and the islander exchanged clothes. The islander's grandparents had been English, and with his sunburned skin and fair hair, once he had changed, he looked like any English sailor. His name was Ivor.

They drank more to celebrate, and Ivor told him he worked for the James Kirwan Estate. Hugh stared at him.

'Did you say Kirwin?'

'That's what I said. They'll take you on when they hear I've gone to England.'

'Are there other Kirwins?'

'No. Kir*wan*. There are other Kirwans, aye. Bigger estates. This one's small. Easy to work.' Ivor looked nervously at Will, who gave him the nod.

'Fancy a black tart?' Will asked Hugh, pleased with himself as Ivor slipped away. 'I'm going out back myself.'

'What?' Hugh asked absently, adjusting his hat.

*

He found himself on a cart with five slaves on the road to Kirwan's. An indifferent white youth rode behind, a gun resting across his saddle. Hugh was so uncomfortable in their company that he didn't care where he was going, but the mountain range forced its presence on him and the deep green trees and bushes along the dirt track seemed to grow as he watched them, so that at any moment they might reach out and swallow him up.

The young man rode off to the big house, and the slaves were no help when they arrived at the plantation quarters. They unyoked the mule, ignoring Hugh, and when he asked where he should go they walked away, leaving him stranded like the fool he knew himself to be. The big house was some distance from what were the stables, outhouses and slaves' quarters, but he was too inhibited to announce himself and stood, looking around him, wondering what he could do.

Another white man on horseback, a coiled whip hanging from the saddlehorn, rode into the compound.

'Who in the hell are you?' the horseman asked, his face knotted in hostility.

Hugh could deal with hostility. He stood square and looked him in the eye.

'Byrne. Hugh Byrne. I swapped places with Ivor.'

The horseman stared in disbelief, then threw back his head until his laughter was cut short by a spasm of coughing.

'Who are you?' Hugh demanded.

The horse shifted its feet and its rider considered the question with a faint smile.

'Cash. Mr Cash, to you. I'm the overseer around here. The boss.' He caressed his whip to emphasize the point.

'Well, do I have a job or not?'

Cash showed his yellow teeth, but didn't manage a smile.

'A job? What job? Young Sir Ivor was indentured here. In your language that's work without wages. A white slave, you might say. He was paying off a debt.' His eyes narrowed. 'He had two years to go and you were fool enough to step into his shoes.' His horse shifted again. 'He went off on your ship.'

'He did.'

'You try a caper like his and I'll flay you alive.'

Hugh gazed at the whip and then looked steadily into Cash's eye.

'I'm not afraid of you, Cash.'

'No? You will be. Irish, with a name like that, I suppose. Wexford, I'd wager.'

'I'm a county of Wexford man, yes.'

'A county of Wexford man. A rebel? Yes, a rebel. A killer. Am I right, Byrne? Yes, yes, I'm right. A killer. What the English would call a murderer. Isn't that so? Well, this may be an Irish island, young feller, but it's English law that runs here. Do you get my meaning? It was French a while back, which would have suited you better, but alas, no more. Now, Sir Ivor sheltered in that shack over there. Tell the negars to get you some food. We start at dawn.'

Cash rode away.

Hugh got his meaning, all right. He stood where he was, trying to take in his situation. Two years. He looked towards the slaves' quarters. They were openly watching him, sizing him up. Two years with no pay, or else he'd be handed over as an Irish murderer. He'd mull over it, and having decided this he strode to Ivor's shack, and the slaves turned back to their own quarters.

Ivor's room was little better than a shelter for an animal, but at least there was a hammock, and lying back in it, his alcoholic drowsiness overcame him.

*

When he opened his eyes a black woman was standing before him. She had been looking at him, probably for a while, and although she feared him she did not drop her gaze.

A shout from the slaves' quarters broke the spell, and she turned, then beckoned him to follow her. She led him to a long shack. In one corner was a bench, with a tin plate. She signalled that he should sit there. The slaves were silent in his presence. They ate with their fingers from large communal skillets. She returned with a pot and poured out thick stew with a type of potato. He looked at it as she left him, then did as they did and ate with his fingers. There was no bread, but it was good, and he licked it clean.

He made to leave, then stopped halfway across the floor, wanting to nod to her or somehow indicate his thanks, but no less than the others she ignored him. As soon as he was outside he heard the buzz of their talk and presumed it was about him. He walked a few steps and stopped, considering the possibility that they weren't talking about him, after all.

Darkness fell suddenly. He couldn't find a flint to light the candle, so there was nothing to do but piss outside the shack and feel his way to the hammock. He stared into the darkness, thinking of the black woman who had come to him and given him his meal. She was of an age with himself, he guessed, and almost as tall. He had never seen such a tall and ... *burning* woman. She burned with fear – or was it anger? Or just the heat of the fields? And when she'd turned away from him, he was surprised to see how much flesh she carried behind.

Sweating, he listened to the sounds of the tropical night for a while, then reached through the darkness for his bag and, rummaging through it, he found the jar and ran his fingers over the seal. He had had the cork sealed with beeswax in Hamburg. Reassured, he left it there and, lying back, he thought again of the fight at Ballyellis.

Was he a murderer? Didn't he help to kill Anthony King in the heat of battle? Didn't King delight in torturing and killing a white man like him? At the back of his mind he believed that King most likely took his chances of licensed revenge. That was what Hugh had done at Ballyellis. That was what he had done. He swore he would never kill a man again.

He turned awkwardly in the hammock, cursing the dead

heat as he stripped. The last thing he thought of was Cathleen pushing him to the ground.

*

He was woken by the sound of a whip cracking. Cash was standing beside the hammock, leering at his nakedness.

'I saved you, didn't I?' Hugh didn't respond. 'I saved you from being gobbled up by one of those negar bitches.'

Hugh ignored him and reached for his britches, pulled them on and, in standing, forced Cash to stand back.

'They tell me you were quiet as a mouse in the eating shack.'

Hugh pulled on his boots and reached for his shirt.

'Order them around, Byrne, or they'll crucify you. Did they give you bread? No, I thought not. You're entitled to bread. I don't eat their stuff myself, but it'll do you. Follow them down to the field when you've eaten.'

Cash hesitated at the door, but if he wanted to say something he left it for another time. Hugh was about to leave when he saw the jug of milk, with bread and cheese, left on the barrel that served as a table. It could only have been Cash who left it there. Puzzled, he broke fast on the bounty, and it was good.

He looked outside for somewhere to relieve himself and saw that a mass of green bushes grew behind the huts, but as he squatted and was beyond the point of no return, he heard the negars laughing, men and women, as they performed the same necessity only bushes away from him.

As he cleaned himself with grass and covered what he had left, he caught their collective stench hanging in the air, and pulling on his britches he slunk away in confusion, almost colliding with a line of women carrying water on their heads. They ignored him and carried on to the negar shacks.

He needed water himself. It was a woman's job, he knew, but he had no woman and the negars showed no signs of bringing him any. Cash had called him a white slave, but even the negar men didn't draw water. What did he care? He got a bucket and went up the track. Within moments he was surrounded by a green world, an intense peace holding the small noises of the forest. A strange bird sang and its companion replied. He watched one feasting on red berries. He wanted to stay here, but he came on the sound of water and a few steps further a mountain stream fed a crystal pool hollowed from the rock.

*

He resolved to submit himself to his fate, however harsh it might turn out to be, until Ivor's indenture ran out. He should have been angry with Ivor, but he wasn't. Ivor would find his own hardship.

He followed the line of negars on a track through the forest, the rear taken up by a horse and cart with the implements and provisions, and Cash on horseback behind that. The negars were well enough dressed in white cotton, even the children. If he closed his eyes he could have been with a column of United Irishmen in Wexford the June before, but he was in a place he could never have dreamt of. His father had maintained there was no place in the world more beautiful than the county of Wexford, but now Hugh wasn't so sure.

*

Cash watched over them from horseback, casually holding his blunderbuss, his whip at his knee. At least one of them would be caught by the buckshot, Hugh reasoned, but, armed with machetes, they could hack him to pieces in seconds.

The bossman rode into the field with three younger men, evidently his sons, and stopped alongside Cash. He was dressed in a top hat and cravat, which seemed madness in this heat. They, too, had guns and whips. Like the negars, Hugh paid them no heed and kept working, until he heard horse's hooves tread softly on the light soil.

'You, boy,' an Irish voice said.

Hugh turned to see the boss.

'Did you like the bread and cheese I sent down?'

'Aye. It was very tasty.'

Kirwan's face darkened.

'I'm the boss here, Byrne. A gentleman. So you address me as sir.'

Hugh felt the veins in his neck thump as he fought against spitting at Kirwan. He wanted above all to keep the promise he had made himself the night before.

'Yes, sir,' he said.

'I hear you fought the good fight in Wexford,' Kirwan said. 'We didn't hear about it until lately.'

Hugh didn't answer.

'I have respect for a man who fights. Especially against the English. So I'm not going to horsewhip you for insolence.' Satisfied he had made his point, Kirwan turned his horse, then stopped. 'You're Catholic, of course.'

'Yes, sir.'

'Well, clean yourself on Sunday morning and be at the path by the stream when the sun tops that hill,' he said, nodding towards the hill. 'Father O'Brien will be glad to have another pure Irish soul in his flock.'

'Yes, sir.'

Hugh didn't wait for him to ride off but hacked the cane with all his pent-up anger. By mid-morning it was hot, sweat was blinding him and his back was aching terribly, so when the white backs were turned, he rested. There were about fifty negars, including women and older children. Yet a handful of men lorded over them. Even Cash on his own was not in danger. He took a hack at another cane and watched it as it fell over. A man would not fall over so gracefully but he would fall all the same. But where would it lead? He shook his head, realizing he was falling back into a military state of mind, seeing himself at the head of the slaves, charging the oppressor with machetes instead of pikes. He thought of how many of the county of Wexford men he had seen die, charging musket and cannon. He himself had cheated death by the width of a hair.

*

As the sun's disc rose above the hill on the Sunday morning, Hugh was waiting by the stream path, as clean and tidy as he could make himself. Then he heard the sound of wheels crunching into the cart track, and Kirwan appeared in a pony and trap with his wife and two daughters, his sons following on horseback. There was no sign of Cash. Kirwan stopped the trap, and nodded curtly towards the back. Hugh held onto the back, his foot on the step, and they continued. Without warning Kirwan left the road and went upwards into the forest, the branches snapping at them as they passed, strange birds flying across their path, until they came upon several ponies supporting empty traps, grazing contentedly. They walked from here until they came to a clearing where a priest and about a hundred people were waiting for them. Up to the last moment Hugh had expected a chapel, thinking the mountainside was a strange place for one, but this was it. The rich leaves of the trees formed the chapel ceiling, and a fine one it was.

He knew without thinking that for all their grandeur, even the plantation-owner Irish were subject to the same penal laws as Catholics in Ireland. Or in England too, he had discovered in Hamburg. They showed no fear of being discovered and kept no watch. Evidently, as in Ireland, despite the law even the worst bigots had long accepted that a man should be allowed to worship if nothing else. Yet it was odd to think that in Ireland they could have a chapel now, yet in this place so remote from England they could not.

After Mass the old priest mingled with the families of the plantation owners. Hugh could see that both classes were curious about him, though perhaps they knew all there was to know. It was a small island, after all. Before the war, these poor Irish were the type of people he would have looked down on, though not as brutally as Kirwan did on him. A different side of the world, a different climate, made little difference.

The trouble with the world, he mused, was that every place was local, a small parish where men with small hearts could crunch their neighbours into the dust and think themselves big men for it. He had come a long way to learn that.

Then the priest came over to him and Hugh felt the eyes of the common Irish bore into him.

'I'm Father O'Brien,' he said. 'I hear you were a rebel in Wexford.'

'I was, Father.'

'Are you a Jacobite? Do you mean to cause trouble?'

'No, Father.'

'What you did was a terrible sin. Have you been shrived?'

'Yes, Father.'

'Good.' His stern face relaxed into a pleasant smile and he touched Hugh's shoulder warmly. 'Good,' he said with emphasis, and returned to the Kirwan family.

Hugh walked back to his shack. Halfway there, the Kirwans passed him. Mrs Kirwan and her daughters sat stiffly, pretending not to see him.

The priest's words had made him uneasy, not because he had lied to the old man about been shriven, but because they had made him remember Anthony King's dying whimpers again. In the hut, he took the earthen whiskey jar from his bag, broke the seal and fished out the ear, the ring still gleaming on its lobe, and propped it against the jar. It had shrunk, he thought, and was more grey than black.

He stared at the ear as he reached over and took a swig of whiskey, then spluttered when he realized what had been in the bottle, but it was too late. The fouled spirit burned in his stomach.

He would never have gone after King had he not been mad with grief. But why was the black drummer any different from the unfortunate Welshman Hugh had slaughtered at Ballyellis? Was it because he had been black? No, the Welshmen were on horseback, with swords in their hands. King was already dying, and helpless, when Hugh plunged his pike into him. It was like killing a child.

He held his head in his hands and wept. He had dishonoured his father's memory. That was the worst of all. He took up the ear and held it to his lips.

'Forgive me, Anthony King. If you managed to avoid hell through what you suffered in the end, then forgive me.'

He thought of Cathleen. He'd had King's ear in his pocket when he last saw her. He longed to turn back time, to take her in his arms and bring her to some peaceful place.

*

He hated Sundays after that. He had too much time to think, to torture himself with going over what had happened in Wexford time and again. He threw himself into work for relief in those early months in Montserrat, and over time he relaxed enough to learn something about the strange place he had come to. It was a small island, about twelve miles by seven, and a mountain range travelled like a spine along it. A forest climbed their side of the mountains, and whenever his eyes grew sore from sweat he turned to look at it, enchanted by it as if it were his own native ground.

*

Twice a week he was sent to the kitchen of the big house with vegetables. The kitchen was run by a white woman, good-looking, half English and Irish, but she ignored him and kept harassing the two negar kitchen maids. Once, when she wasn't there, one of the maids let him taste coffee, and when he spat it out because it was so bitter, she laughed and gave him sugar with it, saying he shouldn't turn up his nose like that because everyone knew that Montserrat grew the best coffee outside of Africa. Did she remember Africa? No, she said, her smile vanishing. She was born in Montserrat, and Montserrat was her home.

He grew fond of her on his trips to the kitchen. When her white boss wasn't there, which was often, she laughed a lot.

'What's your name?' he asked her several times, her infectious laughter making him smile in spite of himself. 'Tell me your name!'

But she just turned away and laughed again, as if he were a small boy who had asked her an intimate question.

137

'I'll have to call you something. If you don't tell me your name, I'll have to call you – what will I call you? Agatha, that's what I'll call you!'

They laughed and she waved her finger at him as she left.

'Agatha it is,' he said to himself, smiling.

His friendship with Agatha opened him up to the negars. Instead of nodding or making signs, he said what he wanted and acknowledged help. He was curious about where their ancestors had come from in Africa. There had been no new slaves in Montserrat for years, so most of them were born on the island. He had heard about the slave ships on his voyage, but couldn't imagine Africa. Nor could he imagine how so many people could be enslaved, until he thought of how easily a small but organized army could subdue a country.

His own subdued country seemed as far away as Africa, as he heard no news outside what happened on the plantation.

He waited for the seasons to change, but it turned out that the only change in the year was the rainy season, when there were high winds and sometimes hurricanes.

*

There were some heavy winds but there was no hurricane those first years. Occasionally he would stop to wonder about passing time, the lack of seasons confusing him. The rainy season would come but there was regular rain in this part of the island, so it didn't seem much different, and one day ran into the next as if the same as the day before.

Apart from Agatha, he never made a friend among them, but he grew easy with the negars, mixing with them on Sundays when they were free to have a life outside the fields. Cash noticed and warned him about it, but both he and the negars ignored the warning when Cash wasn't about. One of them showed him how to reinforce his shack against the wind with fresh palm leaves and branches.

He grew to love the light soil and the strange crops it grew in such abundance. Sugar cane and cotton were the first ones he encountered but, apart from coffee, he brought limes, sweet potatoes, yams, beans, pigeon peas, aloes, ginger, arrowroot and tamarind to the big house kitchen. Lying in his hammock at night, he'd recite the names to himself as if they were a prayer, until soon it was as if he had grown up with them, and he looked forward to growing them for himself.

*

Father O'Brien died, and no priest came to take his place. Hugh didn't care about that any more. All he cared about was that Cash grew more brutal with the negars. They said it was because he had no woman, and he was getting old and too fond of rum. His gun in one hand and his whip in the other, he forced the slaves to hold the victim down while he striped him.

This happened three times in a month, until the boss put a stop to it as it left the slave unable to work for days. And there were no more replacements, even if Kirwan could afford to purchase more slaves, which he claimed he could not.

*

One Sunday morning Hugh went to get water and found five negar women sitting around the pool, talking and laughing. In all his time here, no one had seen him at the pool. His first impulse was to turn back, but they saw him and fell quiet, and stood back from the pool to let him get his water. He acknowledged this with a nod, intimidated by their quiet, collective sexual presence. One was a beautiful young woman he hadn't seen before. He dipped his bucket into the pool, their reflections meeting the bucket as he drew out the water. He straightened and looked into her eyes and, disconcerted, he walked quickly away to the low but unmistakable sound of their laughter.

His mind went blank as he walked back to the shack, spilling water as he went. When he had calmed, her lovely face came back to him. She was tall, but softer than the others. Soft, yet something burned in her, like it did in the first black woman he had seen. Perhaps it was because of the scar on her face.

Then he realized that she worked in the big house with Agatha. He hadn't noticed her for a long time, not since she had been an awkward child. It was hard to know with the slaves, who aged quickly, but she was about seventeen or eighteen, he thought. Unlike the other negar women he knew, her hair was straight, and cut at the shoulders.

A slave girl was making his heart pound. Cathleen seemed like a ghost from a dream, a memory from another life.

He touched his face tenderly, as he would the face of the slave girl. Lost in a daydream, tenderness flowed through him, making him smile. His fantasy brought him back to the pool, where they were alone, and this time he looked calmly into her eyes. She didn't say anything or move, but waited for him to touch her.

He touched her cheek, as he had his own moments before, and her eyes closed. When he loosened her smock, she opened them again, but didn't move to stop him and the smock fell onto the grass. Then they lay together beside the pool.

He broke out of the fantasy, chiding himself. It would never happen. Then he realized what could happen if it did, and it took his breath away. He filled a mug of water from the bucket and drank it back, then lay on his hammock, trying not to think of it. But no matter how hard he tried, the image always came back. A black child in his arms, his own flesh. His own blood. His own bone. And yet the child would be black and call him father. And he would think of him as his son, or her as his daughter. Maybe they would be mulattos, like the people he had heard of in the north of the island.

No, no, he couldn't. He couldn't accept that happening to him. It would be a betrayal of his family, their way of thinking of themselves all the way back to Adam. They would expect a child in their image, a reflection of themselves. A black child would be the opposite of everything they knew.

But then, his family was dead, wiped out by hatred. There was no one left to betray but himself.

He had never thought of being a father before. Didn't he, too, want a child in his own image? Yes, he decided, that was what he wanted. One day, when the yeos had forgotten him, he would return to Wexford, and if Cathleen had married, he would find another good county of Wexford woman to mother his children. He stretched in the hammock. It didn't matter what he thought. He felt certain it would be dangerous to touch her. Some jealous negar would kill him.

And yet . . . she softened his loneliness.

He didn't see her for months, which allowed his fantasy to thrive. The romantic pleasures of dreaming of her helped to make his solitude tolerable. And then he would see her in the kitchen, but, flustered, she would turn and walk out to some other part of the house. Her white boss noticed but said nothing. Agatha smiled knowingly. This would keep him going until he saw her again, the yearning to see her giving him a sweet pain, so that she was always in his thoughts.

*

He was weeding when Cash called him, saying he was wanted in the big house. He went to the kitchen as usual, but the white mistress told Agatha to bring him to the study. Airily, she told him to sit down and wait for Mr Kirwan.

In front of him was a large desk, behind which was a large, leather-covered chair, and behind that again was a bookcase which rose to the ceiling, crammed with ledgers and some finely bound books. He waited, alert for any sound, but no one came. He went to the window and looked out on a large garden, filled with small trees and shrubs he had seen in the forest, and hundreds of bright flowers.

'I have some news that you might be interested in, Byrne.'

He turned to see Kirwan standing at the door. He was light on his feet for such a big man, and he went to his desk and sat down, opening a ledger. He leaned back from a page to read. Hugh stayed where he was.

'I thought I'd hear from you.'

'Why is that, Mr Kirwan?'

Kirwan sat back in his chair.

'Well, your indenture is up,' he said softly.

'How long has it been up?' He wasn't angry that he might have worked longer than he was legally bound. He had no sense of time here, and was simply curious. Kirwan ignored the question.

'Times are hard, Byrne. I can't afford to pay you cash. Or in tobacco. However, one of my tenants has gone to Virginia. He left it, lock, stock and barrel, so you can move in, if that suits you. You've been a good worker, Byrne, and I want to be fair to a decent Irishman. I can give you two pounds to get started and you can have it rent free for two years.'

'Can I buy it from you then?'

'Well,' Kirwan said, looking away, 'it's not so easy as it was to earn a living here, but you have that option.'

'How many acres?'

'Five statute.'

'Five. Barely enough to live on.'

'I'll throw in some food and drink to get you started. I can't do better than that.'

Kirwan stared at his ledger. The interview was over, and Hugh turned to leave.

'Tell me, Byrne, how do you feel now that Britain and Ireland have united as one nation?' Kirwan looked up.

Hugh looked at him blankly.

'You hadn't heard.'

'No, sir.'

'It happened last year. I thought, having fought the good fight, you might have views on it.' Kirwan smiled.

Hugh didn't know how he felt. His life here had made Ireland seem unreal. He walked out, glad to be back in the open.

NINE

Montserrat, 1802

Agatha brought him to the holding and cleaned the house, which was built of wood and had two rooms. He teased her and she struck him playfully with the broom, but still she would not tell him her real name. Her presence reminded him of the other maid, whose name he had not asked, so he fled outside to the ramshackle outhouses, which were built of palm branches and leaves like the shack he had left behind.

He had inherited a white horse. It was a thin, weak animal which had been badly treated.

It was a much drier part of the island, so the holding's crucial asset was a mountain stream, which fed a pool not unlike the one he was used to. He brought the horse to drink from it, and then to grass which wasn't too rich, in case the animal would gorge and bloat. In a few days he could tether it beside the richer grass at the edge of the forest. In a moment of humour, he called the horse White Heaps.

When he got back, Agatha was gone. He looked about him, not knowing what to do. There was a barrel of rum already there, whether it had been left behind or whether it was the one Kirwan had promised him, he did not know, but he poured half a mug of that and sat on the porch, drinking and trying to absorb his new situation. He was very poor, but he was a free man. Looking around him, he saw that the field which bordered the house was overgrown with weeds, but cassava bloom showed through here and there, so he left the rum aside and started to weed. He worked till dusk.

The next morning he brought the horse to the stream

again. Back at the yard he found a saddle but no plough. Fed up with weeding, he saddled the horse and took a ride around his holding. It was no match for the gentleman's horse he had seen on Vinegar Hill, or even Kirwan's, but it was his, and he vowed that one day he would legally own a horse worth more than £5. He rode back to the house, and taking off the halter he looked into the horse's eyes, and the horse returned his gaze.

He met his neighbour, who remembered him from the Mass in the forest. Ryan told him the land wasn't fertile any more, it had been worked too hard without rotation, and predicted that Hugh wouldn't last a year.

Maybe he wouldn't, maybe he would.

Ryan invited Hugh to visit him. He had a daughter to marry off, he said with a laugh. If they joined forces, maybe they could survive. Create a dynasty, that's what they should do. He laughed again, but he was serious all the same, and Hugh was interested. A man couldn't stay on his own all his life, but Ryan walked off without saying when Hugh should go to his house.

After he'd had something to eat, he lay down for an hour out of the mid-afternoon sun. Then he went back to the field and finished weeding. The weeds had absorbed a lot of moisture, leaving the crop stunted, but maybe they'd come on now with some rain. He looked up hopefully at the gathering grey cloud.

It rained overnight, which delighted him. He listened as it struck the roof, imagining the roots of the cassava sucking it up as it filtered down through the parched soil. It was still raining lightly when he got up, and everything looked fresh. But after breakfast he was at a loss. He could start digging, but what would he sow? On the plantation, he'd been told what to do, but despite all his time there he was feeling his lack of experience in this climate. It was an odd thing, but he didn't know what month or even what year it was. The lack of seasons meant that one month slipped into another, and so one year slipped into another. What age was he? He had agreed to work two years as an indentured labourer, and it seemed a lot more than that. All he could think of was to ask the tavern keeper. He saddled his horse and rode to Kinsale.

After he'd had two rums, he asked the keeper what month it was.

'November, the eighth day.'

'And the year?'

'The year of Our Lord, 1802,' he said, as if answering the most natural question in the world.

'And when was Ireland joined with England, can you tell me?'

'The year gone. 1801. God blast them.' The innkeeper looked at him, expecting another question he could easily answer.

Hugh fell silent. All of this was confusing him as he realized that the date meant he was already four years in Montserrat. He went over it three times in his head. He had not gone to Cash or Kirwan when his time was up, because . . .

It was too painful to think of his stupidity. They'd cheated him of two years of his life, but his rage was confused and stoppered by shame.

*

Depression took over his days, and he drank till the rum ran out. He didn't bother looking for more. The thought of killing himself sat in his head but he was too lethargic to make the effort. The years of working with the slaves, of working harder than any of them, had kept the nightmare of that '98 summer at bay but with time on his hands it returned. He didn't shave for weeks, or wash, and his own smell became one of the many reasons to hate himself. It always returned to why he had not died with the rest of his family and so many of his friends. At least then Cathleen could have mourned him.

He stood on the porch and pissed into the dust.

As he turned to go back inside, he staggered. It frightened him how he could be so weak, a strong man like him, still young despite all he had seen that made him feel old. Food.

He needed food, but his bread had gone mouldy. How long had he been like this? The fruit was rotten. Even the bucket of water looked bad, a haze of small flies hovering over it. He threw it out, went to the pool and, kneeling, he drank till he was sated. Then he stared at the water, trying to make out his reflection. He could only see a blurred shadow, but the face of the young kitchen maid came to him in its stead, and he smiled. He lay back on the grass, his eyes closed so he could see her eyes the better. Her eyes, as near to black as made no difference, and her straight black hair and even the scar on her face were a wonder to him. She was lovely, and it was a relief to lie there and dream of her again.

He tried to think of an excuse to visit her, but couldn't. So what was the point in dreaming of her? He would have been better off staying a white slave. At least then he could have seen her in the flesh from time to time, maybe even have touched her, kissed her.

He rinsed out the bucket and filled it. Back home, he saddled up White Heaps and rode to Kinsale for provisions. He would dream no more childish dreams, but he wasn't going to destroy himself either. He would harden and hold out and life would offer him something.

*

He took up Ryan's invitation. Ryan tried to welcome him, but the house was too chaotic, with children running every-where. His eldest daughter was pretty, but she was too young. In another year, or three, perhaps, she would make a wife. Ryan knew as much. In the bedlam of his own home, he was adrift.

*

Hugh met Ryan along their boundary maybe one day in ten, but he missed the negars, and rode over one afternoon to the plantation. The negars noticed him, but kept working as if he were a bird in a tree.

He didn't see what had happened to make Cash mad. He had been looking at a mountain peak, bigger but not unlike the Sugar Loaf in the county of Wicklow, when Cash started shouting. Maybe a negar had answered him back, but whatever it was Cash got off his horse and ran over to the cowering slave and hit him across the side of the head with the butt of the gun. Hugh had seen it all before but this time he dug his heels into the horse's flanks and rode hard down the hill and, as Cash raised his whip for the third time, he threw himself at him and knocked him to the ground. Cash dropped the whip but had somehow held onto the gun and, leaning on his elbow, he pointed it at Hugh. The two men stared at each other. Hugh's mouth dried up.

'Lucky for you you're a free man, you whore's bastard.'

He got up, keeping the gun trained on Hugh, and rode off, leaving one of the young Kirwans, who was pointing his gun nervously now at Hugh, now at the slaves. Hugh was shaking as he realized what had happened. The negar, whose mouth was bleeding and whose shirt was stained with blood, looked up, his eyes like a blind man's. Hugh reached out and pulled him to his feet. He stumbled, and Hugh caught him. He looked into Hugh's eyes but all Hugh could see was pain.

'Back off, Byrne,' young Kirwan said.

The negar turned away and did his best to resume his work.

'Get out of here, Byrne,' young Kirwan shouted, 'before I shoot you for trespassing.'

But fear had left Hugh, and he ignored him as he got on White Heaps and rode away.

*

That evening Kirwan arrived with two of his sons, including the one who had threatened him. They stayed on their horses as Hugh came outside and stood on the porch. Old Kirwan kept his head bowed.

'I hear you interfered with Cash's right to chastise the slaves.'

'He was beating a man to death.'

'That wasn't a man, Byrne,' Kirwan said, looking up. 'That was a slave.'

'Then I saved your property.'

'So you did. I thank you.'

'I want a slave.'

'Could you say that again? I don't think I heard you right.'

'You owe me two years' work, above and beyond what was agreed. I want a slave. I want the girl in your kitchen. The one with the straight hair and the scar on her face.'

Kirwan grinned.

'These savages mutilate themselves. Did you know that?'

'No.'

'Cash threatened to shoot you.'

'Yes. He did.'

'You tackled a man with a gun and a whip.'

Hugh didn't answer.

'I should have you horsewhipped in front of the negars. And if they give Cash trouble, then by Christ I will. You can have the girl. She's more trouble than she's worth and I'm tired of her. And so are my boys.'

He turned to his sons, and they laughed before old Kirwan led them away.

*

She came alone the next evening and stood in the doorway, her head bowed. She no longer seemed beautiful to him, but empty, and frightened.

'What's your name?'

'Alice.'

'What?'

'Alice!' She stared hard at the floor.

'Alice what?'

'Alice Kirwan.'

'Is Kirwan your father?'

'No, master.'

'You have an African name?'

She looked at him stupidly, and he knew he had asked a stupid question.

'I'm sorry. I have some stew,' he said, looking outside to the fire.

'Ama,' she said so softly he barely heard her.

'What did you say?'

'Ama. My mother called me Ama.'

He liked it, and smiled, and made to take her by the arm, but to his surprise she drew back from him.

'Come, Ama. I won't hurt you,' he said as he would to a child, and led her outside to the fire. He ladled stew into a bowl and handed it to her, and she waited until he had filled his own and put it to his lips before she moved away from the fire.

'Ama,' he called softly as he sat on the ground. She turned. 'Ama, where are you going?'

'To eat, master.'

'Come and eat with me.'

'Yes, master.'

'And stop calling me master.'

She sat opposite him, and they both slurped at their food.

'Call me Hugh,' he said. 'I haven't heard my own name in a long time. I want you to call me Hugh.' He looked up. Her bowl was suspended at her mouth. 'Go on. Say it. Hugh.'

'Hugh.'

'Thank you, Ama.'

She calmed a little, but still he could not enjoy her. She seemed blank and closed off from him. Frightened. Maybe he should expect that in the beginning. Still, getting questions like these sorted was useful as a middle ground.

'Why is your hair straight?'

She looked up in alarm again.

'The other women – the other negar women – their hair is short and curled, but yours is straight and down to your shoulders.'

'I don't know,' she said.

'Have you white blood?'

Blank. He was suddenly weary. Would it not be better to

fill her with fear and pain, as she expected, than to try to offer regard, when she had no idea of what that was? Perhaps he should beat her – whip her, even. The idea, the power of it, gave him a surge of excitement, but he stopped himself. He didn't need to find out what power was like. He had seen too much power, had paid too high a price in trying to defeat it.

Yet again he thought of his father half choked. It was disgusting to think of the pleasure it gave them to see a man choke, his hands clutching at the rope tightening round his neck, his feet kicking the air, and they laughing to see a poor man they hated totally in their power.

But the excitement he had felt at the thought of whipping Ama made him wonder if he was any better, and what he had done to Anthony King was always there to assure him he was not. Could he do what they did to his father to another child of God? He looked across at Ama and forced himself to imagine stringing her up between the shafts of his cart, until she was almost dead. He had heard a law was passed against chastising female slaves, but who would know? He looked at the sky. It would be bright for another while.

He got up and took a rope from the stable and beckoned her to follow him. She stared at the rope, sweat standing out on her forehead, but followed him as if he were tugging an invisible string which joined them. He placed her between the shafts of the upturned cart, and he was filled with sadness as he imagined his father's ghost swinging between him and the negar girl, his legs kicking the air, his tongue pushed out of his mouth. He looked back at the negar girl. Ama, that was her name. She stared at him in terror, but he knew she would not move unless he told her to.

Terror.

At least he knew she felt something he could understand, something which had a name. He dropped the rope, vaguely conscious of the little cloud of dust which rose as it struck the ground, and he ran his fingers along her dry, open lips until he touched where they were moist. He closed his eyes. Tears slipped onto his cheeks and he shook, slightly at first and then like a man with palsy.

He felt her take his finger from her mouth and lead him inside and lay him on his bed.

*

Darkness fell quickly and in the gloom she left him and he slept till dawn. He couldn't make out the strange sound at first, but it was her snores. He lay where he was until she brought him breakfast.

'Ama ...' he said, taking her hand, but she was still frightened and would not look directly at him. He wanted to tell her that she was not a slave any more, that he wanted to be her friend, but that would be meaningless. 'Ama, say my name.'

'Hugh.'

He smiled. She looked at him warily. She was puzzled, to be sure, but puzzlement was a noble thing to feel in a strange world. He let go her hand to sit up and eat his breakfast, and she slipped away.

When he got up, she wasn't about so he went out to look for her. He looked around the yard, but no sign. Then she appeared from between the trees with a bucket of water on her head. His mouth dropped. How could such a graceful creature not be a queen?

Later, as they worked together in the field, he thought desperately for some way to converse with her.

'Ama,' he said, straightening, 'if you had the chance to be a free woman, would you take it?' As soon as the question was out of his mouth, he was nervous. He knew he was asking her to be his wife, but he didn't know if her refusal or acceptance would be worse.

She stood up, but to his irritation she still would not look at him.

'Well, would you?'

'Where would I go?'

151

That was true. He reflected on her question and then went back to the yard, put a saddle on White Heaps and rode into the forest to think.

A slave did not resist and the Kirwans had soiled her more than once, he knew. But he also knew that even a slave can keep a part of herself that is hers to give at the time she chooses, and that is what he craved, so that when he lay on her, as he had so often imagined, she would ride him back and pull him into her. He thought about having a child with her, and somewhere at the edge of his soul he knew it was all connected in some way. By all, he meant what had happened in Wexford, his voyage here, his bondage, his wanting Ama and her child.

'Maybe,' he said aloud as White Heaps shifted under him, 'maybe, in the way the world is patient, things might be put right, long after I'm gone, and what was done can be repaired.'

*

It was tempting to go to her at night and take her, but it would be worth less than dust if she did not want him, so although he stared at her when she wasn't looking, his eye lingering on the curve of her breast or hip which filled him with luxurious blood, he waited. Nothing else mattered. Nothing. Patiently, he tried to get her to talk about herself, what her history was, what she wanted from life, but it was no use. There was nothing to tell.

'Have you no dreams?' he asked, wiping sweat from underneath his hatband. She thought for a moment. Her face and neck glistened, and droplets trickled between her breasts. He clenched his teeth.

'No.'

'No?'

She shook her head.

He told her about his life in a green, rainy country like this, but not so hot. He told her about how his family were tortured and killed, and it was a mighty relief to be able to do that. She listened patiently, every now and then straightening up to look at him. Encouraged, he told her about the battles he had been in, and then, as if to fill the silence, about his happy childhood roaming the fields he loved with his brother and sisters.

She seemed unmoved by what he told her, as by everything else he said, but he didn't mind. She listened, and that made both her and his memories more real, more outside his imagination, more themselves.

She was astonished when he accompanied her to the pool, carrying the spare buckets. But like everything else she accepted it. He hadn't forgotten that first glimpse of her coming from between the trees with her bucket of water on her head, and going to the pool with her intensified the pleasure which had possessed him that morning.

She showed no sign of affection, but he lived in hope. At least she was not afraid of him now, and was comfortable in his company, though she never spoke unless she had to, and though the only times they were not together were when they went into the bushes to relieve themselves and when they slept.

*

'It is Sunday,' she said one morning. 'Can I visit my friends?' She was fidgeting with her fingers, and licking her lips as he hesitated, and when he nodded, she left slowly, as if at any moment he might change his mind.

He went to the porch and watched her walk down the path through the trees, wanting to call her back, to keep her from going to where she might smile at a man of her own kind, and give her love and her body to him. She disappeared. He had only to call her and she would come back, he knew that; but he also knew she would hate him then, and that he could not bear.

She returned in the late afternoon in time to prepare his evening meal. There was no change in her as far as he could see and as usual she did not say anything beyond what was necessary. They sat outside by the fire as they did every evening and he was almost finished when she spoke.

'In the plantation they say you saved Bobo's life.'

He stopped eating and looked up at her.

'Bobo?'

'He tells them stories. They love him. He says you saved his life. He says your children will be story-tellers, like him.'

She went back to her food and he knew she would not say any more about it. He stared at her, trying to see his children in her, his children who would be story-tellers, but he finished his meal feeling lonelier than he had been in a long time. In his longing he would have preferred if Ama had softened towards him as she found him, but now, if she did so at all, it would be because of someone else. Because of Bobo. He left his bowl aside for her to wash, then went to bed, staring into the darkness, and thought perhaps he should try to follow the previous tenant to Virginia, where a broader country might give him a chance to make his life. There was no use trying to love a woman who wasn't free. A slave was locked into her own world, which he knew nothing of and could never touch.

By morning he was composed, and life went on as before, except the glow of hope had gone cold. For want of conversation he asked her about Bobo. They counted him venerable and old, though he had been only fifteen in the slave uprising, which Hugh knew was on St Patrick's Day 1786, when they had tried to burn their Irish masters alive.

*

One evening he left her and rode over to the plantation, pretending to look for something in his abandoned shack. The negars were around the fire and at first they went quiet and then a murmur of recognition passed among them. He went into his old shack and stood still for a while, listening hard, but they had gone quiet again. Then he went out and made to get on White Heaps, but turned, and, as he had hoped, Bobo was standing in front of the slaves, waiting for him. Hugh walked over to him. Bobo still had a large scar across the side of his face where Cash had clubbed him. He was a tall man and it was easy to see he had been strong once.

'Hello, Bobo.'

'Hello, Master Byrne.'

'I'm not your master, Bobo. My name is Hugh.'

Hugh wanted to tell him that he wished to marry Ama. He had been foolish enough to imagine that Bobo was a father to her, but now it seemed ridiculous. He turned and, mounting White Heaps, he galloped away.

*

Again he tried to think of leaving Ama and Montserrat, but he would catch himself staring at her as if in a dream and a reverie of their happiness would make him believe that all was well, until, in an instant, bleak reality returned.

He hadn't been to the pool with her for a long time. He suspected that when she was with her friends they had laughed at him because, to them, carrying water was women's work, but now they needed water to irrigate the cotton field and went to the pool together. When she bent to dip the bucket in, and then raise it to her head, she was so beautiful that he forgot to breathe. This happened more than twenty times until he could stand it no longer and as she was about to raise the bucket to her head again, he stood behind her and, taking away the hair from the side of her neck, he kissed it. Startled, she dropped the bucket, and half looked around at him, and then, incredibly, she smiled.

At last. He turned her around. Her eyes were almost closed. He brushed her lips with his fingertip, remembering when he had done this before, this time conscious of their weight, and he loved how they rested in his mouth as he kissed her lower lip and then the upper.

She withdrew then, her teeth showing in another smile, and filling her bucket and taking it onto her head, she walked away. Her tattered cotton dress marked her out as a slave, or pauper, but she walked with one hand flowing slowly at her side, the other keeping the bucket balanced on her head, her hips moving like a calm sea.

He filled his bucket and followed her. He loved her, simply.

They were shy with each other for a while. She would catch him staring at her, besotted, and she would laugh nervously and look away again. They still had to go to the pool together, a place now charged, and it was here, a week later, that he kissed her again, and this time her eyes looked into his, breaking his heart, and she did not resist when he raised her dress over her head, leaving her naked before him. Her breasts were scarred, and her belly and inner thighs were scarred, but he was lost in her lithe beauty. When he looked into her eyes again, they were full of tears and, as one dropped onto her cheek, he held her close to him, appalled by her sadness. She resisted him then, but only to unbutton his shirt and run her fingers through the black hairs of his chest. He looked at himself. There was a V of brown where his shirt was open at the neck, but his torso was still white as he had never bared it to the Montserrat sun. Her finger made a circle round his left nipple and to his surprise it hardened. She hunkered down and took off his boots and then his britches, her hand lingering on his white, hairy thigh. She lay back on some dry moss, and looked up at him, deeply serious. He knelt where he was, his hand moving from her knee until it rested on one of the two scars coming in semicircles, a half finger's length from her sex. She turned her head away, lost in he knew not what dreams or memories. He took her nearest hand and ran it over the scar on his forehead. Her rough fingers were like a breath of air across it as she traced it, frowning in concentration. His fingers traced the scars on her legs again, both of them, and she opened her legs to reveal the deeper darkness between them. The hairs of her sex were wet as he touched them, and his finger reached inwards and pulled aside the swollen lip and a deep pink was revealed. He stared, at last privy to the lovely secret hoarded by the darkness of her outer self. When he looked up she was smiling broadly. He stretched along her, on his elbows, and caressed her face in amazed tenderness. Then as they kissed deeply he hardened and she pulled him into her.

TEN

Their first child was a girl; black, like her mother. Ama disappeared one night into the forest and came back the next day with the child. Men were not to know of such mysteries, unlike in his childhood home, where he knew that the screams of his mother had produced his two sisters. To his bewilderment she was angry with him for not giving her a white boy. But she softened when he asked her what they would call the girl.

'Oriole,' she said, stroking the child's head. 'I heard the bird when I was borning her.'

He made her rest, but after a few days she was in the fields again, the child strapped to her back. When the child cried she sat in the shade and suckled her, but without the lost look of contentedness he remembered on his mother's face as she fed his sisters.

Hugh hated the smell of milk, and it was only when frustration drove them together that he lay with her in a blind passion that blanked out the milky smell. Then he got used to it, and settled into wanting her thickened body again.

*

Once, when he was in town, he was challenged about keeping his slave in his dwelling house. His first impulse was to hit the man, but looking over at Ryan, who must have been spreading the word, he held back and said she had no special comfort. He should get a white wife, the man grunted. There were too many mulattos on the island as it was. Hugh replied that white women were scarce for a poor man like him.

He was angry, especially at Ryan, but then he decided he didn't care what they thought. He would be vigilant, all the same.

*

Some of the slave women had a vegetable patch, and Ama asked him for a patch of her own, and he marked out an area with her which he would not touch. She wanted to work on it only when the other work was done, as the slave women were forced to do, but he told her she should work it whenever she wanted. She smiled faintly when he told her that, and he walked away to let her dream, pleased that life was good.

That autumn of 1804 a hurricane hit Montserrat. Ama knew the signs and was terrified. She remembered the previous one when she was a child and had kept her hands over her ears to try to block out the noise. She was angry because he was calm about it, which sobered him into taking her seriously. He boarded up the house, his hair whipping into his eyes, but Ama told him to leave the flimsy outhouses as they would be blown away like twigs.

She went to collect the goats grazing by the forest, and he went to the field where he thought White Heaps would be grazing, but the horse was running in circles. When he caught him he reared with a whinny, fear in his eyes. He managed to mount him and ride to meet Ama driving the nervous goats to the cave. They waited for what seemed like hours. Birds flew by at great speed. The sky darkened, cloud swirling in from the south-east, the sun becoming a faint yellow disc before it disappeared completely. Then it struck. Even in the shelter of the shallow cave, they gasped for breath amid the terrified animals, their clothes flapping. In the dull light, the debris of the island was tossed about like a scattered flock of birds, but the birds had disappeared. Darkness came down like a curtain. They had forgotten the flint and had no means to light a fire, but it didn't matter as they had no fuel. They huddled together all night, afraid to lie down in case they were trampled. The wind roared on and seemed to grow more powerful as the night passed. Ama shouted to him, asking if he heard the roar of the sea above it all. He shook his head.

'Tell us a story,' she shouted.

'What?'

'Tell us a story.'

'But you won't be able to hear me.'

'It doesn't matter. Tell a story.'

This was madness, but he looked around as if he could get inspiration from the cave. He tried to think of stories from his childhood, but the roar of the wind distracted him. And then he thought of the Voyage of Bran an old story-teller had told in his house in Wexford. It was perfect.

So he told them of Bran's journey from Ireland to a Western Isle in the sun. Ama could not hear a word he said, and he could not hear himself, but he spun out the tale as long as he could. Oriole fell asleep, and Ama and even the animals calmed as he spoke about Bran's voyage which became his voyage, Bran's meeting with Manannan Mac Lir, the god of the sea, becoming his own meeting with the gigantic storm off Spain, and Bran's journey to the Western Isles, the Island of Joy and Mag Mon, the Island of Women, became, in his ever-wilder fantasy, his own journey to Montserrat.

By morning the wind was still strong, but the strength of the hurricane had weakened enough for them to venture out. From this height they could see the sea and the ships wrecked along the shoreline, and in between the battered houses and amputated trees, but he was too tired to care for anything other than his own family and animals and home. They drove the goats back to the edge of the forest, having to negotiate their way across fallen trees and tortured brush, the goats stubbornly halting to munch leaves.

Only the porch remained of their house, and they could see at a glance that their modest crops of sugar cane, cotton and coffee were badly damaged. They looked around them, numb. Their bed was in a surviving tree, swaying in the wind.

'Where are you going?' he asked Ama.

'My pot,' she said, her eyes wild. 'I have to find my pot.'

She found it, and discovered her vegetable patch was intact, which restored her morale, taking it as a sign they would survive, and although the rain came and made them miserable, they built a temporary shack of fallen palm and palm leaves, and found most of their belongings on the hillside. Ama was resigned to what was lost.

The gods hadn't spared the Kirwans. One of their sons had been killed, and their house was badly damaged – the roof blowing away, Ama heard from the slaves, like a cassava bloom. Holding Oriole, Hugh forgave them everything. What could matter to them if their son was dead? They sold out to another planter and went to Virginia, Ama heard, and Cash went with them.

*

Oriole was three when Bridie was born. It was Ama who insisted on the name. Since the hurricane she had asked him to tell Oriole the story again, and then more stories, as Bobo would tell them. He had fallen back on talking about his childhood, and Ama made him tell his stories almost every afternoon, when they rested from the sun, and once Oriole could talk, she wanted to hear the stories about his sisters again and again, so that Mary and Bridie became heroines in adventures they had never had. Ama was intrigued by the name Bridie, thinking it meant a little bride, but no, he told her, it was short for Bridget, who was a saint and, before that, an old goddess.

A goddess? She insisted on knowing about the goddess. In truth Hugh knew very little about her, except that she had three faces, but that was enough for Ama, and soon she was telling Oriole stories about the three-faced goddess as they worked together in the fields.

Calling Bridie after the goddess was Ama's consolation. She had hoped for a son, a white son. She was consumed by this dream, and while she looked after the girls, Hugh could see that her mind was always elsewhere, yearning for her white boy.

Ama didn't go back to the plantation much any more, and on some Sundays they took to walking the cliffs instead, because the children loved the sea. Hugh had to tell his sea stories again, and Ama talked about the sea once, of how Bobo had told them of the voyages from Africa on the slave ships, when the captains made the women dance and the men sing. Many of them jumped into the sea, he'd said, rather than dance or sing, so they could travel home through the dark waters and be free again.

*

It was another two years before a son was born, and to Hugh's amazement he was white, as white as his father, and Ama returned from the forest with him in triumph. They called him Mongan, from the story of Bran, but the slaves corrupted this to Mungo, after a Scottish minister who had been among them, and the name stuck, being easier to say.

After Mungo was born, Hugh daydreamt of returning to Ireland. He knew it was a fantasy. Ama was full of hope, but her joy sprang from her son, and she now thought little of her daughters. Oriole was five and Bridie not yet three. They had taken for granted Ama's distant care, but when they saw the attention and laughter she lavished on Mungo, they clung to Hugh even more than before, trying to help at every turn, Bridie copying Oriole in everything, and hindering him as they did so, but that didn't matter. He had become an indulgent father and he loved to make them laugh, often at Mungo. Sometimes he worried about Ama's neglect, but their affection made him forget about it most of the time.

Oriole had objected once to her name, screaming that, like Bridie, she wanted to be called after her aunt.

'Oh Mary Oriole,' he had chanted, and she laughed. Thereafter Mary became Mary Oriole, who could become a bird at will and fly over the hills and mountains of Wexford.

One afternoon when Mungo was almost two, Oriole and

Bridie snuggled into Hugh's arms, and settled for another story.

'Save your white stories for your white son,' Ama said quietly, so quietly that he almost missed the hardness in her voice. 'Don't give black girls a white boy's dreams.'

Bridie didn't notice, but Oriole's mouth fell open, and she turned to look at her mother, her eyes awash with tears.

'But Mama . . .'

'Hush, girl,' Ama said without looking at her.

'Well, tell her your stories, so,' Hugh said, dismayed.

Ama inclined her head to him.

'I have no story. You know that I have no story. This boy,' she said, looking back at Mungo, 'this boy will be my story.'

Oriole wriggled around in his arms to look up at him, horrified.

'Mama has no story,' she whispered. 'She's forgotten her stories. But I remember them.'

'Hush. You can tell them to me later.'

Oriole's face haunted him. He thought about it all afternoon and for several days and nights. Ama had told the girls stories about a goddess with three heads, and told them well, but they weren't hers. Or were they? Had she an epic tale she wanted to forget? He had always wanted to hear it, and took her silence to be a reluctance to speak of her slavery, but now he thought he knew what slavery meant. A slave, he was sure, was someone without a story of her own. As Oriole now helped him weed, now played with Bridie, he vowed that this would never happen to his children.

There had been a slave rebellion in Montserrat twenty or thirty years before. They had tried to burn their Irish masters to death, but had failed and many of them were executed. Having been through a rebellion himself, and having had his leaders executed, it was confusing for Hugh to think of it, but he knew one thing. Those men must still have had a story in their heads which told them they were men and not beasts of burden. Bobo was one of the survivors. He knew his story. He told it to the others when the day was over.

They loved him. Ama loved him. She must have heard his tales many times. Then why did she refuse her daughters the same wonders? And then, after pondering it for a long time, he thought he understood. She loved her daughters, but saw the world they would grow into more clearly than he. She did not want them dreaming of something they could never have. He fathomed the truth of it, but not the justice.

Hugh could only imagine Africa from what he had heard from his shipmates, some of whom had sailed on the slave ships and knew the Slave Coast. He could only dimly remember what they told him, except that they also knew the Gold Coast and spoke of the wealth of the African kings in the interior.

One very hot afternoon, when Ama brought Mungo to the stream to bathe him, Hugh asked Oriole and Bridie to sit before him. They had not heard a story in weeks. Oriole had been having nightmares and Hugh thought he knew why.

'Would you like to hear a story?' he asked.

'But Mama . . .' Oriole said.

'A black girl's story?'

Bridie threw her fists in the air and laughed. Oriole, so like her mother, smiled, her pleasure quiet, tempered by something deep within her.

'A long time ago, before your mother's mother's mother was born, there were two little girls called Bridie and Oriole, who lived in a country where there were only black people.

'The country was called the Country of Gold, because it was so rich. Bridie and Oriole had no gold, but they lived in the forest with their mama and papa.'

'Was their papa white?' Bridie asked.

'No, their papa was black and so was their mama. They had lots of animals, and everything they wanted to eat, so they were happy until one day some bad people came and took away the people of the village to a strange country across the sea. Bridie and Oriole saw their mama and papa taken away in chains and they were very frightened and they ran into the forest until they were lost. There were lots of animals in the forest. Some were bad and some were mad but most of them were good, just as people are. Some were stupid and some were clever but often stupid, and most knew enough to get by and bring up their children, just like people do. They found this very interesting to learn, but after a day they got hungry and they didn't know what to do.

'Just then they met a beautiful bird, which looked very like an oriole, but because I'm not from the Country of Gold, I don't know what it's called. But Oriole was called after a bird, so she knew bird language, and she called the bird OriOri, which turned out to be its name. So Oriole asked OriOri if he knew where they could find food, and he said, in bird language, which Oriole understood, that he did and that the girls were to follow him. So they came to a stream in the forest and at the head of the stream was a well, and around the well was lovely fruit of every description, and the girls ate their fill. When they were finished eating, they were thirsty, so they drank their fill from the well. While she was drinking, Oriole noticed her reflection in the well. She got a fright as she had never seen herself before, and then she looked across at Bridie's reflection.

'"Look, Bridie," she said. "That's your soul looking back at you from the water." And Bridie said, "Look, Oriole, that's your soul looking back at you from the water."

'When they were finished drinking, Oriole told OriOri what had happened to their parents, and OriOri thought for a moment, then said in his bird language, which Oriole understood, "Come with me. There is a great King and Queen not too far from here, and they have no children. They will look after you."

'So they walked for half a day, because it was a big country . . .'

Ama was weeding again, with Mungo by her side. The girls looked around apprehensively, then back to Hugh.

'We'll finish the story another day. Now we have to get back to work.' They nodded, and went with him, weeding in front of him, then breaking off to play, then weeding again.

That evening, as he sat on the porch worrying about the price of sugar cane, Bridie stood before him.

'Papa, will you and Mama be stole by bad people across the sea?'

'No, my dove. What I told you is just a story. We won't be stole across the sea. We'll be with you here, always.'

She smiled and ran her tiny finger along his nose, before trotting happily inside, and he laughed, shaking his head.

In the absence of seasons, the children marked out the passing years. Ama grew more obsessed with Mungo and didn't care any more what he told the girls. Mungo returned her love while he was dependent, but from the age of four he started to break free of her and seek out his sisters' company. At first she vented her jealousy and anger on the girls, and beat them for no reason. Hugh fought with her over this, until once, in a fury with Oriole, she hit Hugh and in reflex he hit her back with such force that he knocked her down. Her mouth was bleeding and she put her fingers to the wound.

The girls huddled together in fear and Mungo was wailing. Hugh and Ama stared at each other in shock. The slave had struck her master and the lover had wounded his love.

He turned and walked away, leaving the children to their distress. How could he ask a slave for forgiveness? He strode up the hill and into the trees, grateful for the chatter of birds, but still couldn't drown out the storm that raged through his head. He had fought for, and his family had died for, the right to be equal. He knew now, after all his years of trying to forget, that he hated a world where a master ruled over his slave. He had known it with clarity as he stood on Vinegar Hill expecting to die, but too much suffering had clouded it, as if he didn't care so long as he could live in peace. His indifference had brought him to this. What mocking deity had made him love a poor slave? In his helplessness, he wept. He knew that Mungo would break her brittle heart. The boy had spirit, and he knew without thinking it that he would grow apart from her, maybe leave them behind if only to break free of her, and where would his poor Ama be when that happened, as happen it surely would?

He walked to the stream, where it ran steep and fast, and

washed his face, then went back down along the boundary with Ryan's land. Across the field, he could see that Ama and the girls had returned to work, and Mungo played among them as if nothing had happened and they were a happy family.

'Good morrow, Byrne.'

He turned to stare at Ryan as if he had appeared out of the ground.

'Your fields is doing well, I see.'

'You know they are not, Cathal. So why do you say they are?'

Ryan laughed it off.

'Why we bother, I don't know. Sugar, cotton, there's no demand, and the soil is bet.'

'Well,' Ryan said, his face clouding, 'the soil is bet, true enough. The one thing that isn't bet is the price of slaves, since the Act.'

The English Parliament had forbidden the importation of slaves, and while no slaves had come to Montserrat for years, the market being too small, the Act had driven up the price of slaves throughout the Caribbean colonies. Ryan always seemed to be abreast of such news.

'You have a good investment there,' Ryan said, nodding towards Ama and the girls.

'Them's my wife and daughters, Cathal. How often do I have to tell you?'

Ryan laughed again, but his face was grim.

'If you want to make them free coloureds, that's your business, Hugh. But times is hard. The Irish is leaving and going on to Virginia. The only thing that's keeping me is the price of slaves. It will get higher, mark me. It has to. When the price is right, I'm off. I'm sick of this island. And I don't trust the mountains,' he said, looking up. 'There's too much sulphur around the place. Them volcanoes could rip this place off the face of the earth, so they could. Or an earthquake. I felt something last week. And the hurricanes, God blast them.'

Ryan ranted on, and Hugh looked at the mountains.

When he looked back, Ryan was striding through his scrub, still giving out, but to himself. For all his talk about slaves, he was harmless enough and Hugh liked him. He was probably the only friend he had.

When he got back to the rows, the girls glanced at him and Ama ignored him. He smiled at the girls and, nervously, they smiled back, and he settled into work, grateful for it.

That evening, after they had eaten, Hugh looked up at Ama, trying to find an opening to talk again, and saw that dust had caked over the blood on her lips, like parched earth. He found a rag and soaked it in water and, stopping her in midstride, held up her face to bathe it. Their eyes met, then she looked away.

In bed, she turned her back on him. He was tempted to give in and play the master, but it was anger and when his anger faded he looked for a while at her outline in the faint light, and listened to the crickets. He was sweating heavily, and knew it would be raining by morning, or at least he hoped it would. It was strange that on such a small island it rained every other day just over the mountains, but here there were days he prayed desperately for rain. He thought about what Ryan had said about going to America. If things stayed the way they were, then the only alternative would be to starve. Yet even if he wanted to, how could he go? Ryan could sell his slaves, but would even that be enough to bring his wife and six children to America and survive? Hugh's holding was better, and he could sell his interest in it to the landlord – maybe – but the fertility of the land was failing by the year. Perhaps they should go now, while they still could. Ama stirred.

'Ama . . . ?' He reached out to touch her shoulder, but stopped short. 'Ama . . . if you want Mungo to look after you in your old age, you must let him be now.'

She half turned.

'If you watch his every move and spoil him, he won't grow into a proper man. He'll be useless.'

She stayed half turned for a time and his hopes rose that she would see he was right. But she turned back again and soon he could hear the steady rise and fall of her soft snore.

She never said anything but seemed to pay him heed, and Mungo ran wild like a little animal, so that it was Hugh who had to rein him in, sometimes, and it was Hugh who curbed him when he challenged his parents, who thought he was old enough to help a little. Hugh made him work. Ama did too, but he was lazy.

When he was five, he discovered the young Ryans, and as soon as work and eating were over, he'd run across the scrub to be with them. Hugh was foolish enough to suggest that Oriole and Bridie go too, to play with the older Ryans, but a flashing look from Ama stopped him in mid-sentence.

'Who would they play with?' Ama hissed. 'The slaves?'

Oriole ushered Bridie out to play, pretending not to notice, and Hugh felt his heart splitting in two, knowing that Oriole was old enough to feel such injuries deeply. He turned to Ama.

'I'm bringing you all to America,' he said, his voice caught between rage and grief.

'It's no better there,' she said, shaking her head, 'not for a black girl. Your heart's flower, Oriole, she be a slave there too.'

'How do you know?'

'I know. She can marry a free coloured. I hear there's free coloured up north.'

'Here, or in America?'

'Here.'

'Huh.'

He went out to the stable shack and, taking down the saddle, called White Heaps.

'Where you going?' Ama called.

'I'm going to bring my girls to meet some free coloured children.'

Oriole looked up from her game with Bridie, panic-stricken, and shook her head vigorously.

'No?'

She shook her head again, her eyes wide.

'Why not?'

Oriole swallowed hard and looked from Hugh to Ama and back again. Ama was glaring at him, he knew.

'Jesus, what can a man do?' He threw the saddle to the ground and stomped away to the fields, White Heaps walking slowly after him. It had started to rain.

'Put the saddle away,' Ama told Oriole.

*

Mungo worked with Hugh on a row. By cajoling and threatening him, Hugh had got him used to work. He was slow, but at least he did it. It was getting hot, and Hugh straightened to rest for a moment. He had noticed Mungo looking back at the others all morning, and had thought nothing of it, but now he noticed that Mungo was frowning at them.

'What's wrong, boy?' he asked him.

'If they's black, how can they be my family?'

'What? What did you say?' He grabbed him by the shoulders and shook him violently. 'Don't you ever ... Don't you *ever* mention or even think of that again.'

But Mungo stared at him defiantly.

'What colour are my eyes?' Hugh asked him sharply.

'Blue.'

'And your mother's eyes?'

'I don't know.'

'Brown. Dark brown. Nearly black. Like yours. You have your mother's eyes, Mungo.'

'I have not!' he shouted, and broke away. He ran across the field and sat under a bush, sobbing.

Ama stood up, looking from Hugh to Mungo and back again. Hugh shook his head in bafflement, then calmed himself with effort and went to Mungo.

'Come on, lad,' he said quietly, reaching for his hand. 'Come on, be a good lad,' and, sniffling, Mungo went back to work with him and, it seemed, all was well. He was a child, Hugh reasoned, and had heard about these things from the worldly-wise Ryans, but, he felt sure, he loved his mother and sisters, who treated him like a god.

A few hours later, Hugh stopped and turned in the middle of the field, the buds a stark white in the heavy air. Mungo was growing fast, he noticed, his straight black hair shoulder-length. The sky looked like polished steel one moment. The next it was a dirty grey. The ground was spotted with rain. It seemed as if his family, absorbed in their labour, was stooping slowly through a dream. He thought he had put Mungo's question out of his mind, but the more he tried to forget it, the more it insisted. He wanted to hold his daughters in his arms, wanted to tell them a story, to give them something special to make up for the insult they knew nothing about, to say to them that they were his daughters and that they could hold their heads high, and that Mungo and even Ama could listen and learn that much.

But when the work was finished for the day and he followed them into the house, it was Mungo who leaped into his arms and held him tight. At that moment, the rain fell with great force.

A week later they judged the cotton to be ready and once the sun had burned off the light dew, they set about the harvest. They worked well all morning and were in a good mood when they broke to eat, their aching backs a subject of fun.

'Oh,' Hugh said, stooped and holding his lower back, 'it's terrible to be old,' and the children laughed and, to his gratification, Ama laughed too.

'Oh you are very old,' she said, giving him a light push and he fell over, to the delight of the children.

'Oh, I need a stick. Will someone make me a walking stick?'

'I will, Papa!' Mungo said.

'Good man,' Hugh said, sitting up. 'You're good with your hands. Good man.'

Mungo was pleased, and Ama's heart was full, but when she reached out to touch Mungo's head, he stiffened and her smile vanished.

'Come on, let's eat,' Hugh said quickly. 'We need our strength for the afternoon.'

*

They were almost finished when Mungo sat down in the row.

'I'm tired,' he moaned, his face hidden under his straw hat.

'Come on, lazybones,' Ama said. 'We'll be finished in a little while.'

'Yis're the lazybones!' he shouted, looking up, his face blazing.

Before Hugh was upright, Mungo was on his feet, his body tense with anger.

'I shouldn't be working,' he screamed. 'Yis are the slaves. Yis should do the work. Yis, yis, yis!' he shouted, almost choking, pointing in turn to Ama, Oriole, and Bridie. 'Yis are the slaves.'

Hugh turned in horror to Ama, who clutched her breast as if a knife had pierced it. Her head was rolling. Oriole and Bridie stared at their raging brother. 'I hate yis. I hate yis all,' Mungo shouted.

He ran towards Ryan's land and that was his mistake, as the anguish that roared through Hugh turned to fury and he ran after him, catching him by the hair in a few strides and lifting him with one hand so that Mungo's feet kicked the air, and unbuckling his belt with the other.

'I've had enough of you, you little pup,' he said as if to himself, his breath short. 'I didn't see my family die to raise a tin master like you.'

His belt released, he threw Mungo to the ground so hard that the boy swallowed dust and was coughing and spluttering and crying out as Hugh bore the belt down on his back and backside and legs. He didn't care where it landed so long as it hurt him badly, and by the sound of the boy's screams he was hurting him.

Then Mungo wasn't crying out, but his body was shaking violently. Hugh had seen the bodies of chastised slaves tremble in the same way, in awful silence, and it dawned on him what he had done. Wiping sweat from his eyes, he looked around to see Ama almost beside him, her cheeks drenched with tears, her eyes red as she stared at the prostrate body of her son, her daughters clinging to her in dread and fascination. He did not know whether she suffered more because of what her son had called her, or because of what his father had done to him. Hugh replaced his belt without taking his eyes off them. She leaned over Mungo, crying quietly, and nervously touched his head.

'Son?' she pleaded, her voice breaking. When he did not resist, she rolled him over and gathered him into her arms. All Hugh could do was gather his daughters to his side and stare at Ama and Mungo, lost in each other as Mungo's trembling ceased. Then she stood and, lifting Mungo into her arms, she carried him back to the house.

Hugh and the girls watched them as they disappeared.

'We'll finish it ourselves,' he said, and they set to work, but they were so dispirited, what should have taken less than an hour took almost two.

*

When they got back to the house, Ama was kneeling beside Mungo's bed, staring at him.

'He's sleeping,' Hugh said.

'I gave him rum,' she said. She had taken rum herself, but he knew her slurring was not because she was drunk. He touched her shoulder and she turned her haggard face to him. 'I gave him rum,' she said again.

He helped her to her feet and led her to the table and sat her down.

'Sit in with us,' he beckoned to the girls with his head.

He poured a mug of rum and held it to Ama's lips, and she drank. He poured some into a mug for the girls and told them to share it and, spluttering and coughing, they did. Then he drank his own, grateful for the fiery warmth in his belly.

'He was only repeating what the Ryan children told him. He didn't mean it. He has no sense.'

'Will you beat sense into him, Papa?' Bridie asked.

'I think I did that today, my dove.'

'Because I am not a slave, am I?'

'No, love. You are not,' he said, glancing at Ama.

Ama looked at Bridie, and then, to Bridie's surprise, reached across and stroked her hair.

'Do you want to lie down?' he asked Ama. She shook her head.

He looked around him, not knowing what to do. Oriole and Bridie were staring at him.

'Help me get White Heaps,' he said.

'Where are you going, Papa?'

'To Ryan's.'

They leaped up, grateful for the chance to escape. Ama looked at him quickly, but said nothing.

He cast an eye over what they had saved before he left, and it was a consolation to see that most of it was good. Ama wanted some spun to make clothes, and they could use the lesser quality cotton. The price had fallen since the year before, and had fallen the year before that. He looked at the sky. The clouds which had threatened rain had broken up and it would be a beautiful evening. He felt a love for the island, but as much as he loved it, the time was coming fast when it would no longer support them. He stuffed the cane knife in his belt and held out his arms to the girls. They came to him, and he leaned down to kiss them on the forehead.

'I won't be long,' he said, mounting White Heaps. 'Be good to Mama.'

He rode towards Ryan's. He had only been in their squabbling house the once, when Ryan had tried to marry off his eldest daughter to him. He thought of how a little time could change a man's life, for better or worse. If he had waited a year or so and accepted Ryan's offer, he wouldn't be riding now to kill him.

Looking around him, his thoughts drifted to Wexford.

There was a time when he never wanted to see its blood-soaked fields again. But he told himself that he wanted to go back, just the once, maybe when Mungo was older, and find Tom's grave and bury him where he grew up, where his spirit could have happy memories. That woman, the one who had a fancy for Tom, she would remember where he was buried, and he'd bring him home and bury him in his own land, under the noses of the Orangemen if he had to.

He pulled on the reins and headed to the forest, and once deep inside, where the light was emerald, he turned White Heaps and stopped. He had sworn he would kill no more, and Tom's ghost, he knew, had reminded him of that oath. The thought crossed his mind that he should cut his own throat instead, and it was easy enough to think of it, but he wouldn't leave his children fatherless. He would never return to Wexford. How could he bring his poor Ama, his innocent Bridie and Oriole, and equally, how could he leave them, even for a time? He had only to think of Ama's face as she turned from Mungo's bed to know he would never be happy again, not as he had been. All that was left was to love Ama and his children as fiercely as a man could, and hope for that as consolation.

*

All was quiet when he returned. Inside, Mungo was still asleep, a light sheen of sweat on his forehead. Hugh reproached himself again. Unable to dwell on what had happened, he sat at the table to have a drink. When he tried to pour from the jug, it was empty. He frowned and went to the barrel, but hesitated. Puzzled, he went outside. There was no sign of them. He almost shouted Ama's name, but stopped in case he woke Mungo. Then he saw the footprints in the dirt, unmistakably those of Ama and the girls either side of her. He followed them around to the back of the house, and saw they led through the brush and up the hill past the windbreak trees towards the cliffs, and he knew with blasted clarity what was happening. Desperation propelled him onto White Heaps and he urged the horse faster up the hill through the brush and trees, the young branches snapping into him until he reached the barren ridge near the cliffs.

They were gone. He knew it as surely as if he had seen them fall.

He moaned as he stared at the sea boiling around the bluff, hoping that somehow they would surface and live. But Ama had dragged the girls to the bottom, he was certain of this, and though his eyes never left the water, it was into the emptiness of his soul that he stared.

Darkness fell and White Heaps nudged him. He looked around at the shadowy horse, and considered it. The moon had risen and its light was like eerie daylight. Then he mounted and let his faithful animal take him home.

Part Three

DAN

ELEVEN

Dublin and Wexford, June 1998

The train pulled out and crossed the Liffey and avidly Dan looked upriver. Architecturally, Dublin seemed a hotch-potch, and yet somehow it held together. It had been a long time since he'd been here and it had changed a great deal. The new money had yet to acquire taste, as far as he could make out, but that would happen over time.

A mobile rang a few seats away from him, and he took out his own and dialled Hugh's number. An answering machine clicked in, with Mungo's voice, asking to leave a message for Nuala, Hugh or Mungo. He told the machine that he would be in Gorey on the afternoon train.

Why was he here? What had driven him to a bog in Ireland? It was hardly to cry on his father's shoulder. It was forty years since he had been to Wexford as a baby. His mother had talked about it every chance she got, especially as she grew older, so much so he sometimes thought he could remember it himself. She had always boasted that the reason he had rarely been sick as a child was that she'd bathed him in the cold mountain stream. He could ask Hugh to show him where it was. The old fellow would do that for him, at least.

The train passed through Dun Laoghaire and, spotting a sign for the ferry port, he presumed that this was where his grandfather's remains were landed on their last journey from London to Wexford. He felt as if something in his life was coinciding with something else he couldn't name. As his parents had brought him with them to bury his grandfather, he would have travelled along this same track in his mother's arms. How normal, and yet it made him feel strange and baffled.

He paid more attention to the houses, the wild embankment flowers, the sea, the cliffs – everything. He couldn't think why, unless it was to say to his hidden baby self, this is what you missed, you milk-drunk little stink. His baby self. Oh God, what a phrase. What a thought. What a disgusting thought.

*

Just a few weeks before, he was preoccupied with being a man, a father, a husband. Why was it so painful now even to let those descriptions of himself slip into his thoughts? He had read once about men who acted out their reversion – nappies, soothers, even baby food, for Christ's sake.

He turned his head in disgust and gazed at Killiney Bay as the train wound around the track on an overlooking cliff. How lovely it was, how peaceful and perfect, and he felt himself calm. A mountain punctuated the southern side of the bay. Was that Croghan Kinsella?

The train stopped in Bray. No, of course it wasn't Croghan. They were miles away yet. A lot of young people got off and a few dozen replaced them. A woman with two young children, a girl of about six and an infant, struggled on with a buggy, and he almost got up to help her, but with a deft push of her knee, the buggy behaved itself and slid into the luggage compartment. She sat across from him, her daughter at the window.

The baby started crying, and he watched openly as the woman gave it her breast. Then he looked beyond her at the swans idling on marsh water, the mountains looming to the west.

Those regressives sucked breast milk too. The thought of a grown man drinking his fill of mother's milk, his eyes closed in pre-erotic contentment, was revolting for some reason.

When I was a child, he thought, trying to remember the

Pauline quote. What was it? *When I was a child, I spake as a child, I understood as a child, I thought as a child: but when I became a man, I put away childish things.*

It was the Protestant version, from the King James, but he preferred it to the insipid Catholic one. He had picked it up at college. His flatmate was unfashionably religious and read the King James.

As if by putting away childish things, one became a man. Was that all it took? Others perceived you as a grown male animal, true enough, and supposed that one had put away childish things. Yet how come it only took one betrayal to scatter his confidence? It wasn't that he questioned everything, but that he trusted nothing any more. He didn't know what the questions were, and maybe that was why he had come to Ireland. It began here, somehow.

It was humid, and he was relieved to see the catering trolley. He bought some good coffee and a chicken sandwich which stuck in his throat.

He dozed for a while, then went to freshen up. Trying to keep his balance, he splashed his face with one hand and dried it with the rough paper towel. The train slowed as he tidied his hair in the mirror, and he returned to his seat. They were crossing a road bridge. To his left was a supermarket and a large new-looking school, and beyond them an interesting cluster of nineteenth-century buildings, including a church.

'Where's this?' he asked a man.

'Gorey.'

'Oh. Thank you.' It was sheer luck he hadn't missed it.

He joined the holiday crowd and crossed the station bridge. They hadn't met since they were babies but he recognized Mungo from photographs and, in any case, the family resemblance was so strong they might have been brothers. Mungo spotted him and they smiled at each other.

'Dan.'

'Mungo.'

They shook hands.

'You're very welcome.'

'Thanks, Mungo. It's good to be here.'

They drove up the tree-lined avenue and out the Holly-fort road, Mungo describing the route for him, and suddenly they were in the countryside, but there were many new, large houses on the outskirts of the town.

'Hugh's very excited about you coming,' Mungo said.

'Really? That's a new one on me, I have to say.'

'Oh, yes. Proud as punch.'

'Proud?' Dan laughed. 'Can't wait to show me the solar house, more like. He never stopped talking about it while he was in London.'

'Oho. He's proud of that, all right,' Mungo said in a way which suggested he was proud of it too.

Mungo reminded Dan forcefully of Hugh. Maybe it was the accent, the leisurely, deceptive way of saying things. This was his family and they shared some impressive genes, but thinking of this only reminded him of Kate's child back in London and he looked out of the side window to distract himself.

'This country really is incredibly green. Or have I lived too long in a city?'

'It's lush all right, this time of year. There was a time it just passed me by, but now . . .'

He seemed moved as he took in the luxury of the hedgerows.

He laughed self-consciously. 'A certain kind of woman can make you see things in a new light.'

'I see you've found your heart's desire,' Dan said, trying to suppress another wave of hurt or self-pity or whatever it was.

Mungo took his eyes off the road for a moment to look at Dan, then looked ahead again. They were only travelling at about forty-five miles an hour. There was no hurry, Dan thought, none, and he took a deep, invigorating breath.

'Well, let's say it took a long time,' Mungo said. 'But yes, you're right. I'm content with my lot. I hope you'll get on. I'm sure you have a lot in common.'

'She'll probably despise me, Mungo. I'm just a hack. From what I hear she's a visionary architect.'

Mungo laughed again.

'Don't talk rubbish, Dan. She has to do her bread and butter stuff too.'

So. They lived in the real world, after all, and not in some Celtic mist. That helped, and he relaxed even more. They turned over a bridge and around a sharp corner, passing a nice stone-cut pier. It seemed that Mungo laughed a lot, but far from irritating him, Dan was beginning to feel grateful for his openness.

'That's Mount St Benedict,' Mungo said, continuing his tourist-guide role. 'Used to be a Benedictine monastery, as the name suggests. Before that it was called Mount Nebo, the home of a notorious yeoman. I'm sure you've heard of the Rebellion of 1798.'

'Probably. This is the bicentenary, then?'

'It is. And it'll be hard to avoid hearing more about it in the coming week or so.'

'I see.'

They climbed a steep hill which levelled at the top into a pleasant road lined with mature trees. A couple of miles away there was a long hill and beside it a small mountain, blue in the late afternoon heat.

'Is that Croghan Kinsella?'

'That's her,' Mungo said.

Dan stared at it, fascinated. So this was the mountain which captivated generations of Kinsellas. Were mountains feminine?

'The hill beside it is called Annagh.'

They passed a hamlet called Hollyfort and descended into a valley again, and the road rose gradually towards Annagh and Croghan. Then they turned onto a long lane. Distracted by the hypnotic shimmering of Croghan, he didn't see the house until the last minute. They drove around the wind-break of young evergreens to the front where the full glory of the house was revealed.

'It's glass,' Dan said to himself.

'Mostly,' Mungo said. 'Don't worry, it's not like living in a glasshouse.'

'I know,' Dan said dryly. 'I'm familiar with the literature.'

'Sorry,' Mungo said. 'Hugh and I forget that other people know more about this than we do.'

'That's all right, Mungo. I'm used to it.'

'Well, this is The Moor, Dan, and you're welcome.'

The front door opened and an old sheepdog preceded Hugh, who was stripped to the waist like the bricklayer he once was. Father and son faced each other but didn't embrace or shake hands.

'Well, you made it,' Hugh said.

'I did.' Dan looked the house over. An array of solar panels faced the sun, making the house look more like a spacecraft. He made a quick mental comparison of similar places he knew and with what he had seen on the Web. Looking around him as he went in, Dan noticed three small wind turbines in a field not far from the house. 'Nice place you've got here.'

Hugh laughed mildly and turned back. 'Come in, come in.'

It was cool and shady inside. A long wooden table was laden with salads and fruit. Hugh sat at the table and opened his arms wide to emphasize the plenitude. The dog clambered onto the chair beside him.

'Come on, there's loads,' he beamed, 'fresh from the garden.' He mixed a salad dressing from a small bowl into the large one and tossed the salad like an expert. Of course he gave Sarah credit for teaching him that, back in the fifties.

'Your own garden, I take it,' Dan said, sitting in.

'Whose garden do you think? Now come on, tuck in. It's all organic stuff. Lettuce, three varieties, peas, carrots, broccoli, even nasturtiums,' he said proudly, pointing them out in the large salad bowl. 'The cheese, well, it's home made, in Cavan, but Aidan and his girl got it in a market in Dublin. Nuala gets some on her travels too.'

'She won't be back till tonight,' Mungo said. 'She sends her best.'

'Raspberries,' Hugh continued, pointing down the table, 'strawberries to bate the band, blackcurrants and gooseberries. The best in the world. The cream is in the fridge.'

'I don't know how he does it,' Mungo said, turning to Dan, 'in this boggy soil.'

'Not a bother on it. Drain it, lots of compost, Bob's your uncle.' He reached over to serve Dan. 'The bleddy snails got most of the cabbage and lettuce, but I'll get something to blast the bejesus out of them next time round.'

'This is very good,' Dan said. 'Did you make the bread too?'

'I did, by Christ. In the solar oven,' he added, collapsing into silent laughter, before recovering suddenly and going to the fridge, producing a bottle of white wine and expertly uncorking it. Dan's heart sank.

'Here, get that into you,' he said, pouring a glass to the brim.

'And here I was expecting cabbage, bacon and potatoes,' Dan said, raising his glass.

'Ah, that was ould God's time,' Hugh said, still unable to suppress his delight.

Dan looked on him in wonder. Here was a man who had worked hard all his life, a labourer, a brickie, a truck driver, a builder, used to and happy with the plainest fare – and now he was like a boy let loose in Aladdin's cave. He looked around him. There was something magical about the place with its light-sensitive glass – the entire house, he could see at a glance, designed to conserve and generate electricity. He made an educated guess as to how it was stored. Odds-on heat storage was a combination of rock and water. Despite the bog, he was sure there was rock not too far from the surface. The solar array and windmills generated the electricity, with maybe some oxygen and hydrogen generation for fuel cells. There was so much money put into it that he was sure Nuala had employed the latest technologies. Yes, a pity the office didn't do much work like this. It had the people, including himself.

The wine was good, but already he felt the heartburn.

Mungo worked as a carpenter, so the conversation turned to a comparison between the building trade in Ireland and London, on to what Nuala was doing, and then to what Aidan was doing. When Hugh was fetching the cream from the fridge, Dan asked Mungo how he felt about a house built without carpentry.

He shrugged.

'It doesn't bother me. I made the furniture – the beds, the table here, the chairs, and the kitchen units. Nuala wanted steel for the kitchen but Hugh insisted on wood, so they compromised. She designed it. I made it.'

'It's very pleasant.'

'Yes. Nice bit of wood that. Beech.'

'Locally grown, I suppose.'

Mungo smiled, but didn't reply as Hugh prepared the mixed-fruit dessert.

Afterwards they brought Dan on a tour of the house, and yes, it was pleasant, each room bathed in muted light.

They said they'd leave the technical explanations to Nuala, and Hugh brought Dan to see his garden, which was indeed ravaged by snails.

'The little bastards,' Hugh muttered to himself. 'Anyway,' he rallied, 'none of it is wasted. What I can't use I put on the compost heap.' He looked darkly at the damage. 'I was up half the night on the Internet looking for an organic way to nail the fuckers.'

Dan could restrain himself no longer and laughed out loud. It was such a relief to laugh that he let himself go. Hugh looked at him askance but started laughing too, and the permission that gave him made Dan double up so that in the end one was laughing at the other, the original reason forgotten.

Dan recovered, wiping his eyes and sighing.

'It's easy to make you laugh,' Hugh said, pleased.

'All that white wine, I suppose.'

'Come on. I'll show you these windmills.'

They walked across the field.

'Is that Hollyfort over there?' Dan asked, pointing to a tree-covered hill. Because of it, the sun seemed to be low in the sky, though it was a few hours to sunset.

'Yes, that's Hollyfort,' Hugh said.

To the east of Hollyfort, in the valley, was a line of snaking brush and young trees, probably ash and willow.

'I take it that's a river down there.'

'Yes, that's the Bann.'

'The Bann?' Dan turned to him and Hugh looked steadily into his eyes. 'You mean . . . ?'

'The very one,' Hugh said. Elizabeth was suddenly the unmentioned presence between them.

Elizabeth had bathed the infant Dan in the Bann, near the source on Croghan mountain. It was the single event of his childhood that she had talked about. And her face would change as she spoke, as if it had been a religious experience. He could picture it so vividly that sometimes he was sure he must have witnessed the scene as an adult.

They walked on to the wind turbines, and he listened dutifully while Hugh explained the technicalities to him. They admired the leisurely spin of the rotors in the light breeze before Hugh made to return to the house, and then stopped.

'But you're not here to put up with me bragging about the latest technology, are you?'

'No. Not really.' Dan put his hands in his pockets and absently kicked at a clump of rushes.

'So what's up?'

'Kate and I . . .' Dan swallowed as a rush of emotion left him inarticulate.

'Bad patch?'

'The child is black. I thought you knew.'

'I did. I just needed to hear you say it.' Hugh smiled.

'So you think it's funny?'

'When I was a child we had to collect money for the Black Babies. You didn't have that, of course, having been brought up in pagan England, thank God. But, by Jesus, we spent every penny we didn't have on the bloody Black Babies in Africa.'

'I'm glad you find it so amusing.'

Hugh rubbed his face.

'Did anyone die? No. Well, then, somewhere at the root of it, it's funny. Your job now, I'd say, is to find that big joke at the heart of it, and laugh, mostly at yourself. Perspective, Dan. It gives you perspective.' He squinted against the evening sun, the soft whirr of the rotors the only sound.

Dan looked after him bitterly as Hugh walked back. No one had died. The phrase brought back Charlie instantly. He was the unspoken benchmark of tragedy in the family. Everything else was a joke beside Charlie's death, unworthy of being taken seriously. He had a black grandchild, for Christ's sake, and he didn't give a toss.

Dan stopped in his tracks. What had he just thought?

No. The reason Hugh didn't care was because he knew his genes weren't involved. His son's betrayal didn't mean a thing to him. Nothing new about that, of course.

He turned, drawn to the river, and followed it for a while until he was below a house surrounded by trees. It was a delightful walk, the river full of green, wavy weed and rather small brown trout. He sat on the bank and tried to cross his legs but winced. The damn wound. He thought it felt wet and he prayed it wasn't bleeding. He took off his shoe and sock and, gritting his teeth, raised the plaster. It wasn't bleeding, just oozing a clear fluid, but it was worrying all the same. He stuck back the plaster, and was startled by three black faces staring at him from the opposite bank. His heart pounded. Bloody sheep! For an instant he'd thought – oh, he didn't know what he'd thought, and he strode away only to be pulled up by worry about his foot. Fuck it, was there no way he could turn! He was swearing more in the last week, and worse, to himself, than he had in the past year. He limped to the house to discover that Nuala was back, having collected Aidan, Mungo's son, and his girlfriend from the station on her way.

Nuala looked tired, but she made an effort to be pleasant, which warmed him to her. She was a small, calm, dark-haired woman of about forty. Aidan was tall, thin, with a lot of nervous energy, friendly but with his mind elsewhere in the end. His girlfriend, by contrast, was small and shy, but when Aidan introduced her as Siobhán, she dazzled him with a smile.

While Nuala went to have a shower, Aidan handed out glasses and poured some more white wine.

'I hear you've your own computer business, Aidan,' Dan said as his glass was filled. His heartburn was bad already, so another glass couldn't make it much worse.

'Well, with two other fellas,' he said. 'It's software, actually, rather than computers. Middleware, to be precise.'

It was interesting stuff. Dan noted with satisfaction that Hugh was mystified, but Aidan explained it with remarkable clarity. The conversation turned to technology in general, a natural subject in this household, with Hugh throwing in his thruppence worth. He was talking through his hat some of the time, but what matter. Nuala came back, and the conversation took them to dinner, which Mungo served.

'Are you in software too?' Dan asked Siobhán, who had just listened.

'No,' and she smiled that stunning smile again. 'I'm doing my doctorate.' She sat into the table.

'Oh,' he said, sitting in beside her. 'How impressive.'

'Not really.'

'In what, may I ask?'

'Physics.'

'That sounds impressive to me,' he said, but she just smiled and started eating.

How he envied their easy confidence and natural ability. They thought nothing of it, as if it were the most natural thing in the world to be like that. But then, his own children were the same, or so he hoped. He, however, had always had to work hard for everything he'd achieved. Perhaps they did too, he conceded.

After dinner, at Hugh's insistence, and to their mutual

embarrassment, Nuala showed Dan the technical side of the house. As Nuala knew well, there wasn't anything in it he wasn't familiar with, and he longed to be alone. The place was too lively – too damned extrovert. Luckily, Aidan and Siobhán went away soon after, first to see Aidan's mother and then on to a nightclub. The rest of them were whacked and, having watched satellite TV for a while before they talked over a good brandy, mercifully it was an early night.

At least the brandy had cured his heartburn, but the strangeness of the room unsettled him at first and he tossed and turned. He got up and slipped outside. The stars were huge. That idiocy annoyed him and he corrected himself: the stars looked bigger in this clear atmosphere than he was used to in London. Warily, he leaned his weight back against the glass wall, and once again he was annoyed with himself. He should know better than most that the glass was stronger than any brick wall.

Think straight! he chided himself. Think! Even here, he thought, growing ever more irritated with himself, even here his thoughts meandered. He was here because ... He was here because he wanted to start from the beginning in order to somehow discover who he was now.

He was born in Citizen Road, off Holloway Road, in 1955, at home, like – what was her fucking name, anyway? Mag? Meg? Meg. Like the little black bastard Meg, he was born at home.

He was born at home in Citizen Road in 1955. The terrace was demolished in the 60s, and his family moved to the house he lived in now. A big step up, but he still missed Citizen Road. He often went back and looked at the blank where their house had been. The terrace had been replaced by two tower blocks of flats. Along with Karl's encouragement, it was what made him become an architect, really, the idea that you could so radically change a street which had seemed permanent. That had struck him when he'd gone back to the street in his teens, and the gleaming concrete and glass towers had stayed in his mind as symbols of possibility, of breaking free.

His best friend had been an older girl next door, or she had been for a few years. Then she disappeared into her own pubertal life. It was Nancy who had told him about Charlie, and for a long time he had thought of him as an imaginary companion. He hadn't understood that Charlie was his physical brother, who had once been alive. So he never asked Hugh or Elizabeth about him in those early years.

It was strange how one could forget these things, but he remembered now why he hadn't made the connection. Was he imagining this? Both Elizabeth and Hugh had always referred to their dead son as The Fisherman. They never mentioned him by name, a fact that puzzled him all through his youth, but he had only to look at his own children to understand now. He could not contemplate their loss. It was literally unspeakable.

He had imagined The Fisherman as a tall, shadowy man in a sailor's jacket and woollen cap, sitting in a boat on the lake in Finsbury Park because, sometimes, when Hugh told him stories, he told about how he used to fish with The Fisherman on a big lake in Ireland. As a child he couldn't imagine a lake in Ireland so it became the one in Finsbury Park. They had fished, Hugh said, for the Great Salmon of Knowledge, which, if you ate it, gave you wisdom and a knowledge of all things. They never caught it, but the patient fishing gave wisdom of a kind.

He shook his head, moved that he remembered that closeness with his father, Hugh's face full of joy and his eyes full of sadness.

Even if he knew that once he'd discovered the real identity of The Fisherman, it was obvious the story was not for him, that he was outside its meaning – even as he knew this, he still clung to that precious closeness with him. He had to, seeing as it was all he had.

Speak of the devil, he thought as Hugh came out and, looking up at the sky as he had done, let loose a modest stream with a grunt of satisfaction. Even as his waters hit the ground, Dan knew that Hugh was aware of his presence.

'You might well ask,' Hugh asked rhetorically as he shook

free the remaining drops: '"What's an en suite for in the middle of the night?" And I would have to reply that, at my age, it's hard to beat the pleasure of a good piss under the stars.'

TWELVE

Wexford, June 1998

That night, the image of Hugh with The Fisherman on the
lake, the lake bordered by a mountain which came down
to its shore, wouldn't leave him be. It was like looking at
photographs taken from different angles of the same, timeless
scene. They were there, not saying anything, not doing
anything but fishing. They never caught anything.

He woke slowly, puzzled at first as to why he was in
Japan. It must have been the soft quality of the light,
combined with the minimalist décor of the room. He looked
around for a bonsai tree, but no, that would have been too
neat.

He padded into the kitchen, bleary-eyed. Mungo was
already up, reading the Sunday papers, a pot of coffee, which
smelt delicious, in front of him.

''Morning,' he said. 'Sleep well?'

'Not really, to tell you the truth,' Dan said, looking for
some orange juice in the fridge. There was some filtered
water so he opted for a large glass of that instead. 'Very
comfortable, mind you, but, you know, first night in a
strange bed and all that.'

'Coffee?' Mungo smiled. 'Help yourself.'

Dan drank back the water and felt better. He poured
himself a cup of coffee, buttered a large slice of coarse brown
bread and dripped some honey on it.

'Any news of note?'

'Ahm . . . the Tour de France is coming this way, if you're
into that sort of thing.'

'Here?'

'Well, Arklow, Enniscorthy ...'

'The Tour de France in Ireland? That's a bit Irish, if you don't mind me saying so.'

'Yeah, I suppose it is.' Mungo smiled. 'It's part of the 1798 commemorations.'

'Oh, that.'

The bread and coffee were wonderful and, combined with this diversion, Dan felt in better humour.

'Forgive my dim wit, Mungo, but what has a bicycle race to do with 1798?'

'I suppose it's because the French Revolution inspired the Rebellion here in '98. Maybe cycling symbolizes liberty, equality and fraternity. I wouldn't know, but there you have it. There was a battle in Arklow, and the decisive one was on Vinegar Hill in Enniscorthy. I presume that's why the race is going to those two towns.'

'I see. So how long is this commemoration going on for?'

'It's been going on all year, actually. There was a fair bit of activity around here too, by the way – in '98, I mean. If you go out the back and look at Croghan – the rebels had a camp beyond that on a hill called White Heaps. A couple of our ancestors were involved.'

'Really?'

'That's a fact. There's been such excitement about '98 all year that we decided to do a bit of research, and sure enough, we tracked down Hugh Byrne.'

'You mean this man is my ancestor too?'

'Yep,' Mungo said, folding his paper. 'Him and his brother Tom, they were up to their necks in it. Tom was killed, actually, above in Carlow. A place called Hackets-town.'

'I'm amazed. I never knew anything about this.'

'Ah, sure neither did we. Siobhán is typing it all into a genealogy program for us. They're coming down next week-end again for the pageant in Craanford. She should have it then.'

'How interesting,' Dan said.

'Apparently, this Hugh Byrne character escaped to France and then on to America, but he was one of the few to come back. It's a sad story, actually, if it's all true. Apart from Tom getting killed, they say that while the boys were out fighting, the militia burned his family to death. He went mad at the battle of Ballyellis after that, and killed all round him.'

'But he came back?'

'Yes, he brought back a son, who was born in America. The son was called Mungo, as it happens.'

'Aha. And his wife?'

'No, she died in America, it seems. I can't remember her name now,' Mungo said, leaning back. 'Irish or Scots, I think. It's all in the family tree yoke.'

'So we might have Scots blood.'

'A wee drop, aye,' Mungo said.

'What's this about Scots blood?' Hugh demanded, taking the kettle and filling it. His hair was still tossed and he was in his bare feet.

'Mungo's been telling me about our ancestor in 1798.'

'Oh, him! I'm called after him,' Hugh said, switching on the kettle and picking up a newspaper.

'You mean you're called after an ancestor who was called after him?'

'Whatever. I'm going to eleven o'clock Mass in Ballyfad,' Hugh said to Dan. 'Fancy coming?'

'Sure. What about the others?'

'They won't surface till the afternoon,' Mungo said.

'Heathens, all of them, God bless them,' Hugh said, brightening.

*

'I didn't think you were religious,' Dan said in the car.

'Ah, just in my own way. The ancestors and all that stuff.'

'That's sort of Japanese, isn't it?' Dan said as he looked ahead towards Croghan, and remembering the sensation he had when he woke.

Hugh snorted.

'The Japanese for cars and Walkmans! My religion is my own.'

'You're talking about my grandfather, then.'

'And grandmother. They're in the same grave.'

'Speaking of cars, I see you don't have an electric one,' Dan said, weakly trying to score a point.

'Not yet, not yet. It's early days for battery technology. But we've high hopes for these fuel cell jobs.'

Dan shook his head. It was bad enough listening to this sort of thing from his son.

'Fuel cells ... A year ago you'd have said that was the name of a racehorse. Where have you got all this ecobabble?'

'Ecobabble? That's everyday speech, Dan. Haven't you heard of the bleddy World Wide Web? Switch on, man!' and he guffawed so heartily that Dan kept an anxious eye on the upcoming corner while silently cursing his stupidity for walking straight into Hugh's conversational high ground. Maybe he should have asked how the blight was affecting the potatoes this year.

It made Hugh feel young, Dan conceded. But then, he thought gloomily, his father was making him feel old. The order of things was out of kilter. He was the sad, embittered old man, and his father was the exuberant, iconoclastic youth. It was all a bit too much.

Fed up with rubbishing himself, he tried to empty his mind, and was grateful that the hedgerows were lush and pleasantly distracting. The car struggled up a steep hill.

'I suppose you know all of this area well,' he said to make conversation, though Hugh seemed perfectly at ease in the silence.

'Not really,' he said, and the ordinary mildness of his tone was a relief. 'I left too young. And you have to walk a place to know it properly.'

Nevertheless, he spoke about families he had known, who lived in houses along the way, which he remembered from his boyhood. It was marvellous to hear him talk like this – no jokes, or put-downs. No showmanship. Just the ordinary remembrance of an ordinary man. He couldn't remember when he had been so happy in his father's company. Or maybe he was just relieved.

'Thanks,' he said as they got out of the car at the chapel.

'For what?'

'For being yourself.'

'I'm always myself,' Hugh muttered as they went in.

Dan paused, taking in the spectacular view to the sea and, to the south, the lowlands beyond Gorey.

After Mass, Hugh stood outside the door talking to some old farmer he knew, ignoring Dan. Then they made some joke and Hugh slapped the old farmer on the shoulder.

'You go ahead to the grave,' Hugh said then, pointing. 'It's about three from the end over there.'

Dan took his time and found the grave. The inscription was odd.

MÁIRE KINSELLA,
beloved wife of Brendan, mother of Hugh,
went to her rest
January 15, 1943.

BRENDAN KINSELLA
53 years,
Died August 17, 1957.

No mention of Máire's age, he thought, tracing the incised words with his finger. Hugh knelt by the grave with a tray of young flowers.

'What have we got here?' Dan asked, settling on his hunkers beside him.

'A bit of wild colour.' Hugh grunted as he dug with the trowel. 'Some cornflowers, baby blue eyes, larkspur, black-eyed susan and a few poppies. A mix to keep the old pair happy. I've been meaning to do it for a while.'

Some of them were in flower already, and very delicate and pretty they were too, Dan thought.

'From wild seed, you say?'

'Wild seed. There's too much shop stuff. Wild flowers

hardly get a look in these days. Considered weeds. But you've got to have wild flowers. Variety. You've got to have diversity. It's the way of nature.'

'How do you know all the names?'

'From the packet.'

'The packet? I thought you said they were wild.'

'If you put a pound of farmer's butter in a fancy packet, it's still a pound of farmer's butter.'

'True.'

'Are you trying to question my eco-credentials?'

Dan threw away a blade of grass he was fiddling with. He stood and looked down on his father. He knew the old boy was driving home a point about the child in his own subtle yet not-so-subtle-at-all way, and felt angrier than he should have been. Hugh glanced at him and saw that he'd got the message.

Dan looked seaward. The sea was several miles away, but he could make out a ship heading north. Hugh grunted and groaned as he kept planting, and Dan calmed. Why should he be angry with his father? He had come here to work things out, and at least the old fox was offering a point of view. Hugh finished and Dan offered a hand to help him up, which Hugh accepted.

On the way back, Dan noticed that the mountain seemed near and barely a mound. Of course they were quite high at this point.

'Mungo mentioned that the rebels camped somewhere over here, if I'm not mistaken.'

'In White Heaps. We'll have a look if you like.'

Hugh stopped and turned, and they went back the way they had come, turning uphill from the post office. They reached it in a few minutes. There was a commemorative boulder on the roadside and they stopped to read the simple inscription.

'White Heaps,' Dan read aloud. 'After the battle of Vinegar Hill the Wexford Army under A. Perry camped here, June to July 1798.'

It was a plateau, with spectacular views. Foxgloves grew in profusion, and through the artificial rows of the evergreen forestry there was a gap through which he could see Croghan Kinsella.

'That's Gorey down there,' Hugh said, pointing south. 'That's Tara Hill,' he continued, pointing to a hill to the east near the coast. He turned. 'That's Arklow. They could see every damn thing from here, that's for sure.' Apart from the commemorative boulder, there was nothing to indicate that it had any significance. Yet as they walked about the plateau, Dan was touched that their ancestor had camped here before a battle, probably wondering if he was soon to die.

'When you think of it,' Hugh said, obviously moved too, his hair tossed by the wind, 'it was only a few lifetimes back.' He thought for a moment. 'My great-great-great-grandfather. It's that close.'

'When you put it like that, one can understand how it's so immediate in people's minds.'

'At a time like this, anyhow. Come on, I'm starving,' he said, heading for the car.

*

It was a dull but very warm day, so after lunch the young people wanted to go to the beach at Courtown. Nuala was all for it.

'Will you come, Dan?' Siobhán asked.

'No, I think I'll just laze around. Thanks.'

'I'll keep Dan company,' Mungo said, as Hugh traipsed to bed, yawning. Nuala made no attempt to persuade them, and in minutes she was gone with the young couple. The two men brought out the newspapers and sat on deckchairs, reading for a while, but soon they both lost interest.

'I take it you know why I'm here,' Dan said out of the blue.

'To see your father, I suppose.'

'Not really, though it's good to see him, the old bollocks.'

Mungo laughed.

'No, it's a bit of marital bother, to tell you the truth.'

'Well, you have my sympathy,' Mungo said, folding the paper by way of a gesture.

Dan had thought of asking advice of some kind from Mungo, but now he saw it was a stupid idea and had only opened old wounds for his cousin. But advice on what, exactly?

'Did she throw you out?'

'No. I bolted for a while to try to sort things.'

'Maybe that's not so bad, then. Another woman?'

'Nothing like that, no. And you?'

'Yeah. She saved my sanity.' Mungo smiled to himself, then he looked at Dan. 'Tess was one good woman, and I owe her a great debt. But Connie and I were finished before I met her, though I didn't know it at the time.'

'You just grew apart?'

'Oh. You don't know the story, then?'

'No – I don't mean to pry.'

'That's all right. It's old news now. I got drunk one night, when Aidan was about nine, and set his bed on fire with a cigarette.'

'What.'

'Accidentally, I hasten to add. He still has the scars.' Mungo's face darkened. 'When I think of what might have happened his face!' He groaned, trying to laugh it off, but couldn't. 'I thought it was ... but I suppose you never get over it, really. The guilt.' He reflected for a few moments. 'He's fine, though. Got a nice girl, which is great. I used to worry about that aspect a lot.'

'Did you leave when he was small?' Dan asked as he suddenly missed his own children very badly.

'No, I stayed till Aidan – and his sister, Ethna – were in their late teens.'

'And – what's her name – Tess?'

'Tess has a solid, decent guy in her life. We're still friends.' He smiled. 'We meet the odd time in Dublin. We helped each other out at a bad time for both of us, so that's still a big thing between us. But then, my mother died and left me the farm, so Connie and I moved down here – I mean, to the farm beyond Monaseed, and Tess and I sort of drifted apart. Shag it,' he said, smiling in spite of himself, 'I missed that woman for years.'

'My wife's had a black child,' Dan blurted.

'Christ! Sorry,' Mungo back-pedalled, putting up his hand. 'Sorry, Dan.'

'They say it's possible that it was dormant in the genes.'

'Well, that's something,' Mungo said, relieved.

'Do you think? To tell you the truth, I don't know if I want to believe that, or can't face the thought that she slept with a black man, or which of the two is worse.'

'You could have a paternity test, couldn't you?'

'I don't want one,' Dan said quietly. 'In my head I love her so much, and yet if I loved her properly, this wouldn't matter, would it? So maybe I don't love her after all, maybe I just love what I wanted to love in her. It's bloody confusing, I can tell you.'

'I can see why you need the space,' Mungo said, rising. 'Do you want a beer?'

'Yeah. That would be great.'

He had said it. Why had it taken him so long to say it? There it was, the real question: did he really love her, or had he indulged in some adolescent fantasy all along? He could see that she was ageing, the wrinkles and loosening flesh were becoming more obvious all the time – but no, he could truthfully say that that didn't matter a damn. It didn't matter at all, no more than she cared about his slack belly and grey hairs. So that question, too, was answered. It wasn't a mid-life crisis, at least not in the clichéd sense of looking for another, younger woman to make him feel young. No, it was probably much more pathetic than that.

Mungo handed him a beer and, gratefully, he took a few mouthfuls.

'Tess and myself,' Mungo said, sitting, 'we told each other stories – you know, yarns. Lied through our teeth. Before we knew it, we were getting to the root of things through the stories. It's a funny thing: telling a good lie can make you see the truth a bit clearer. Still,' he said, taking another drink, 'that's probably not much use to you. You'd have to find a woman who was good at telling stories to start with.'

'I'm no good at telling stories. Don't have the knack. But it's an intriguing idea.'

'Yeah, well. I was in denial, I suppose. No, I don't suppose it, I know it. It was too painful to admit the reality of what I'd done to Aidan. But I can tell you this much: you can know something happened, objectively. But if you don't feel the thing, it might as well be a dream, or worse, something that happened to someone else. But it was too painful to feel it, and the yarns helped. Yeah, they helped a lot, actually. They helped me to face what I'd done, and ask Aidan to forgive me.

'And he did. That brave lad – he was only eleven or so at the time – came up to me and said, "Da, it's all right. I forgive you." Those very words. I'll never forget it. It released me, you know, into feeling like a human being, a man.'

Dan was intrigued by the idea of forgiveness having anything to do with feeling like a man. He had never felt like a man. Not really. Not in himself, by himself. With Kate, he was half of something. Without her, he was nothing.

It was different for women. Or maybe not. He didn't know. How could he? But he was beginning to realize that a man didn't become a man by reaching a certain age, not even by becoming a father. There was something else.

'Mungo, am I right in thinking there was a time between the asking and the saying, so to speak?'

'Yeah. Yeah, there was. I asked him to think about it, and not just say it out of loyalty. I was in bits, of course. He might have said no. But I wanted him to really know what he felt about me. That's why I brought him fishing. You can think when you're fishing, you see, so I thought it would give him time to think.' He laughed suddenly. 'In an hour or so! I was so naive I thought an hour would be enough for him – half an hour, even. But the child was wiser than the man and he took his time, thank Christ. It was hell, but it

202

was the only real way. There's no getting around these things. They take time, above all.'

'Was it on the Bann?'

'Yes, it was, actually. Further down from here. There's a big island – for the size of the river, I mean.'

'Would you mind if I went there?'

'Why should I mind? As long as you respect the place, I'm sure the Websters wouldn't mind either.'

'Can I follow the river from here?'

'In theory, yes, but you'd get into all sorts of bother. You should follow the river until you find a footstick—'

'Yes, I've seen that.'

'Good. Cross that and go up the brow till you get to the road. Then go down the road till you come to a T-junction. In Donnelly's field, to the left, you'll see woodland just beyond it. In there you'll find Webster's island. It's covered in mature oak. The pool is halfway down the island on the left. Get on the island itself.'

'Thanks.'

'It's a nice spot.' Mungo got up to go inside. 'A good place to think. Do you want a rod?'

'No. I'd just like to see it.'

'Enjoy yourself, so. I'll get you some wellingtons.'

*

Dan found the island easily enough and, crossing shallows, fought his way through the thick grass and fern beneath the massive oaks. Mungo's directions were good and he reached the pool quickly. There was no mistaking its serenity and within seconds he spotted the shadowy trout flitting through it. He thought of Mungo in this place with his ten-year-old son. A perfect place to ask a serious question. The simple, correct question. He sat down and looked into the water.

Since coming to Ireland he had come to see that some places – maybe most places – were haunted by ghosts as scary as in any story. He felt it now. Rebels before a battle, lovers making love, a heart breaking, begging for forgiveness.

A place, perhaps, where a man might find the courage to be himself.

It was hard to credit that this was the first time in his life that he saw how a place could have deep significance for someone, or why a pre-industrial people might think that the earth was their mother. He'd had very little time for that way of seeing things because he'd been unable to feel it. What had Mungo said? You can know something happened, but if you don't feel it, then it might as well have happened to someone else. Something like that.

If only he'd been prepared for that child. Meg. 'Black Meg,' he said aloud. She had caught him unawares, unprepared, a hollow man. If he'd been sure of himself, what would he have done? Most probably he would have had the paternity test – not to prove anything, but to put Kate's mind at rest that he had no doubt. So he believed her? No. No, he didn't believe her. What he was trying to get clear in his head was that if he was the man he thought he should be, he would believe her. But that was wishful thinking.

It was also too hard on his head. He went back to thinking about the ghosts which inhabited land, knowing that out of habit he had come to see land as a building site and little else. True, he loved a green space as much as anyone, and he had tried to incorporate as many plants into commercial buildings as he could without turning a shopping centre into a garden centre. But they always looked alien, somehow, beneath the strip lighting.

Why hadn't he cared about anywhere? Yes, he took into professional consideration the effect a development would have on its surroundings, but that was different. That was caring about his company's reputation, not about the essence of a place, its history, the meaning of its name – its soul, dammit. He didn't have to be a rice-eating ecology freak to consider that. It wasn't even so much about a place as about himself. Relationship. Making a connection.

Try telling that to the boss with a client breathing down his neck. Function. Get the damn thing done as cheaply as possible and get out.

His thoughts had drifted, as ever. He had come here to think of Kate and himself. Relationship, again. Maybe, though, the two had something in common – the attitude to his profession and what he thought of his wife. He had become an architect because of the difference he thought he could make. He had gone one better than his brick-laying father and Hugh had been proud of that when he graduated. And Kate? He had married her because she was the first person to convince him he was worth loving, and he was grateful. But he never believed his worth himself, not really. Kate, he saw now, had protected him from any challenge to that worth. It took an innocent child with black skin to bring the façade tumbling down. Pooohh, he blew, so hard that a faint ripple appeared on the pool. He let his head fall back and looked up into the canopy of oak leaves. It wasn't about Kate, or the child. It was about him.

He lay back into a cushion of fern and closed his eyes, thinking how lovely it would be to stay here until he merged with the earth, forgetting everyone and everything, until – and he smiled as he thought of this – the millennia had made a fossil of him.

THIRTEEN

Wexford, June 1998

As he crossed the river, something – a stitch – seemed to tear in his foot. He had forgotten his injury and had become careless. He sweated a bit at what the consequences might be, but there was nothing for it but to be a big boy and walk back the way he had come. At the road he glanced into a luxuriously overgrown garden. Two men were walking out the laneway and he waved to them, as he thought people did in the country, and they waved back. He laboured up the hill, and then down the lane towards the footstick, and it dawned on him that the two men were the Donnelly brothers, who owned the land he was walking through, and from whom the site for the solar house had been purchased.

Nuala's car was parked in front of the house. So they were back from Courtown. He tramped in to find them around the table, eating a cold supper. Nuala asked him to join them but he made his excuses and went to the bedroom to check his foot. He got out the first aid kit he had brought with him and gritted his teeth as the hairs were torn away with the plaster. How he had done it he didn't know, but a stitch was loose and the wound was open just above the ankle and oozing a clear liquid beneath it. He opened the tube of sterile water and emptied it into the tray. Then he took the plastic tweezers and, dipping sterile cotton wool into the water, washed the wound, dabbed it with dry cotton and bound it tight with hypo-allergenic plaster to close the wound. He stood up and it was comfortable. Just to be sure, he reinforced it with another layer of plaster before joining the others.

Aidan and Siobhán were going back to the train station immediately after supper. Siobhán invited him to stay with them in Dublin if he didn't mind a pull-out futon. No, he didn't mind, he didn't mind at all, and he keyed their number into his mobile. Mungo and Nuala were dropping them into Gorey and he was tempted to go with them, but he wanted to talk to Hugh.

'I hardly ever see this woman,' Mungo said, putting his arm round Nuala's waist and hugging her to him, 'so I better make the most of it.' Nuala laughed.

'Will you join us, Dan?' she asked. 'Check out the Gorey nightlife?'

'No,' he said, 'thanks all the same. I hardly ever see this man,' he tried to joke back, inclining his head towards Hugh.

'True enough,' Hugh said dryly, and sucked on his teeth.

Dan joined him outside to see them off. Mungo rolled down the window and Aidan did likewise.

'We nearly forgot in the rush,' Mungo said to Dan. 'We were talking about it earlier but got side-tracked. Siobhán has nearly finished the family tree.'

'Please come to Dublin.' Siobhán beamed.

'I will,' he said.

Hugh grunted as they drove away.

'So she's worked it out on the computer, then.'

'I'd like to see it.'

'Me, too.'

They went inside.

'Tell me something,' he said as Hugh reached for the remote control and the TV came on in loud stereo. Hugh looked around, startled, and turned it off.

'Is there something special you want to watch?'

'No,' Hugh said unconvincingly.

'You probably watch it every Sunday.'

'The usual stuff. Out of habit, more than anything else.'

Dan sat beside him on the designer sofa.

'Did my grandfather, Brendan, ever know me?'

Hugh looked serious for a moment, then smiled faintly.

'You were the apple of his eye. Did I never tell you that?'

'No. And I always meant to ask.'

'I must have told you. Sure you were the last one he kissed before he died.'

'What?'

'On his deathbed in the Royal Northern. The Northern's still there, you know. Closed now, though.'

'You brought me once to show me. We stood on the opposite side of the road, and you pointed out the ward where he died. And where Charlie died. But go on,' Dan said, unable to take his eyes off Hugh, his ears keen in case he missed a nuance.

Hugh nodded, remembering.

'Your mother brought you in to him. We were all around the bed, your mother, myself, Sarah and Deirdre, and Elizabeth held you in front of him, and you laughed to see your granddad, and his face lit up and his eyes . . .' Hugh turned away to compose himself. 'He said that the hardest thing was to leave us all. That's what he said. Then Elizabeth lowered you to him and he kissed you.'

'I knew it.'

'That was an hour before he died. He just slipped away then.'

'I knew it,' Dan said again, this time in full voice.

'I must have told you. You were too young to remember otherwise.'

'Maybe.'

'Or maybe Elizabeth told you. Sure you were only nine months old. You couldn't possibly remember.'

'Maybe not. Do you remember telling me stories about The Fisherman?'

'Oh, them. Do you remember them?'

'They were about Charlie, weren't they?'

'Yes. I suppose they were.'

'Why?'

'Why? Lordy, you're doing a lot of catching up tonight.'

'Well, you might be dead in the morning.'

'True. So might you, of course.'

Dan couldn't help but look away and smile.

208

'Indeed, I might.'

'Would you care for a whiskey?' Hugh said, rising.

'I'd love one.'

'I only have Irish,' he said, finding the bottle. 'Will that do you?'

'I like Irish.'

Hugh got two glasses, handed one to Dan and poured until Dan stopped him with his hand. Hugh sat, they clinked glasses and drank. Then Hugh stared ahead, lost in thought, his glass passing from one hand to the other.

'I suppose . . . I suppose it was too hard for me not to be able to see him grow into a man. So I made up these yarns, as if . . . Ah!' He scratched his head. 'Do you remember any of the others?' he asked nervously, glancing at Dan.

'Others? No. Just that one. The Fisherman.'

'Not The Builder? The Farmer? The Soldier? The Foot-baller?'

'No. Were all of them about Charlie?'

Hugh didn't answer immediately.

'You liked them, didn't you?'

'I liked The Fisherman, obviously.'

Hugh took a large mouthful of whiskey and was silent again.

'Maybe I shouldn't have used you like that,' he said at last. 'It was only that one evening you put me on the spot for a story and after that, well, I just thought you liked them.' He drank again. 'You were a child. What could you know of grief? I know what you're talking about, Dan. I'm sorry.' He looked old suddenly, his usual spark gone.

Dan bowed his head. He didn't know quite what he felt, except that the acknowledgement meant a lot.

'Do you remember I used to bring you to Finsbury Park?' Hugh rallied, brightening at the memory.

'We used to play football.'

'I was worn out at the weekends, but I thought, well, I had to get you away from your mother for an hour.'

'Freedom.'

'Freedom. Get your knees cut like any boy. You couldn't

go upstairs to the lav on your own but she'd be fretting. It's a wonder you turned out as sane as you are.'

More subtle praise.

'That's Kate's doing, of course. She made a man of you, thanks be to God. Till she came along, I feared the worst.'

'And what was that?'

'That you'd turn out a nancy boy.'

Dan hooted.

'No, all my dreams were of hot women. You needn't have feared. But I see what you mean.'

'Ah, it was hard on your mother. When you lose a child, the way we lost Charlie, it's hard to rise above your fear. Sheer, mind-stopping fear. That's what it was,' and he lapsed into reflection again.

'I know. I mean, I know now. I can't even bring myself to think of losing Jim or Sara Mae.'

'Or the little one . . .' Hugh looked at him straight on, and Dan couldn't return his gaze. 'You were wanted, Dan, in case you're worried. Is that what you came here to ask?'

'I don't know what I came here for.'

'Well, maybe it should be said, anyhow. I know you grew up in Charlie's shadow, and that can't have been easy. Your mother and myself may never have got over Charlie, but you were wanted, and you were adored. I guarantee you that.'

All the sadness he had ever felt as a child lodged in his throat because, he remembered, once he knew about Charlie, he had always doubted what his father had just told him.

'I'll never forget what Elizabeth said when she found out she was pregnant with you. I couldn't bear the thought of another child, to tell you the truth. Not so soon after losing Charlie, anyhow. I was still a young man and, as the young fellas say today, I couldn't handle it, and I walked out when she told me. Couldn't handle it,' he repeated, nodding to himself. 'And then I heard her say it. She said: "I want this child, with or without you." That's what she said. Hmm. Yeah.'

Dan stared in fascination at his father.

'Did you . . .' he asked as if he was prying, 'did you say anything back?'

'Ah, I said . . . I said something like "We're in this together", or something foolish like that. You know the way it is. You never remember what you say yourself.' He turned to look Dan in the eye again. 'Elizabeth had many faults and, as you know nearly as well as I do, they got worse as she got older – though no worse than my own, of course. Our faults grow fat on us unless we catch them young, and we seldom do. But I'll say this for her. She made that act of faith in life. That made up for everything else in my book.' He took another drink of whiskey, just a sip this time, and Dan took a mouthful too. Hugh grunted and leaned forward to rest his elbows on his knees, and held out his glass to study it.

'God, or Life, or whatever you want to call it, took Charlie away, but we got you in his place. And I'll thank God for that till my dying breath.'

Dan strained his jawbones to stem his emotion.

'Why didn't you tell me this before?'

'Why?' He twirled his glass. 'I don't know. If you'd have asked, I might have. Would have. It's different now. A man from my generation – ah, we weren't brought up to talk about stuff like that. Karl was the only man I could talk to about anything apart from football and work, and maybe the odd time about politics. The usual oul' rubbish that men talk about in pubs. It's amazing how a grown man can tell you where a team is in a bleddy league table and he couldn't tell you the name of his grandchild.'

'Well, you can't talk about private things in a public place.'

'True enough. Women manage it, though.'

'Karl told me that you should never question life, just accept it as it is.'

'Well, Karl had his reasons for that. When you've suffered as much as Karl, you're grateful to be alive at all.'

Dan reflected.

'Can I watch my programme now?'

'Oh go on,' Dan said. 'I think you've earned it.'

*

Dan went to his room with a new respect for his father. On impulse he picked up his mobile and speed-dialled home. As he rang he panicked and was about to hang up when Sara Mae answered, and he crumbled at the sound of her voice.

'Sara Mae? This is Dad.'

'Hello, Daddy. Will you be home soon?'

'Soon. I promise. You're up late, aren't you?'

'Granny was here. She's just leaving. Mammy—'

'Dan? Is that you, Dan?'

'Kate. I'm sorry, Kate. I'm sorry for messing you about like this. I need a little more time. Not long.' He pressed the off key and clenched his eyes shut. 'I miss you. I fucking miss you.'

Or did he only miss what had been their normal life, once, a short time before? He had to answer that, because the cosy life was gone. He should have asked how she was. He pressed his forehead into his palm. Dammit, he should have asked her how she was. He was a bloody idiot. A bloody idiot.

Here he was, in a perfect room, in a beautiful place, but he was an idiot. Why? Because he wasn't acting from a central point in his life. It was so obvious that the insight wasn't dramatic. It was just there, simple and obvious.

He thought of Karl again, how he had advised him not to ask questions of life. Maybe that was fine, once you knew what the questions were. Yet Karl had been a good teacher, and as he acknowledged this, the day which changed his life came back to him. He had forgotten all about it. They were in Karl's garden in Putney. Yes. They were all there, the two families, the adults easy and familiar with each other, the two teenagers, Karl's daughter Liz and himself, wary and self-conscious. Mortified, actually, because both sets of parents expected a match. God-awful, that, the way parents casually torture their children. Kate's mother had done something similar with her, but at least it was with another girl. And Liz felt foreign then, on top of everything else, because of her German and Romanian parents. She told him that years later. But Karl saved him that day by bending down and picking up a daisy, and asking him to examine it. He saw nothing special. It was a daisy like a thousand others in the garden. Karl asked him, in that slight German accent he never lost, to count the florets which grew clockwise.

There were twenty-one. And anti-clockwise. There were thirty-four. Not only was every daisy like this, but even the nebulae of distant outer space had the same underlying structure. Dan remembered vividly how his jaw dropped. Karl smiled, patted him on the shoulder and went back to talk to the adults. That night, instead of wondering about Liz and her increasingly obvious new shape, his mind was engulfed by the beauty of creation, from the smallest flower to the largest cluster of stars, and he felt the overwhelming beauty of connectedness which he longed to express. It was that night he hit upon the idea of being an architect. He could draw fluently and well, even then. He was good at maths too, and had thought of being an engineer, but not any more.

Why had he forgotten that? In school he had discovered the Renaissance and had had become immersed in the past. The Fibonacci Series, which explained the daisyhead structure, was formulated in the Renaissance, and he had been interested in it as a teenager, but somehow he had not identified it with Karl and his daisy.

He lay back on the bed and tried to visualize the daisy. He could probably find one outside, but he wanted it in his head.

She had turned out to be a beautiful woman, Liz. They had gone out together when they were seventeen, but it had all ended abruptly when he had groped her one night, thinking it was what she expected. He didn't go to her house after that, of course. When they met again several years later it was as if his indiscretion was forgotten, or forgiven, and they were friendly and easy together, perhaps because there was no sexual chemistry.

His other relationships were forgettable, a series of affairs which began pleasantly but ended quickly. It seemed that women were attracted to him superficially, but soon backed off. He had noticed that with his male friends, those who were offhand and casual with women were the most successful with them. Perhaps he had been too earnest, too attentive. Smothering, really. He had always been told that women needed attention, but that was bull as far as he could see then. Enough to reassure them they were important, perhaps, but what most women wanted was the space to get on with their lives. Of course, as soon as he had decided this, along comes a woman to contradict his theory. Marie was a French architectural student who seduced him at a party, and for the first time he discovered that sex could be as glorious as some people claimed. He could never figure out why, but she couldn't get enough of him. He became arrogant enough to enjoy her for the moment, not caring if she was going to be with him the following day or not. It was she who kept ringing him, insisting that he pay her attention, and he'd amble over to her flat, sure of his welcome. What a luxury it was, all that London summer until she had to return to Paris. He missed her but wasn't really upset. She had given him such confidence that he couldn't believe it wouldn't carry over to another woman. Instead, the old pattern asserted itself. He decided it was Englishwomen who made him insecure.

But then he met an Englishwoman who changed everything. He had known her all her life, having met at family gatherings almost until the time she went to Barcelona when she was eighteen, but for several seconds he didn't recognize her.

'Hello, Dan,' she'd said as he was paying for a round of drinks. He turned to see before him the most beautiful woman he had ever seen. She smiled, and slowly it had dawned on him, but as they talked on and the evidence slipped into place, he still hadn't been completely sure he was talking to Kate.

She had grown tired of teaching English in Spain, and was living with her parents for the summer before she settled into her job in London.

She'd gone back to her friends, three women and a man, and he back to his, but for the rest of the evening he was conscious of her. They were related, but only by marriage. No problem there. It just seemed odd that he had searched all his post-pubertal life for a soul mate, and here she was, someone whose adolescent awkwardness and shyness had repelled him, and whose grandmother had married his grandfather. Already he could hear the jokes about incest – and he hadn't even decided to ring her. He knew he was about ten years older but, he reasoned, she'd lived abroad and was obviously mature. More than he was. And yet it wasn't any of those questions which stopped him ringing her for more than two weeks.

In another man it might have been a tactic to seem blasé, but with him it was terror. Terror. He relived it now. It wasn't just nerves about asking a woman out. He had been through that a thousand times. No, this time he was afraid of losing her before he'd even touched her. They hadn't even shaken hands. He had passed it off as part of the love at first sight syndrome, but now he wondered if it had been something more, some deeper, hidden source of terror.

He had often wondered how, out of billions – well, he thought, let's say thousands – of people out there, how two people could come together and decide they were deeply in love and made for each other. No one else would do. He'd heard that a lot of people just made the decision. That's how they did it. This will be good for me, they said, give me a productive, stable, safe life. Love will come in due course. That sort of thing. He had thought of doing that himself when out of the blue Kate was there and obliterated all possibility of there being anyone else.

To his amazement, she'd always wanted him, though she didn't tell him that until they were married. She had been too scared to approach him, convinced he was aloof. She'd even thought of him in Barcelona, and had written letters which she'd torn up.

But if he couldn't stand the sight of her when she was seventeen, how had he fallen in love with her in that pub when he turned and looked into her steady blue eyes?

He hadn't heard their car, but Nuala and Mungo's laughter brought him out of his reverie. He pulled aside the glass door to the en suite, ran the cold tap and splashed his face. He let the tap run a few moments more, idly watching the water flow away before switching it off and drying himself. He switched on the shaving light and looked in the mirror. Tired, but otherwise unremarkable. He tidied his hair with his hands and went out to greet the jovial couple.

He was too tired to match their good spirits, and when Mungo offered him a drink he declined, saying he wanted some fresh air before retiring.

'Good idea,' Nuala said. 'I might do the same before I quit.'

It wasn't quite dark, with strips of deep red and white fading in the west. There were still crows settling in the treetops, and the last *caw, caws* were faint, and lonely somehow. And then, in a little while, it was deep black apart from the brilliant stars.

He was right to come here, whatever drove him to it. He looked over his shoulder to where Croghan Kinsella lay and thought he could see its outline, though probably he could not. *Fancy having a mountain called after your name.* His mother's words came back, her absurd pride in the notion evoking pity in him, whereas before he had just laughed at her.

He stayed where he was for a while, thinking of nothing, and when Nuala came to the door for a few lungfuls of fresh air he was confident he was too far away for her to see him. When she went back inside, he took his father's example and had a satisfying piss beneath the stars. Then he leaned back against the elm and listened to the deep silence of the night.

FOURTEEN

Wexford and Dublin, July 1998

He had slept deeply and stared at the bedside lamp, trying to wake properly. This country air, he thought. It can't be good for you. He lay on for half an hour or so, fantasies and vague plans for returning to London blending with half-conscious musings about those he knew and barely knew. Then he tired of it and got up. Once he'd had a shower and dried himself he opened the first aid kit, and clenched his teeth as he pulled off the dressing in one go. His ankle should have been hairless by now but there always seemed to be enough hair left to make it unpleasant. The wound hadn't quite healed but it wasn't too bad, and he put on a fresh dressing.

Over the past few days he had kept to himself a lot. Hugh, to his credit, had indulged him.

He had thought about his life, his childhood, the time before he and Kate had fallen in love, sure that the key to all of this mess was in the past, but it was impossible to put a coherent shape on it. Everything was sucked back to his fear that chance had robbed him of his wife and children. And yet he had to face that probability, and get used to being without them. It was hard, but it was right. Wasn't it? Wasn't this what people faced up to all the time? He yearned to ring the children, if only to hear their voices, but what would he have to say to Kate?

It was a dull morning but the kitchen was lit by pleasant, soft light. He made himself a cup of coffee and browsed through Nuala's architectural journals. He never thought he'd be anxious to get back to work but, having slept like a simpleton since coming to The Moor, he was getting restless. He thought over what still needed to be done. Fittings, really, the small details. Builders always seemed to fit the wrong things, or in the wrong way. You just needed to be on top of it, that was all. Nothing strenuous. In short, he needed to get back.

Hugh surfaced around ten, and Dan offered to make him breakfast, but all he wanted was some porridge, which he made in the microwave, and brown bread and tea. Dan waited for the right moment while Hugh plastered butter on his bread.

'It's been great here,' he said.

Hugh looked up, reminiscent of a sad old clown for a moment.

'You're not going already, are you?'

'Well, I thought I'd take up Aidan and Siobhán's offer and stay with them overnight, and fly to London in the morning – or as soon as I can get a seat.'

'Oh. Have you and Kate made it up, then?'

'No. Not yet. I thought maybe I'd get a small place for a while.'

'You're not going to tell me you're leaving that lovely girl.'

'Well, I'll support her, of course, while—'

'Support her. You mean pay her money.'

'Yes. That's what men do, isn't it?' he said, angry now.

'Jesus. Look – if you're not going back to her, what's the hurry? Stay here. Get your breath back. Then at least we won't have to worry about you.'

'Worry? About me?'

'Yes. About you. Ah, fuck you,' Hugh said, pushing his plate away. 'You've ruined my breakfast. Do what you like.'

'I just thought I'd get a little place in London to think things through. I'm—'

'Well, think it through here, for Christ's sake. Fresh air, good food, Mother Nature – what more could you want to recover, instead of locking yourself in a dingy bedsit where all you'll do is make yourself more depressed than you are already.'

'I'm not depressed.'

'No, of course not,' Hugh said, rising and going to the bathroom. 'You're the life and soul of the party.'

He knew how to hit home, as usual. It was true he'd have to kip on a colleague's floor till he got a place, but he needed to work. He exhaled heavily in irritation, and flicked through the journal again, but couldn't concentrate. The fact was he wanted to believe that Kate was innocent but couldn't, and he couldn't face her like this. It was his own fault as he wouldn't take the damn test, but it was demeaning – for both of them. It said that he would only believe her if science proved him wrong. Yes, that was it, he thought, his mind suddenly clearing. It wasn't just an excuse, it was a clear, good reason. Somehow, he had to believe her out of his own resources. If he couldn't do that, he didn't know where he could turn.

He went for a walk along the lane. Cloud obscured Annagh and Croghan, but that was good. He didn't want to be distracted by beautiful scenery. He had understood something important, a basis to start on the way back to Kate, and he wanted to grasp it. Even if she didn't want him back. Even that. The thought of her not wanting him brought on a rush of hurt so intense that he bent over, hands on knees, breathing heavily.

'Oh Jesus,' he panted.

He recovered and looked around him. The moor was too damn desolate without the softening effect of Annagh and Croghan. Too much a damn reflection of his soul, if he had one. He turned back to the house, intent on leaving but had only gone a few steps when he stopped and looked around him again. Surely it was too coincidental, too obvious. Had he subconsciously sought out the very external image of himself? He hadn't noticed it with the sun shining, the blue of the mountain, the maroon of the long hill, the green of the rolling high ground. But that was all cut off now, or dimmed by cloud, and all that remained was the bleakness of the moor. He faced it, convincing himself that he was facing the essence of himself, and that that, too, was a beginning.

Ever since he had come here, he had thought he was making a beginning, but every time it happened it never seemed like step two, only yet another step one, as if he was beginning on several fronts or in several ways.

He walked out to the road and on towards the Wicklow Gap. If he wasn't mistaken his father had gone to school somewhere up there. Insofar as he had gone to school. He had come to admire his father. Here he was, a man who old Sarah had more or less taught to read, and yet he was living in an architecturally advanced house with a sophistication his son and grandchildren were hard-pressed to match. And it wasn't as if he had always been like that. People can change, even in their seventies, he thought, and the novelty of it all was keeping him young and fit. And he suspected that Hugh's sophistication – or was that another word for experience? – was subtly guiding him, in the way old fathers were supposed to be wise, but seldom were as far as he knew. What was it, this wisdom? Like so much else, it was obvious once he stopped, not so much to think, but to see. Hugh had grown compassionate. He supposed it extended to his plants and flowers, to everything he touched, really.

His mobile rang and without thinking he answered it.

'Don't hang up on me, Dan, please.'

'I won't,' he said as he recovered from the surprise. He could hear her breathing nervously.

'How are you?' she asked.

'Better.'

'Are you?'

'Yes. I'm . . . I'm learning a lot.'

'About what?'

'My father,' he said.

'Mammy, let me . . .' Sara Mae pleaded in the background and Dan smiled.

'Your father . . .' Kate prompted.

'About me too, I suppose. How are you?'

She didn't reply, and for a moment he thought she'd hung up.

'Sara Mae wants to talk to you,' she said then.

He forgot himself as she told him about her important life. He was smiling again, feeling light, unwittingly charmed. When she had exhausted her news, Sara Mae handed him over to Jim who told him he had scored a goal in a match in school. This was normal enough, and yet strange, listening to his son speak about football on a mobile phone in the middle of an Irish moor.

'Why aren't you in school, Jim?'

'It's lunch hour. Mum brought us home to ring you.'

'Dan?' Kate had taken the phone from Jim.

'Could you not wait to ring till this evening, instead of taking the children out of school?'

'No,' she said. 'It couldn't wait. Not another five minutes.'

He caught his breath. A direct hit about his disregard of her. She was right, of course.

'Ring me, Dan, if this is to go on. Or if you can't face ringing me, at least ring the children.'

'Yes. I will.'

He pressed the off button, and stared into space. Yes, he should ring her, and speak to the children. Keep the channels open. But equally, he was certain, he should stay here for another while. He rubbed his jaw. It felt like he had been to the dentist.

Already he had been away a few hours and it was lunch hour. When he got back, Mungo's car was parked in front of the house.

'Ah, there you are,' Hugh said, his mouth full. 'I thought you had put your bundle over your back and gone off with yourself.'

'Naw,' Dan said, shaking the coffee pot to see if there was any left, 'I'll stay a few more days.'

'Good. Good.'

He was surprised that Mungo was back but it turned out he was doing a roofing job outside Gorey.

Dan found himself enjoying the male talk which went from food to the building site to the 1798 commemoration.

The thing about organic food, Hugh said, warming to his favourite subject, was that it was grown in exactly the same way as it had been when he'd been a child.

'No differ,' he said.

All he was doing was going back to his roots, pun intended.

'Once you stay the way you are,' Mungo said, 'you're bound to come back into fashion.'

It was inconsequential, yet intelligent and funny, and it took him out of his head. He had decided that he wouldn't quiz his father again, bothering both Hugh and himself with his soul-searching. He would just be with him, help out a bit, maybe, though in truth there wasn't much to be done, and try to talk like they were talking now, just being ordinary men together. His ankle hurt him again after his long walk and he knew he should rest that too.

He enjoyed the next few days, learning to cope with silences between them, and trying to be still in himself, so that he could speak about ordinary things and do ordinary things without fuss. Hugh even stopped making jokes at his expense, perhaps because there was no need to, and he felt the peace of mutual respect.

That was no small thing.

*

'I've been wondering about what you said about Karl,' he said to Hugh over a cup of tea. ' "When you've suffered as much as Karl" was how you put it, if I remember rightly.'

Hugh was silent.

'Oh, yes,' he said then. 'Oh, yes. What he went through. You know he was imprisoned in England during the war?'

'Yes, I knew that.'

'His family in Germany were wiped out. The Russian front, the bombing in Hamburg. The big one in '44.'

'The firestorm?'

'Yes. That played on his mind.'

'I remember something about that.'

'The only one in the world he had was Elizabeth. And then I came along.'

'Karl and my mother were lovers?'

'Yes. She loved Karl. And so did I, to tell you the truth. It was the nearest a man could get to loving another man without being a nancy boy. But your mother wanted me in the end, and he went to pieces.' Hugh sniffed and shook his head.

'How—?'

'He was the last one to see Charlie alive.'

'Say that again?'

'He was the last one to see Charlie before he fell down the stairs.'

Dan felt his head tighten.

'Are you saying – are you saying that Karl pushed him?'

'I don't know.'

'You don't know. But you stayed friends.'

'Yes.'

'If you knew for certain that he had pushed Charlie, would you have stayed friends?'

'Yes.'

'You'd have forgiven him.'

'Yes.'

Dan was stunned, and neither of them said any more.

*

He was now ringing home every evening, mainly to speak to the children, enduring the fact that he and Kate could only exchange a few strained words.

He was sure this was the steady road back to sanity. His ankle was healing quickly, which in his new mood didn't surprise him.

*

On Saturday, Siobhán and Aidan came from Dublin again. Dan went with Nuala to meet them in Gorey, and they had a drink in Browne's pub, a hair of the dog, Aidan said, before going on to The Moor.

Aidan had received the photos that Hugh had asked Deirdre to send, but apologized that he hadn't got the photographic paper to print out the touched-up picture of Dan's grandfather, as he had promised. Siobhán had finished the family tree and had it with her on disk.

After dinner, Siobhán produced her disk and they trooped into the workroom. To Dan's surprise, it was Mungo who sat into the computer and opened the disk's genealogy program.

'Now . . .' Mungo murmured, with Hugh looking over his shoulder. 'Hugh has given us your unique side of the tree. We just have direct ancestors here. Right. We'll start from the beginning with your children, Dan, and go back. If you see a mistake, shout.'

Dan noticed there was no mention of the black child.

'Here's your grandfather and namesake, Brendan Kinsella, whose second wife was your wife's grandmother, Sarah Considine. His first wife was Máire O'Connor from Galway. She's buried with Brendan above in Ballyfad. You know that much. We don't know anything about her family, unfortunately.

'Now, Brendan, your grandfather, was born in 1904. He had four brothers and two sisters, but they all emigrated when he was a child, presumably to England or America. A family tradition, it seems, as that's what happened with my brothers and sisters. We haven't been able to trace them, as yet. Anyway,' he said, 'as you can see here, Brendan's father was James Kinsella, born in 1880, died 1925, and his mother was Mary Kavanagh of Monaseed, 1882 to 1948. She went back to her people when your father married,' he said, turning to Hugh. He turned back to the screen. 'It's her we're interested in, from the point of view of 1798, right?'

'Her father was Brendan Kavanagh of Monaseed, born about 1836 – that's a guess – died 1912, and her mother was

Marie Byrne, also of Monaseed, 1842 to 1905. Now Marie Byrne is interesting because she survived the cholera epidemic in the Gorey workhouse in 1851. Her mother, who was a Nora Cullen, died there. Do you follow?' he asked, turning to Dan.

'Yes. Yes, I follow.'

Mungo turned back to the screen again.

'Nora was married to Mungo Byrne, who is interesting because he was born in America about 1805. His mother was, we think, an Alma Kirwin, from somewhere in Scotland or Ireland, we don't really know. It got a bit vague in family letters, it seems, but she died when Mungo was about six. One of the reasons we think she was Scottish is because Mungo is a Scottish name. Anyway, that's how it entered the family.'

He cleared his throat.

'Where are we? Oh, right. That brings us to Mungo's father, Hugh Byrne, who fought at Vinegar Hill as a young man – and at most of the other battles as well, including Ballyellis. We can drive up there tomorrow before the pageant in Craanford, if you like.'

'So Mungo came back to Ireland from America?' Dan asked.

'His father brought him back when he was about ten or twelve, and they took over the old place Hugh's family had been burned out of. The Protestant tenants who rented the holding from 1798 had emigrated to Canada. A lot of the poorer Protestant families emigrated from the area, it seems. These ones left about 1818. Hugh came back at the right time.'

'This commemoration is a good thing,' Nuala said. 'We're discovering it wasn't all black and white. Terrible things were done on both sides.'

Hugh sucked his teeth.

'True,' Mungo said. 'Anyhow, the family story has it that he looked up his brother's old girlfriend, who had been with the rebels at the second battle of Hacketstown, and they dug up Tom's bones and buried them with the rest of the family above on my land. Well,' he said ruefully, 'my wife's land now, I suppose. They say he buried a jar of old whiskey he brought back from America with him. People did that, sometimes. My father ploughed up one, once.'

'Really?' Siobhán asked. 'Do you still have it?'

'Ah, it's above in an outhouse, somewhere, gathering dust. There was no whiskey in it anyway. Just a little heap of dust. It's likely that Mungo Byrne got through quite a few of them as he drank himself to death and his wife to destitution. That's how Nora and her daughter ended up in the workhouse. The Kavanaghs took over the tenancy, and took young Marie out of the workhouse when her mother died.'

'I see,' Dan said pensively. 'And who was Tom again?'

'Hugh's older brother. He was killed in the battle of Hacketstown, remember? Hugh was at that too, it seems, and when he came back he discovered that his family had been burned to death by the yeos. They say he went berserk at Ballyellis because of it, and made bits of a black drummer.'

'What was a black drummer doing at Ballyellis?'

'He was with the Ancient Britons, who had got themselves a bad name in Wicklow, and they rode into an ambush.'

'It seems the drummer always got the job of flogging, and the bould drummer had a black reputation, if you'll pardon the pun, among the people, and he got his comeuppance at Ballyellis.'

'Yeos. That was the landed volunteer cavalry, the yeomen, wasn't it?' Dan asked.

'The very ones. The end of it all was that the Rising was a disaster. Forty thousand people died in the space of six weeks. Hugh escaped to France, and from there to America, where he married and made a few dollars.'

'Funny how the names come down the generations, isn't it?' Aidan said.

'Well, that's the way with families,' Hugh said.

'What strikes me about this,' Siobhán said thoughtfully, 'is how close it all is.'

'There's old men that talk about it like it was yesterday,' Hugh said. 'They could tell you the colour of the Redcoats' eyes. That black drummer's name was Anthony King, by the way.'

'Really?' Dan said, impressed.

'Come on, print that out,' Aidan said to Mungo. 'I've a drouth on me. We can talk about this in the pub.'

'No need to ask where you were last night,' Mungo said.

'In my sweetheart's arms,' Aidan replied, and Siobhán slapped him on the wrist. 'Where'll we go? The Gap?'

'The Gap's just fine,' Hugh said.

*

Mungo and Hugh drove Dan to Ballyellis early the next morning, leaving the others to go to the pageant in Craanford later. They passed the road up which Mungo once lived, and stopped in Monaseed to have a look at the new plaque in memory of Miles Byrne. Hugh read it out.

'Erected to perpetuate the memory of Miles Byrne, 1780 to 1862, Chef de Battalion, in the service of France, Officer of the Legion of Honour, and Knight of St Louis, buried in Montmartre Cemetery, Paris. And all from this area who fought, suffered and died during the Rebellion of 1798. Unveiled by the Right Honourable James Boger, ONZ, former Prime Minister of New Zealand. Erected on 30th May '98. Well, how about that.'

Mungo pointed out the theatre hall named after Miles Byrne, and Mungo's old school, just across from it.

At Ballyellis, they parked on the verge of a narrow road, flanked on one side by a high ditch and on the other by a crumbling wall. There was a Celtic high cross as a memorial to the battle, the inscription in Gaelic and English.

'Read that out to us, there, Hugh,' Mungo said.

'This cross was erected to perpetuate the memory of the men of Wexford and Wicklow who defeated the Ancient Britons and other British forces at Ballyellis, June 29th, 1798. Grant them eternal rest, O Lord. Erected by the Askamore and Ballyellis '98 Association, June 29th, 1941.'

There was also a less partisan modern granite, rectangular plaque erected a few weeks before.

'So this is where it happened,' Dan said, looking around him.

'Yes,' Mungo said. 'A lot of blood was spilled on the road you're standing on. The musketmen hid behind this wall over here,' he said, indicating an ivy-covered wall about a metre high, 'and the pikemen behind that ditch. The carts were used to block the road, so when the Britons and dragoons and yeomen came flying around that corner, chasing the rebels . . .' Mungo made a face and held out his hands. 'The game was over.'

'And the black drummer?'

'He escaped over that field – they caught up with him beyond,' Mungo said, pointing.

As they stood on the road in silence, looking onto the field where the drummer had been caught and killed, a cloud obscured the sun and Dan felt as if the shadow had passed through him. It was an eerie feeling.

'How do you know all this?'

'Well, we kind of knew it growing up, and this commemoration has got people interested again.'

'My God. Imagine the terror of running for your life and then being run down.'

'Well, them boys got back what they didn't mind dishing out,' Hugh said.

Dan and Mungo bowed their heads at that. There was nothing to say.

*

They drove on to Craanford where a large crowd had gathered. There was a long wait, but finally, led by a man on a white horse, the pageant rebels appeared, marching in rank and file down a narrow road to the village. For a while, despite the incongruous modern rebel music blaring from a tannoy, it was possible to imagine these men and women marching towards a real battle in 1798. Or, as the marchers were clean and tidy, to their first battle, perhaps, full of hope and innocent of the ugliness of war. Nevertheless, as they marched past in perfect step, Dan realized that some of these people were descendants of those they were imitating, separated by only a few generations, as Siobhán had pointed out, and the physical resemblance was probably strong – young and fit, middle-aged and pot-bellied, country men and women. Somewhere in there, it was easy to imagine, was his ancestor, Hugh Byrne.

*

As the crowds broke up, they found Nuala, Siobhán and Aidan and together they went to see the eighteenth-century watermill restored by the Lyons family, and had tea and home-made scones in the mill café.

'When we're out, we're out,' Hugh said as they sat down.

'Feck the expense,' Aidan said, and they all laughed.

Dan enjoyed the frivolity. Hugh was enjoying himself too, happy, Dan knew, to have unexpected time with him.

He rang Kate and the children while Mungo left Aidan and Siobhán to the train. It was still an endurance test, but it kept him realistic. His felt less anger towards her. Speaking to the real person rather than to the one in his head kept a sense of perspective. He knew he should go back, but he still hadn't the courage, or the emotional wherewithal. Another few days, he told himself. Just another few days.

He prompted Hugh to speak about 1798, and was impressed by what he knew. Very little of it was from a history book, Dan suspected, but it was vivid, and he could name names, which was impressive. He thought back over the pageant as Hugh spoke. As Mungo had said, forty thousand people, like those he had seen march past him, had died within a matter of weeks.

*

All seemed well when he went to bed that night, but around dawn he woke, struggling out of a disturbing dream.

The sheets were drenched in sweat and, still struggling to wake, though his heart was pounding and he was terrified, he managed to sit out onto the bedside chair. Then he was wide awake as his panic focused and he checked his leg to make sure it was still there. He fumbled at the lamp switch, finally getting it on, and slowly relaxed as he saw that all was well, but the nightmare was still vivid. He pulled away the dressing and was relieved to see that the wound was still healed. He hardly needed it, but replaced the plaster to protect it.

The damp sheets were now uncomfortably cold, so he rearranged them before getting back into bed. He had calmed and was able to think back over the nightmare.

The wound in his ankle had festered and infection had entered the bone. The pain, as his foot grew gangrenous, was so intense that even consciousness of the foot was obliterated. It was a high-pitched noise which deafened him to everything else, cutting through his heart and cleaving his head. He looked down on himself, his spirit detached from the catastrophe, to see men in green masks cutting away his foot from above the ankle. No, don't do that, he screamed noiselessly, that's my foot! But they ignored him and went away. While they were gone, the stump festered and the pain became worse. The stump was giving him agony and now the missing foot which was in the bin was giving him agony too, so that he didn't know where to fight it. The men in green returned and removed the bandages to discover that not only was the stump a mass of worms, but the leg was discoloured to the knee. His heart was caving in with pain as they took their saw to him once again, this time cutting midway across the thigh to be certain to stem the gangrene.

Exhausted, he looked at them from above, as before, and his pain was divided three ways, so that he was bewildered, and he drifted from it far across the sea to a tropical island. There, he was laid on a bed of palm by kind people and left to rest in the cool shack. At dusk two magicians came to examine his leg. They were very gentle and said they thought they could do something for him. While they were gone it dawned on him that he knew them, and when they returned he saw that they were Hugh and Mungo, but they were black.

'What are you doing here?' he asked them.

'We've been here for centuries,' Mungo said.

'We've brought you a new leg,' Hugh said.

They pulled back the sheets and compared a beautiful black leg with his.

'It fits,' Mungo said.

'Perfectly,' Hugh agreed.

Dan looked down on the leg, now sealed into his own. They helped him to the side of the bed, and lifted him to his feet. It took his weight with comfort as if he had been born with it.

'Where did you get it?' he asked them in awe.

'From your daughter,' Mungo said.

'But she's just a child!'

'No, she was grown.'

'Was?'

'She's dead.'

'But she can't be! She's only six weeks old!'

'It's been many years since you ran away,' Mungo said.

He could not argue with that since it was true. He had been running away since Charlie became a man, according to Hugh.

The magicians left and he looked in wonder at the shapely, black female leg. It was strong and his pain was gone. He took off his shorts and tee-shirt and stood naked in front of the full-length mirror of burnished steel. To his horror, its blackness was spreading upwards, and that it was a warm, sensual sensation did not lessen his fear. He watched, unbelieving, as it spread to his hips and across his groin, spreading inexorably up his stomach towards his heart. It was then he could take no more and sat up in bed, sweating.

*

It was too much. He was getting out of The Moor today. There was no way he could face staying in this bed another night. The house was well soundproofed but he didn't want to risk any noise and he stayed in bed until nine, in case he disturbed Hugh. He was determined to act as he had over the past week, and casually tell Hugh it was time for him to return to London. He could take up Aidan and Siobhán's offer of a futon, perhaps, and go to London the following day.

Hugh was disappointed when he told him but then he said yes, that was a good idea and, after Dan had booked his Aer Lingus flight, gave him Aidan's work number from the computer. Dan rang at eleven, apparently a good time for Aidan, and yes, he said it was cool. Aidan was working till eight and Siobhán till about seven, and if he could kick his heels for a few hours then that would be great.

'Perfect,' Dan said. 'I'll get myself something to eat. I'll see you about eight.'

'I'll let Siobhán know,' he said. 'Have you a pen?'

Aidan gave him directions. That was it, then. It was settled.

'I'll drive you to the train,' Hugh said.

'Thanks.'

They looked at each other. Dan felt the urge to put his arms round his father, but something about the old fellow made that seem ridiculous and unnecessary. In any case, their exchange of looks said it all, like an invisible nod.

As Hugh prepared lunch, Dan stood at the window looking at the rain.

'Just why did you come back here, Hugh?'

'Why?'

Dan turned. Hugh was cutting a loaf, but looking at him.

'It's like this, Dan. You and your family have your lives, and I have mine. My family was the one thing that kept me in London, once I had a few bob, but then I thought, supposing you grew up here, in the countryside. Odds are that you'd be living in London, or maybe Dublin, these days. And I'd still be here anyway. Most parents live a couple of hours from their families, if they're lucky. And then, well, I got the chance to live in this palace. I love it, you know. I just love it. It's like coming back to my childhood, but without the poverty and longing and hunger. I've always something to do, and sure these days I can go to London if

I need a holiday, and I'm there in a few hours. I have it all down to a tee,' he said, resuming work on the bread.

'So you have,' Dan said quietly. 'So you have.'

*

They were subdued on the platform at Gorey.

'Why don't you come over when the children are on holidays?'

'I might,' Hugh said. 'I might well do that.'

*

On the train he thought about Hugh having things worked out. To know what you wanted and then to grasp the opportunity, that was the thing. His father had wished him luck on the platform in Gorey, had looked into his eyes, but thankfully had resisted giving him advice. He knew the score, the old devil. Odds were that he learned it with Elizabeth, who was not the easiest of women as she grew older and arthritic. They had loved each other, though, through all the rows, irritations, irrationalities. He thought about what Hugh had told him about Karl, and supposed that she, too, must have wondered about him standing at the top of the stairs as their son fell. She had probably gone over it a thousand times, and died wondering. Karl was most probably innocent, of course.

He felt that he understood his parents better in knowing about it, although what exactly he understood about them he couldn't say. He remembered he had sided with his mother once in a row, and before he knew it they had ganged up on him, all lovey-dovey. What did he know, she'd said, about what they were discussing. Discussing! That taught him a lesson. He could smile at it now. He had been a prissy idiot for a long time, wanting things all neat and tidy, especially the way people behaved to each other, as if that could ever be plain and simple. Kate had cured him of much of that particular vice. Yes, well . . . He could see that it had revived and been writ large in his reaction to the child.

He just didn't want blackness to be part of him. He had thought he was coming round to the idea, in a nice liberal kind of way, to glide over the reality. But as the dream proved, that was a crock of manure. The whole notion was alien to him, it terrified him, as if his body were being taken over. Hugh could sense that, and agree with him on some level. He was sure of it. The dream had gone deep. It had put it up to him.

Where were they? Wicklow. It started to rain again as the train pulled out and new passengers settled. His thoughts drifted. Despite everything it had been a good stay in The Moor and, physically at least, he had recovered his well-being. He had even recovered some sensual feeling, which was an occasion of cheer, and looking at a fine woman, as he was doing now, however discreetly, meant something again. It was liberating – up to a point. Even under these weird circumstances, he was a married man. No harm in looking though. It let him believe that he was flesh and blood and not some miserable ghost.

The swans were still on the marsh water, he noticed. Then suddenly the rain lashed the windows. He closed his eyes and tried to think of nothing.

*

As Aidan had suggested, he got the 90 bus from Connolly station to O'Connell Bridge. Aidan and Siobhán's apartment was west of the Ha'penny Bridge on the far side, beyond – what was it? He pulled out the note he had of Aidan's directions. Beyond The Winding Stair Café and Bookshop. He went as far as the Ha'penny Bridge and, sure enough, there was the café and bookshop. Crowds were streaming across the bridge and through an alley called Merchant's Arch. Heavy lorries and buses made the narrow road noisy and unpleasant, so he walked on and turned left down a cobbled street where it was quieter. He took out his mobile and dialled the apartment but immediately an answering service clicked in, so he turned off the phone. It was far too early. He looked around him. He was in Temple Bar, beside what turned out to be the artists' gallery. Great. There were two things of interest in Temple Bar – new buildings and food.

He wandered around, admiring the architecture and the atmosphere it generated, attracting as it did a seemingly endless stream of young people. On a corner of Temple Bar Square, an artist was painting a child's face. The child was stock-still, her face covered in red paint and silver stars.

He remembered there were some buildings on the southern quays that he wanted to see, having read about them in journals, and he made a mental note of it. Always checking the competition. He smiled at this, then bought an *Irish Times* and found a quiet pub and leafed through it over a beer and some pub food, but his thoughts hadn't strayed far from Kate and the children. Fatalistically, it seemed, he was going back to them, feeling ashamed.

He was an architect, which should have meant something, but he only fulfilled the bidding of others. Not everyone could be a solitary genius, and he accepted that he wasn't one and never would be. And yet even he was entitled to a feeling of being unique, of dignity, of quiet pride. No one else need know. All he was missing was something to dream about that he could think of as his own.

He opened the *Irish Times* again and found an advertisement with some white space and took out his pen. He hadn't doodled in so long – not for himself. Work, always the pressure of work which was always, dispiritingly, the same. The future was solar, Hugh maintained. Well then, let's suppose it was.

Lost to himself, his pen seemed to take on a life of its own. Preoccupied, he paid for another pint and continued, keeping the sketches tiny. He could elaborate on them when he got home. With the white space and several margins covered, he drew over ads, photos, more margins. When his second pint was finished, he looked at his watch. Seven twenty!

Delighted the time had passed so pleasantly and productively, he tore off the pages covered in his sketches, folded them carefully and put them in his pocket. They weren't world-shattering, but he could work on them and they were his. He was going to design his dream building, a solar house, for a city centre. For a particular site in a city centre, a site he knew, whose history he knew. It would never be built, of course, but it would be his dream. And dreams didn't need to come true. A person just had to have one, that was all.

He headed for the apartment, but then remembered he wanted to see those buildings, and he had time to kill. He made his way along the south quays until he came to Parliament Street. The old building on the corner looked Italian. He peered at its name carved above the door. Sunlight Chambers. How appropriate. The stonework base, the stucco work, the tiled roof, the friezes depicting men and women at their work – yes, it was Italian. Lombardo-Romanesque.

He glanced downriver at the Four Courts, crossed the bridge and walked along the quay opposite the new buildings which joined it. They weren't easy to view with the passing buses and lorries and cars driving at a mad speed for such a narrow, badly surfaced road, but they blended quite well with the Sunlight building. This was a pleasant surprise, as they were unequivocally contemporary. There were only three of them, the end one giving way to a recess where older buildings were about thirty metres from the quay, allowing space for a small amenity, seating which mimicked a Viking boat, and a bus stop.

The recess allowed him to stand back and get a good view of the end building, and he could see that the back followed a snaking alley. That was interesting.

A woman screamed behind him and he turned to see a youth running towards the alley with her handbag. He didn't take in what was happening for a moment but then forgotten anger at the mugging in London sluiced through him and he gave chase. The youth looked around as he ran and, seeing that Dan, despite the encumbrance of his bag, was gaining on him, he flung the handbag away as he turned out of the cobbled alley and down a narrow road. Dan's anger drove him on. Then the youth slipped through a gap in a hoarding onto a demolished site. Dan squeezed in after him. The youth looked around again and, panicking when he saw Dan, tried to scale a wall.

'I'm going to kill you, you little bastard,' Dan shouted after him, and he meant it. He paused when he saw they were not alone. Junkies were lying on the ground, five or six of them, in their own dazed world, and there were streaks of blood on the hoarding they were slumped against. Dirty needles were scattered about them. He was in a shooting alley, for Christ's sake. But they weren't going to join in this little party, he was sure of that, and he had this trembling little fucker in his sights.

The youth looked around him and quickly reached down for a syringe. Leaving his bag down, Dan let him. It would even things up, and the youth faced him, pointing the syringe, daring him to come nearer, his face torn between fear and violence. It crossed Dan's mind that the junkie could give him a lucky nick, and that would be that, but it didn't bother him, somehow.

His stare unnerved the junkie and he charged, brandishing the syringe. Dan disarmed him easily. The boy was weak from drugs and sleeping rough, but his fear and rage carried him on and he struck out with all his dwindling strength. Then something happened in Dan. The anger at himself, at Kate, at destiny, all the angers he was venting on this boy were gone. He subtly moved back from the blows, but deliberately let them fall so they were emptied of their power to hurt him, conscious that it was a dance of sorts in the end until, exhausted, the junkie fell to his knees, sobbing, not only not caring what Dan might do to him but, in all likelihood, not even aware that he was there.

The child was damned, Dan thought. Condemned to terrorize vulnerable people. That's all he was, really, a child, fifteen or sixteen, and damned. Malnourished, unwanted, most likely abused, without a chance in hell. And that's where the poor devil was, in hell. He reached down and, taking the boy's hand, hauled him to his feet. The boy was shaking and his sweaty face was grey.

'Listen to me!' Dan commanded, and the boy tried to focus. 'Listen to me. How much is a spot?' He hoped that that was the right lingo.

'Twenty,' the boy said.

Dan looked around him to make sure no one was watching, took out his wallet and gave the boy two ten-pound notes.

The boy looked at the notes, then back at Dan, and back to the notes again.

'I don't suppose you'd get something to eat?' Dan said, handing him another fiver. 'No, forget it,' he said, shaking his head and, picking up his bag, walked away without turning back.

*

Siobhán's voice came over the intercom. He noticed there was dried mud on his shoes, and he cleaned them as best he could. He smelt, he realized on the way up, and supposed he looked a mess, but there was nothing he could do about that apart from a quick flick of a comb. She was waiting at the open door of the apartment when he came out of the lift and gave him her big smile, choosing not to notice his dishevelment, and he felt grateful and relieved.

Her kitchen was tiny. The flat was tiny and he saw that really he should not have inconvenienced them like this, despite their invitation. A quick survey told him that they had one bedroom, a tiny bathroom, the kitchen and a false balcony, and that was it. The door to the bedroom was slightly ajar, revealing a neatly made bed. Everything had to be neat in a place like this. A notebook computer was on the living-room table, showing some complex graphs, alongside some open books. He had interrupted her work. She asked him if he had eaten and he assured her he had.

'Listen,' he said, 'I'm interrupting your work.'

'Well,' she said, embarrassed, 'I want to try to get something done, if you don't mind.'

'Not at all. I'll go for a walk.'

'Oh no,' she said quickly, raising her hand as if to stop

him. 'Stay here, please. I can work in the bedroom, no bother. I often do when Aidan is here.'

'If you're sure. He did tell you I was coming, by the way?'

'No.' She smiled. 'But that's all right. You're very welcome, Dan.'

'I can tell you it's a great relief to have somewhere friendly to rest my bones.' He was surprisingly tired after his tussle with the junkie. 'Thank you.'

She moved her things into the bedroom, and he tried on the cordless earphones and pointed the remote control at the TV. Then he checked the volume without them. Perfect. They hadn't satellite but they had cable and he surfed the twelve or thirteen stations, including English ones, and found nothing of interest on any of them. He ended up watching a nature programme, lionesses tearing stupid gazelles to pieces and the like. Charming. No sentimentality in nature, that was for sure.

He jumped a bit when Aidan tapped him on the shoulder. Siobhán came out of the bedroom to greet him.

Aidan looked tired but he made himself some soup and devoured a roll he had brought home while Siobhán finished her work.

'I'm gumming for a pint,' Aidan said when he'd finished eating. 'Would you fancy one, or three?'

'Somewhere quiet,' Siobhán said, 'where we can hear ourselves talk.'

'Hughes',' Aidan said. 'There's live music but you can hear yourself talk.'

They went the back way to avoid traffic, Aidan naming the streets for Dan's benefit.

'You know the area well,' Dan said.

'I used to live not far from here when I was a child – before we moved to Wexford. I like the place,' he said, looking around him with pleasure.

The pub was behind the Four Courts, and Dan paused to look at the Gandon-designed edifice before going in. There was a red streak in the grey clouds to the west, and for a moment he thought of The Moor. In the pub, there were already musicians in the snug playing a lively Irish tune.

'What'll you have?' Aidan asked.

Siobhán brought Dan to sit down with her and they found a table.

'I saw a lot of junkies this evening. I thought Ireland was a prosperous country now.'

'If you're educated, and the majority of younger people are, it's a great country,' Siobhán said. 'If you're not, it isn't. We're the lucky ones, I suppose.'

Aidan joined them with the drinks, as they continued talking about the new prosperity.

'I talked about it with Da and Hugh a few months ago,' Aidan said. 'I don't think my generation has a clue how tough it was, for Hugh's generation especially. Da was out of work for a long time when we were small, so I know it wasn't a bed of roses. There were rows about money all the time in our house, and I think it's what drove my parents apart, really.'

'Imagine all those Irish, only seventeen or eighteen, going over to London in the middle of the Blitz, or even after it, and most of them from the bog and had never gone further than the parish boundary,' Siobhán said in wonder. 'What must it have been like for them? I suppose some of them were killed,' she mused.

'Brendan was nearly killed a few times, I hear,' Aidan said.

Dan looked from one to the other. He liked these young people, who seemed to know more about his family history than he did. They had no hang-ups, as far as he could tell, and were open and intelligent. And generous. This time it was Siobhán who went to the bar for a round.

'I hope you don't mind my asking, Aidan, but what was it like for you when your parents split up? I ask because, well, I'm going through some marital difficulties myself at the moment.'

'I'm sorry to hear that, Dan.'

He twirled his near-empty glass. 'What was it like? Well,'

he said, leaning back, trying to find the words, 'we were grown up when they finally split, so it wasn't so bad. Da came to us and explained things and it was cool because they both wanted it. But – they were apart for years, really. It came to a head when I got burned as a child, but it was money, poverty, lack of hope that did them in well before that, I'd say, looking back.'

'And did that affect you?'

'Sure. But you live with it and you grow out of it and hope the same thing won't happen to you.'

Siobhán returned with the drinks. In the upper end of the bar, the musicians were tuning and a group was lining up to dance.

The music started and the dancers exploded onto the floor. It was a set dance, Siobhán said, and Dan noticed that an area of the floor was specially inlaid for dancing. There were six of them. They danced from the corners to the centre and back to different corners, as far as he could follow. It was very regular and precise and satisfying to watch. It was satisfying, too, that they weren't wearing costume, and that they were both young and of late middle age, tall and short, fat and thin, beautiful and plain, and they reminded him of the pageanteers in Craanford.

*

'I must show you the images of your grandfather before we hit the sack,' Aidan said as the lift door opened and Siobhán went ahead to open the apartment.

'Yes. That would be fantastic.'

'A nightcap, anyone?' Siobhán asked, putting on the kettle as they came in.

'Would you like a beer?' Aidan asked him, unzipping a bag and putting his notebook computer on the table.

'A beer would be nice,' Dan said, fascinated by what lay stored in this neat machine.

Siobhán handed them uncapped bottles as Aidan launched a graphics program with a double click.

'Do you want a glass?' she asked Dan.

He shook his head and smiled.

'Here, you'll like this one,' Aidan said. 'It's you as a baby.'

Dan's mouth dropped. There they were, his mother and father, Elizabeth holding him, both of them looking so young and happy. And proud. They actually looked proud.

'I don't know who these other people are,' Aidan said.

'That's . . . that's Karl and Marta, and their daughter,' Dan said. 'Karl and Marta were good friends of my parents. So much so, in fact, they were sure that innocent girl and myself would be an item.'

'How romantic,' Siobhán said, her cup of mint tea held in both hands to her mouth.

'Not one bit, I assure you,' Dan said. 'Not for either of us.'

'I suppose,' she said.

'This is your grandfather's wedding,' Aidan said, opening another.

'My God, look at that!' Dan exclaimed. 'I remember this one.'

'You didn't know the last one?' Siobhán asked, surprised.

'No. No, I don't remember it at all.'

'Lord, weren't they handsome!' Siobhán said.

'Strange you never saw that one,' Aidan said, turning to him.

'Yes,' he said quietly. 'Do you think you could print it out for me?'

'Sure.'

'The bride is my wife's grandmother,' he said, rallying.

'Oh, so she's not your grandmother,' Siobhán said.

'No. Sarah was Brendan's second wife. Hugh's mother died when he was about fourteen. She's buried with Brendan in Wexford.'

'Of course. The family tree . . .'

'And this girl here is Deirdre, my wife's mother. And this is Hugh, of course.'

'Hmm! There wasn't a pick on him,' Siobhán said.

'And the two black people?' Aidan asked.

'Ah. They were friends of Sarah and Deirdre. Sarah died several years ago, but her friend died only this year. She was from Montserrat, actually.'

'You mean the island that blew up?' Aidan asked.

'That's it.'

'The next one,' Aidan said, clicking again, 'I'm very proud of. It was full of wrinkles, but I ironed it out, so to speak.'

His grandfather's face appeared, and Dan felt a rush of excitement as Aidan enlarged the picture to three-quarters fill the screen. The photo seemed to have been taken in the 40s or early 50s.

'It blows up pretty well, but look, if you'll bear with my technical wizardry,' Aidan said, and the picture was gone almost before Dan had a chance to take it in. 'I thought this would look really cool.' Aidan clicked.

To Dan's astonishment, his grandfather's head gradually appeared against a black background, as if it were three-dimensional and floating.

'Cool, isn't it?' Aidan said with satisfaction.

'Are you all right?' Siobhán asked gently, touching Dan's elbow.

He didn't answer, unable to take his eyes off the floating head.

'You gave me goosebumps there, mate,' he said finally.

'Hah!' Aidan exclaimed. 'Listen, I was thinking. Why don't I email it over to you, then you can print it out yourself to your heart's content.'

'Thanks. A lot. That would be marvellous.'

'I can do the same for your father.'

'He'd love that. He really would.'

'Why don't we do the same with the family tree?' Siobhán suggested.

'That would be smashing,' Dan said. 'I can download the program from the Web, can't I?'

'No bother,' Siobhán said. 'We can send you the Web address.'

'It's cool, huh?'

'It's very cool, Aidan,' Dan said, gazing at his grandfather and resisting the urge to kiss the image. 'I miss my family,' he blurted.

Aidan handed him his mobile.

'Ring home,' he said, 'like a good alien.'

'Thanks, but I have my own.' He laughed, in spite of himself. 'Listen, you two have to come to London, soon.'

Aidan suddenly looked tired.

'Don't worry,' Siobhán said. 'We will.'

Aidan closed down the program and the computer.

'And now, if you'll excuse me, Dan, I'm knackered.'

'Of course. Of course.'

He helped Aidan pull out the futon while Siobhán got some bedclothes.

'Goodnight, Dan.' Siobhán smiled.

'Goodnight, folks. And thanks again.'

*

He looked at his phone for a while before he rang.

'Is that you, Dan?' Kate asked before he had time to say hello or change his mind.

'Yes.'

'Where are you?'

'Dublin. I'll be home tomorrow afternoon, if that's—'

'Yes.'

'Are you sure?'

'Yes. No. I'm not sure. But come. We need to talk.'

'Yes.'

'I don't even know if I can talk to you.'

'I know. I'm sorry. I'm truly sorry.'

'Well . . . that's a start.'

'I know. I mean, I know it's only a start.'

'Yes. The children keep asking me when you're coming back.'

'How are they?'

'Edgy.'

'And the little one?'

'Cries a lot.'

'You must be exhausted.'

'I am.' Then she broke down and the phone went dead.

He stood, staring at the wall. Then he came to and turned off the phone and left it in his bag. He went to the window and stared at the traffic.

He turned out the lamp and lay on his back. His bladder was uncomfortably full, but he waited till they were finished with the bathroom before going himself. He thought of what Siobhán had said about their being the lucky ones. He was one of the really lucky ones, all told. When he looked in the mirror, he was startled to see how like his grandfather he was.

It was a humid night, and the hum of the traffic along the quays, despite being on the third floor and despite the double glazing, was hard to get used to after the deep silence of The Moor, and indeed his own bedroom in London. He thought of what his father had told him about being the last one old Brendan had kissed before he died. He pushed off the duvet and lay in his shorts.

In his reverie, he imagined his grandfather's head floating a few feet above the end of the futon. He stared until he could no longer hold the illusion, then lay on his side and wept bitterly.

FIFTEEN

Dublin and London, July 1998

The bedroom door opened and Siobhán slipped discreetly into the bathroom, and he heard her use the toilet and then the shower. She returned to the bedroom and Aidan padded out in his shorts, and went through the same procedure.

The sun brightened the room suddenly. Dan reached for his watch. 6.42 a.m.

As Aidan returned from the bathroom, Dan noticed the wide uneven track where his chest hair didn't grow because of his childhood burns.

He wondered what it must have been like having such a scar as a teenage boy, before he met a woman who said it didn't matter, she loved him anyway, scar or no scar. Women were better at accepting imperfection, he thought. There was something in a man, or perhaps a man who hadn't yet been scarred himself, which veered towards the absolute. Women were much better at seeing there was no such thing.

Aidan and Siobhán came out fully dressed, careful not to disturb him.

'It's okay,' he said. 'I'm awake.'

'Good morning,' they said, almost in unison.

'Would you like some coffee?' Siobhán asked.

'I'll help myself later, if that's all right.'

'That's what I like to hear,' Aidan said.

Dan waved them into the kitchen, and with a smile they concurred, and talked quietly as they breakfasted. It was a small apartment, Dan thought, but there was an atmosphere of happiness in the place.

Aidan told him that if he didn't want to break any more Irish notes, and leave himself carrying loose change, he could get an ordinary bus from Eden Quay to the airport.

'Right, then,' Aidan said, gulping back the last of his coffee, and joined by Siobhán, he slung his computer bag over his shoulder. 'Just pull the door after you and leave the key in the letter box.'

'Why don't you lie on?' Siobhán said. 'I would.'

A flurry of goodbyes and they were gone. She must have hypnotized him because suddenly his head and eyes were heavy.

It was after ten when he staggered to the kitchen, found some filtered water in the fridge and drank back a glassful.

He hadn't slept like that since he was at university.

'God, the energy of those people,' he said aloud, thinking of Aidan and Siobhán's drive at such an unearthly hour.

He pulled up the futon into a settee and folded the linen.

*

He went for breakfast in The Winding Stair, and sat by the window, watching the river flow by and the crowds moving over the bridge as he drank his coffee. What would he say to her? What could he say that didn't sound trite? That he was sorry for putting her through what he did, but that he had needed time to accept that the child was his? Perhaps he could now truthfully say that. Her integrity was what he most admired in her, so he would have to be sure it was true before he said it, because if it wasn't, that would definitely be the end. The coffee had cleared his head.

He remembered lying in the fern on the island, and concluding that this whole mess wasn't about Kate, or the child, but about him. And then, in Hugh's house, he had seen it clearly. A paternity test would be demeaning for both of them. It said that he would only believe her if science proved him wrong.

Did he *need* to know? No, not really. He looked out onto the river again. He felt lighter. The hurt at what he had seen as betrayal had blinded him to that simple fact. What mattered was that he loved Kate. He drank back some coffee to choke the rush of emotion as he thought this. Yes, he loved her, he knew that. He loved her, and he loved their children. He couldn't quite bring himself to say that he loved Meg, but maybe, in a few years' time, when she crawled onto his lap and twisted his nose, maybe then it would come without him thinking about it. He still couldn't get his head around the idea that he had black genes. It went against the deep grain of how he thought of himself. The terror of his nightmare underlined that, but the nightmare had also suggested that it was true.

He looked at his watch. He shouldn't go home empty-handed. Maybe Kate would see it as a sop, and maybe she'd be right, but the children, at least, would expect a present from Ireland. He paid for his breakfast and asked for directions to Grafton Street. He walked across the Ha'penny Bridge through Merchant's Arch to the Central Bank. The plaza was swarming with young people – punks, Mohawks, skunks, or whatever – lazing in the fickle sunshine.

He had intended getting some expensive perfume for Kate in Grafton Street, but on the way he decided against it. Instead, he found a little bookshop opposite Trinity College called Books Upstairs, and bought a book on Irish art for her. It was more appropriately neutral, he thought. He bought a book on the Burren for Deirdre, and some Irish children's stories for the children, and felt relieved that it had all been so easy. Outside, he took his bearings, noticing in passing how Trinity and the Bank of Ireland complemented each other, and he squinted, trying to imagine the street without the pollution and constant noise of traffic.

He liked the idea of the bus, so in good time he sauntered along Westmoreland Street to O'Connell Bridge and found the bus on the quays. He sat beside an old, neatly dressed man who after a minute or so struck up a conversation with him about the dull summer weather. Dan had no talent for small talk but out of politeness he did his best. Then a black family, a husband and wife and their lively young son, got on. The old man went quiet, looking them up and down, and then turned to Dan with a strained smile.

'I wonder how long it's been since they came down out of the trees?'

'Pardon?'

'Just when we get on our feet in this country, they march in and live in the lap of luxury at the taxpayers' expense. It's not right, and our own people with no roofs over their heads.' The old man's smile was still fixed.

'Did you ever have to leave Ireland to work?' Dan asked.

'No, I did not,' the old man said proudly. 'I worked hard all my life building up this country. And now look what's happening. Swanning around as if they owned the place.'

The old man was set in his ways, and Dan lost heart, too depressed to argue with him. He would never use such shocking language, but that was a superficial virtue, and lent him a moral superiority he didn't deserve. He looked out the opposite window until the old man got off.

*

It was strange coming back to Heathrow, getting the tube and taking a red bus. It was as if he had been away for many years, in a country much more foreign than Ireland seemed to be. The familiarity alarmed him. He knew it was seducing him into thinking that everything would go off smoothly and he had to fight to remind himself that it wouldn't, maybe even shouldn't.

He walked from the bus stop, as nervous as he had ever been. As he reached his street, he turned back abruptly, unable to face it, knowing he was never so nervous because the reality of what he had risked in walking out on Kate like that came home to him again, as it had on the moor, and he couldn't bear to think he would lose it.

But he had to face her sometime, and he braced himself before he walked back, and again before he rang the bell, though he had a key. His heart was pounding as the door opened. It was Jim who jumped into his arms.

'Dad,' he breathed, holding his neck tightly. 'Dad . . .'

'Hello, Jim. How are you doing? Okay?'

Jim leaned back and nodded, then broke into a smile.

He let Jim down and looked up to see Kate standing in the hall. Jim looked from one to the other.

'Hello, Kate,' he said.

'Did you have a good flight?'

'Yes. It was fine.'

'Shall I make you a cup of tea?'

'Please.'

She went into the kitchen and Jim closed the door after him. He put his bag under the table in the hall and, tossing Jim's hair, he followed Kate, who was filling the kettle at the sink.

'Jim,' she said without turning, 'tell Sara Mae her daddy's home, will you?'

Sara Mae was playing in the garden with her friend Celine, and Jim went away to fetch her.

'I'm sorry, Kate. I'm truly sorry.'

She emptied the teapot and rinsed it, keeping her back to him. In the garden Sara Mae looked up to Jim's call, then ran into the house, followed after a moment's hesitation by her friend.

'Look at her,' Kate said.

Sara Mae burst into the room and leaped into Dan's waiting arms. She said nothing, just hugged him tight. Dan glanced at Kate. Sara Mae's friend came and stood at the door, wide-eyed, unsure of her position.

Jim stood behind her. Meg started to cry, and for the first time Dan noticed the pram. Kate was obviously relieved for the excuse to bring her upstairs, and left without a word.

'Celine,' Dan said to Sara Mae's friend, 'would you mind going home for today?'

She bit her lip and nodded, then went home over the garden wall.

'Well, folks, did you miss me?'

He had intended his voice to be full of cheer, but he couldn't manage it.

'No,' Jim said, pretending nonchalance, and Sara Mae giggled.

Dan shook his head and smiled, relieved.

'Well, I missed you two devils,' he said. 'Jim, fetch me my bag from the hall.'

Their eyes lit up when they saw the books, and some sweets he had got at the airport, and the novelty of his return was forgotten as they went away with them, leaving him alone and at a loss. But then Sara Mae came back and jumped into his arms again and kissed him softly on the mouth.

'I love you, Daddy.' They looked into each other's eyes before she wriggled away and went to read her book.

He cleared his throat and poured himself a glass of water and drank it back. He stood at the sink for a while, the empty glass in his hand, and stared out at the garden. Sara Mae had both knocked him for six and given him courage, the little sweetheart. He took off his jacket and, bracing himself yet again, he went upstairs and knocked softly on their bedroom door. She didn't answer, so he nervously went in.

Her shirt was still open, a breast bare, but the child had finished sucking. Kate looked at him and he held her gaze.

'I know she's mine, Kate. I know that now.'

'Did you find out?'

'No. Not in so many words.'

'Then how do you know?'

'I feel it.'

She looked away, as if considering this.

'Do you want to hold her?'

'Yes. Please.'

He went to her and she held up the child and carefully he held her.

'Her name is Meg.'

'Yes. I remember. She's beautiful.'

'Yes. I think she looks like you.'

'Do you think?'

'Dan, I've been so angry with you that I don't know if we'll ever be the same.'

'I know. I'm not the same and I don't expect you to be either.'

'You've changed? Really?'

'Yes.'

'Because ... I knew you'd come back. But ... I don't want you back if you're the same.'

The tears she'd held back flowed freely now.

He stared at Meg, at the contrast between her brown-black face and his white arm. He didn't know what to say, and looked back at Kate. She was looking at him very closely.

'I don't want you back if you've just swept everything under the carpet,' she said.

He handed Meg back to her and sat on the edge of the bed.

'Yes. I know,' he said. 'I've always done that. That's why I fell apart.'

She reached over and touched his hand.

'I do love you,' she said.

'And I love you,' he said, unable to look at her. He put his hand over hers.

'But I couldn't bear you not loving your daughter.'

She had hit the mark. He was trying to love Meg but he still didn't know how.

'I won't fake it,' he said, and she sighed in what he took to be relief.

She turned his head with her free hand, making him look at her, searching his face.

'I'm very tired,' she said, and he brushed the hair away from her eyes. Then she kicked off her shoes and got into bed, fully dressed, with Meg.

Meg lay in the crook of her mother's arm, and he tried to absorb her features, but mixed with his awe was bewilderment still, and he couldn't help it. When he looked at Kate, she was asleep.

How strange that this lovely woman was his wife. He was grateful that she insisted that he was honest. She was brave as well as beautiful. He covered her with a throw.

He had always thought he had that integrity too, but Meg

had unmasked him even to himself. He remembered the pool by the island in Wexford. Meg had plucked him out of such a dark, unreflecting pool and left him gasping and naked in a world with colour and consequence.

There was a pen and notebook on the side table. Kate most likely had been writing a diary, trying to work out her feelings. He looked about him for some paper before tearing off some cardboard from a box of nappies, and wrote in large letters that Meg was downstairs with him.

He looked at it. Maybe she would panic when she saw it, and he tore it up and stuffed it in his pocket. He gathered her things, delicately took Meg and brought her downstairs to the pram in the kitchen. Jim was sitting under the tree in the garden, reading his book. Dan gazed at him, until Jim sensed him and looked up. Dan nodded, meaning to ask if the book was any good, and Jim gave the thumbs up and they both laughed.

Meg woke, googling away to herself, and he picked her up. She seemed to look at him from a great depth, unsettling him. If he'd believed in God he would have prayed then to be granted some understanding, but all he could do was look helplessly at this mysterious child. He rocked her in his arms, and she seemed content with that.

Sara Mae came in and helped herself to a drink of water, then turned, catching her breath, and took in the picture of her father holding her sister, smiled, then went away happy.

Well, that was something.

The inevitable happened in due course and he got the bag and changed her on the counter. This was like old times, he thought as the smell assaulted him.

He cleaned her and as he reached for the cream and powder, she kicked her legs.

'Hey, that's better, isn't it?' He laughed, and she kicked some more. 'That's my girl,' he heard himself say, 'Daddy's going to make you nice and comfortable.'

Sara Mae came back, looking worried.

'Where's Mammy?'

'She's very tired, Sara Mae. She's having a snooze.'

Jim came in then and she told him that Mammy was having a snooze.

'And Daddy's looking after Meg.' She beamed. Jim nodded and looked away as he tried to suppress a smile.

Dan looked at his watch.

'I suppose you people are hungry.'

They were, so he set them to work peeling potatoes for chips to go with the chops and peas he found.

They were happy, and he allowed himself a little cautious happiness as well.

Things were going fine until Meg began to get grumpy and this time she wasn't tired or soiled, but hungry. He looked about for some baby food but quickly remembered that Kate breastfed her. There was nothing to do but wake Kate, but then, as if she'd timed it, she was at the door and taking Meg from him. She suckled her for a while before she spoke.

'Did she need to be changed?'

'Yes.'

'You changed her?'

'Yep. Like old times.'

She smiled faintly, and looked drowsy rather than exhausted as she had earlier.

*

He slept in the spare room that night, and mid-morning the following day he rang work, and was assured that everything was under control, and that he wasn't to come back until he was fit.

Kate said he should go to the site for an hour to put his mind at rest. She knew him well, and he gratefully accepted her suggestion. He gave her her present from Ireland before he left.

'More bedtime stories?'

He winced. She looked at the wrapped book and tried to laugh, but couldn't, and left it on the table, unopened.

'Well...' he said, and left for work, telling himself that

he should expect this kind of thing in the near future, at the very least.

*

Everything was under control as his colleagues had said. Every last detail was in place, and all that was left to be done was the clean-up. So he went to the doctor and got the stitches out. They should have been out earlier, but it was a perfect heal and just needed a small plaster for another few days.

On the way home he took a detour to Citizen Road. He parked in a side street and walked by the embankment. He had thought about going to the Royal Northern again, to look up at the window of the ward where Charlie had died, but no, that was Charlie's story.

He gazed at where their house had been. It was hard to grasp that as a child he had played in this vacant space, had had nightmares, dreams, jelly and custard within its ethereal walls. It was as if it had never existed, but it still flourished in his head. It would always be there so long as he drew breath. Every detail.

*

When he got home the house was empty. He made himself a cup of tea, musing about the next job at the office, but squeezed the milk carton too hard and milk splashed onto the floor.

'Damn.'

It would leave a stain so really he should wash it and he looked for a mop in the broom cupboard under the stairs. He turned on the light and the mop and bucket were standing against the wall, but as he pulled them out he knocked a box off the shelf.

He mopped the floor and left back the mop and bucket and finally had his cup of tea with a slice of fruitcake, standing at the sink and looking onto the garden. He enjoyed the cake, but as he washed it down he noticed some papers sticking out from where they kept bills and the like. It was the unfamiliar handwriting which caught his attention, and he reached over and pulled it out. He left down the cup as he read in astonishment. It was his family tree on his mother's side, going back to 1872. It was Deirdre's writing, he was sure of that now. The interfering old cow! Trying to prove that the black genes could only come from his side, and his English side at that, but he was fascinated all the same. He should get that genealogy program off the Web, type it all in and casually show it to Deirdre. Siobhán had promised to send him the Kinsella side, which was definitely free of black genes, right back to the eighteenth century.

As he rinsed out his cup, he wondered about the box he had knocked off the shelf, and went back to the broom cupboard to investigate. It was a box of body paints they'd got the children the Christmas before. No doubt it had been forgotten in the excitement over the computer. No, they had been used, he saw. But not the black.

His blackness dream flooded back but in daylight, at least, it had lost its terror.

After all, he had held Meg in his arms, so he allowed himself to reflect on it. The two magicians, on some tropical island – and that awful pain they had snuffed out. But it was obvious that the dream had come from the painting in the Pilgrim's Hospice in Florence. Cosmas and Damian, the saints, healing what's-his-name.

In reverie he was walking through Florence again with Kate, besotted by her, solicitous, stunned at his good fortune that she loved him.

It was sad that their love would never be so easy again, and he yearned for that uncomplicated time. She didn't know any better than he did what a new beginning might entail, but she saw clearly that it was necessary, and it was dawning ever more forcibly on him. His first step was not to fake love for Meg, as he had promised Kate.

He picked out the black crayon from the box and smudged his left hand. He was sweating, because he knew that his rationalization of the dream was just that. His calm, easy explanation had glossed over its molten core, its raw-ness, its . . .

He reckoned there was enough of the black paint, and brought it upstairs to their bedroom, hoping that Kate and the children would be away for another while. He stood in front of the full-length mirror and stripped, then painted his right foot, except the scar, then his leg, front and back. He continued painting until half of him was black and he had reached into what really scared him in the nightmare. The thought of blackness engulfing his body, his lips, his nose, his eyes, his heart, was still terrifying, but as he stared into the mirror he realized that the dream had not wanted to make him something else, but only to reveal who he was.

Acknowledgements

Acknowledgements are due to Eamonn Wall, for the epigraph, taken from the poem 'Tour de France/Enniscorthy', published in his collection *The Crosses*, Salmon Publishing © Eamonn Wall, 2000; to The Arts Council of Ireland/An Chomhairle Ealaíon and Aer Lingus for an ArtFlight to Italy, which allowed me to visit the Museo di San Marco, Florence; to Declan Meade, editor of *The Stinging Fly*, which published an early draft of Chapter One; and to Lorna St Aubyn, in whose home in Co. Meath the novel was thought through.

Certain books, journals, monographs and web sites were of immense value in placing parts of the story in their context. These include *The People's Rising: Wexford 1798* by Daniel Gahan (Dublin, Gill & Macmillan, 1995); *Journal of the Wexford Historical Society*, no. 17 (1998/1999); *Memoirs of Miles Byrne*, edited by Kevin Whelan and Thomas Bartlett (Enniscorthy, The Duffry Press, 1998); *The Askamore Parish Journal*, 1998 (with particular reference to the article on the Battle of Ballyellis by Dr Ruan O'Donnell); *The Slave Trade* by Hugh Thomas (London, Picador/USA, Simon & Schuster, 1997); *The Road to Rebellion: The United Irishmen and Hamburg 1796–1803* by Paul Weber (Dublin, Four Courts Press, 1997); *Caribbean Islands Handbook* by Sarah Cameron (Footprint Handbooks, 1999); *Soul of Africa Magical Rites and Traditions* by Klaus E. Müller and Ute Ritz-Müller, with photos by Henning Christoph (Cologne, Könemann, 1999); *The Holy Grail: Its Origins, Secrets & Meanings Revealed* by Malcolm Godwin (London, Labyrinth, 1994); *In the Blood: God, Genes and Destiny* by

Steve Jones (London, HarperCollins, 1996); 'An Irish Settlement on the Amazon' by Aubrey Gwynn, *Proceedings of the Royal Irish Academy*, vol. XLI, Section C, no. 1 (Dublin, Hodges, Figgis & Co./London, Williams & Norgate, 1932); *If the Irish Ran the World, Montserrat 1630–1730* by Donald Harman Akenson (Liverpool University Press/McGill-Queen's University Press/The Press University of the West Indies, 1997); *The Panorama of the Renaissance*, edited by Margaret Aston (London, Thames & Hudson, 1996); *The Garden of Earthly Delights: Hieronymus Bosch*, Introduction by John Rowlands (Oxford, Phaidon, 1979). Some of the above were gifted or loaned by family and friends, who also gave unstintingly of their knowledge and research. My thanks also to Jeremy Cameron, author of *Brown Bread in Wengen* (London, Scribner, 1999) and *Vinnie Got Blown Away* (London, Touchstone, 1995).

Important web resources were Bill Innanen's Montserrat Index Page, www.mni.ms/index.shtml, which includes a 'Condensed History of Montserrat'; 'The Woman Slave and Slave Resistance' from Barbara Bush's *Slave Women in Caribbean Society: 1650–1838* (Kingston, Heinemann, 1990) at www.math.upr.clu.edu/~wrolke/linda/carslave.htm; 'DNA and the Concept of Race'; the *New York Times*, www.nytimes.com/library/national/science/082200sci-genetics-race.html; and The Web Gallery of Art, www.gallery.euroweb.hu/index1.html.

I'm indebted to the following who contributed directly or unwittingly to the making of the novel: Mick Considine and Mary Manley, and Sean and Kay Halford; Lisa Eveleigh, Mary Mount, Tess Tattersall, Nicholas Blake; Nora Liddy and her colleagues in the Wexford Historical Society; the staff of the ILAC and Wexford libraries; Christine Clear, Suzanne Clear, Ulrike Boskamp, Emer Singleton, Paola Meucci and Paolo Leonardo; Terry McDonagh, Corinne Browne, Grace Wynne-Jones, Thomas Lynch, Eamonn Wall, Florrie McGuinness, Richard Lewis, Jim Greeley, Peter and Aileen Casey, John Casey and Geraldine Byrne; Karina Casey, Pat and Ann Casey, Paddy and Eileen Doyle; the staff of Hotel Lorena, Florence; Billy and Tom Donnelly of Grove Mill and The Moor, Hollyfort; the Webster family of The Grove, Hollyfort; the Lyons family of The Mill, Craanford; Davy Donoghue of Askamore; and the parishes of Askamore, Craanford/Monaseed and Bally-fad, Co. Wexford.

Hunter Gowan, Miles Byrne, Richard Holt, Anthony King and Anthony Perry were actual combatants in the 1798 Rebellion in Wexford. Hugh Byrne and his story, as well as his family and friends, however, are entirely a figment of my imagination, and any interaction with historical persons or fact is not intended to suggest otherwise.